Norman Johnson is a hard man (
brought up in poverty, he ran wil
as a child, before moving to Lor
immediately fell in with the gangs who ruled Soho at the time. Always working alone, he quickly gained notoriety, and was once told by a senior policeman that he was rated amongst 'the top six bad men in Britain', and he served a number of prison sentences for grievous bodily harm and other offences. It was from this unlikely position that he accidentally found himself working as a personal bodyguard and confidant to a Middle-Eastern royal family, one of the richest in the world, and ended up having an intense love affair with the Sultan's sister. When the affair was discovered, he was forced to move to New York, where he worked alongside senior Mafia figures until, on a subsequent visit to England, he was arrested and imprisoned once more. Having now completed his sentence, he has turned his back on his life of crime to concentrate on telling fictionalised accounts of his considerable and remarkable experiences, working in conjunction with co-writer, Andrew Crofts. *The Princess and the Villain* is their first novel together.

Andrew Crofts is one of Britain's most successful ghost-writers. Millions have read his books believing them to be by other people. Through his work he comes into contact with spies and mercenaries, billionaires and slaves, rock stars and actors, courtesans and fraudsters, gangsters and gurus, and sinners and saints of every kind, and he has told many of their stories in his catalogue of varied books. He has also written a selection of manuals and guides on writing and marketing. *Maisie's Amazing Maids,* his first work of original fiction published under his own name, came out in 2001.

BY ANDREW CROFTS
PUBLISHED BY HOUSE OF STRATUS

Maisie's Amazing Maids

the princess and the villain

Norman Johnson

and Andrew Crofts

This edition published in 2001 by House of Stratus, an imprint of Stratus Holdings plc, 24c Old Burlington Street, London, W1X 1RL, UK.
Also at: Suite 210, 1270 Avenue of the Americas, New York, NY 10020, USA.

This edition published in 2001 by House of Stratus, an imprint of Stratus Holdings plc, 24c Old Burlington Street, London, W1X 1RL, UK.

www.houseofstratus.com

Typeset, printed and bound by House of Stratus.

A catalogue record for this book is available from the British Library.

ISBN 1-84232-417-9

CHAPTER ONE

1970

'I'm getting married, Norm,' Len said, obviously nervous.

'What? To that?' Norman jerked his head in the direction of the woman sitting next to his brother. It wasn't that she was ugly or anything, actually she was in pretty good condition for a woman of her age. She certainly looked after herself. The figure was trim and the hair expensively cut. There was a lot of jewellery on her. She obviously had money.

'I heard you had a mouth on you.' Ruby pulled a long white-tipped St Moritz cigarette out of a shiny crocodile-skin case, apparently unconcerned by the insult. Her hand was shaking slightly as she flicked open a Dunhill lighter, making the chunky gold bracelets jangle on her wrists. She offered the case to Norman. Under normal circumstances he would never turn down a smoke, but these had little gold bands round them for Christ's sake. He didn't even bother to shake his head, staring hard into his baby brother's shifting eyes. Ruby gave a little shrug, snapped the case shut and replaced it in her dainty crocodile handbag. She patted her hair and moistened her brightly coloured lips.

'No,' Len said hurriedly, clearly embarrassed by Norman's manner. 'This is Ruby. She's Babs' mother.'

'Babs?' Norman was becoming irritated. When they told him he had visitors he'd been hoping for someone who would bring him news of what was happening in the clubs. He hadn't seen Len for at least two years and suddenly he was sitting in front of him with a woman who looked like she should be sipping her first gin and tonic of the day in a hotel bar somewhere in the West End rather than prison visiting.

'Babs is my fiancée,' Len explained. 'She wanted to come and see you today but she had a hairdresser's appointment.'

'Right,' Norman nodded, as if he now understood. 'Got any smokes?'

'Sure.' Len surreptitiously passed over a couple of packets of Rothmans. Norman took them without bothering to hide his actions. He knew the guards well. They weren't likely to give him any trouble. It wouldn't be worth their while. Len was a 'Category A', top-security prisoner who knew his way round the system. That meant he was treated with respect by most of them, particularly the ones who got something in return.

'I bullied Len into bringing me to meet you,' Ruby spoke without moderating her voice, as if she was sitting at a North London dinner table. 'I just kept hearing your name around the clubs. You sounded irresistible.'

'The clubs?' Norman's eyes moved like lightning away from Len and onto the woman. 'You go to the clubs?'

'I like to play a little kalooki now and then,' she shrugged. 'Some poker. It gives me something to do. A girl needs a hobby, you know.' She moistened her lips again and stared hard into his eyes, apparently not intimidated by the blank look which Norman normally found made even the hardest of troublemakers act like shuffling schoolboys in the presence of their headmaster. 'Your name comes up a lot in conversation. Len here had been keeping quiet about his famous brother. I had to drag it out of him.'

'What sort of "conversation"?' Norman demanded.

'People say you didn't deserve to go down for this one, but you'd done a lot worse and got away with it. You're a bit of a legend in your own time, it seems.'

Len shifted in his seat uncomfortably. Watching his future mother-in-law flirting so outrageously with his brother was not a pleasant experience. He didn't imagine either Babs or her father would be likely to be pleased with him for letting Ruby press-gang him into taking her prison visiting. Not that he had told either of them anything about his big brother. He had been so shocked when Ruby asked him outright if he was related to Norman Dorset that he'd blurted out the truth. She'd seemed excited at the prospect of being related to a notorious hard-man. Ruby had worked out pretty quickly that Len would prefer Babs and her father, Jack, not to know of Norman's whereabouts, and had made it clear he could buy her silence with an introduction.

She was hoping that being able to drop Norman Dorset's name around the clubs would get her a bit of respect, maybe even a bit of credit.

'One man put me here,' Norman said eventually, his fists involuntarily tightening into a ball in his lap.

'I heard that too,' Ruby said. 'Jim Moody.'

The detective constable's name caused a spasm of anger to pass over Norman's face and Len glanced nervously around, wondering if Norman was about to explode into one of his infamous tempers. It was one such explosion that had got him back in prison again. Len willed Ruby to shut up. He just wanted to get out as quickly as possible without giving his brother any cause for offence.

'Moody's as bent as the rest of them,' Norman said after a long pause. 'He makes out he's whiter than white, but none of them can resist the money when it's actually offered. The papers go on about the gangs running London. That's bollocks. Scotland Yard runs the whole bleeding country. They're all on the take.'

But Norman didn't really believe that about Moody. It was entirely because Moody wasn't as bent as all the others that Norman hadn't been able to buy his silence. The man was a little worm of a creature and he showed no respect for Norman, or for the conventions of the business world. Norman found that hard to understand.

Ruby nodded her agreement. 'Who can resist the money, eh Norman?' Her wrists rattled as she swept an imaginary piece of hair back from her face.

Len was shocked to see a trace of a smile twitch at the corner of his brother's mouth. It was as if he was warming to Ruby. God, he hoped this wasn't going to cause any trouble with Jack. Marrying into this family was the best break Len could possibly have asked for. At last he would have access to some serious money and he would be able to start himself up in a proper business. He was fed up with going from one dead-end job to the next while his brother lived the high life in the West End, with the occasional break for a prison sentence. Len could remember what it felt like when Norman was on the outside. Len would be fixing his fourth car of the day, his fingers ingrained with engine oil, by the time Norman even got out of bed. He didn't want to find himself back where he was two years ago.

Mind you, he had work to thank for bringing Babs to him. She'd turned up in her white E-Type, wanting a service, and he had been more than happy to oblige. The other guys had been laughing at her, unable to miss the way she flirted with him, but he didn't care. Lying under the car he had been able to see all the way up inside her tight pink miniskirt. He hadn't imagined she was doing anything more than flirting until she came back the next day, asking him to come out in the car with her because she thought it was making a funny noise and she needed him to listen to it.

The boss had been out at the time, and so Len, accompanied by the suggestive jeers of his colleagues, had agreed. Babs had laughed at him when he put plastic covers on the passenger seat to protect the upholstery from his overalls.

'I don't mind a bit of dirt,' she teased, accelerating away with a screech of tyres.

She drove hard and fast out of London and Len had said nothing. He knew there were no funny noises coming from the engine. The car was going like a dream. In fact the whole experience seemed like a dream. Babs eventually stopped at a pub. There was a garden outside and she sat him down at one of the benches and went in to get them drinks and food. He didn't argue. He hadn't got any money on him anyway.

While they ate she told him about her father, Jack Rabitz. 'He's in show business,' she said. 'He manages all these stars, publishes their music, books them into places, you know the sort of thing. He's out most of the time, we don't see much of him.'

Len hadn't interrupted her. He just stared. Although she had great legs, he didn't think her face was up to much. She had a cute nose, which she later confessed had been fixed by a plastic surgeon as a twenty-first birthday present.

'You should have seen it before,' she laughed. 'Jimmy bloody Durante wasn't even close!'

Even though the new nose still wasn't able to make her pretty, she had a liveliness about her which he found attractive, and a way of stroking his thigh as she talked to him that made him moan out loud. Before driving him back to the garage, she'd told him he would be taking her out the following night. She took his address and told him what time she would pick him up. He'd expected they would go out dancing or maybe to see a film. He hadn't expected to be taken straight home to meet her parents.

The house was large, sitting on the hill in Highgate with views right across London. It was the sort of house that Len only knew existed because he'd seen them on television, and had never dreamed he'd ever actually be inside one. He and Norman and their sisters had been brought up in Liverpool, with a sitting-room just big enough to hold a sofa, a chair and a television. They had all shared a bedroom. The downstairs bathroom in the Rabitz house was big enough for a three-piece suite.

Jack and Ruby were obviously less than pleased to find they had an unexpected guest for dinner. Out of politeness to him they tried to make conversation, but Len could hear them rowing with Babs every time they thought he was out of earshot. They clearly believed she had brought home a garage mechanic just to annoy them. Len was beginning to think they might be right.

Now, sitting opposite Norman, he felt his brother was being as disapproving of his future mother-in-law as they had been of him. Since their father had always been away at sea, Len and the sisters had looked on Norman as a father figure, and when Norman moved to London, Len had followed him, feeling unable to cope with life in Liverpool without him. Norman had quickly made it clear that unless Len wanted to work for him in the clubs he was going to have to get himself a life of his own. The club life was obviously not for Len. He didn't have the front for it. He was basically an honest man and was uncomfortable with the constant scams and dodges and the threatening air of violence that hung in the air whenever his brother was around. The loan sharking and the clip joints, the endless hours of drinking in smoky back rooms that were meat and drink to Norman didn't appeal to Len. He wanted something better. Norman was not the sort of man to allow filial duties to mess up his life. If Len wasn't going to make himself useful, he didn't want him hanging around looking disapproving. He found a job for Len in a garage, organised a bedsit for him in Ladbroke Grove, and then left him to his own devices. After that, Len had drifted from one garage to the next.

'Looks like you've got a couple of pennies to rub together,' Norman said to Ruby.

'We make a living,' Ruby agreed, lighting herself another cigarette, having only smoked half the first one. She didn't bother to offer one to Norman this time. 'I hear you made a good living yourself for a few years.'

'Len and I didn't have much when we were kids,' Norman said, his face stony again. 'I guess he's told you about that.'

'I can tell Babs isn't marrying him for his family fortune,' Ruby laughed, making her earrings swing. She patted Len on the thigh. 'But that's okay. Babs has all the money she needs.'

'So, you're a gambler?' Norman changed the subject, feeling a twinge of pity for his brother.

'My husband works a lot in the evenings. I don't like sitting around the house waiting for him to come home.'

'I can imagine. Where do you go?'

She named a string of clubs and Norman nodded. He asked a few more questions, hoping to discover what might be happening to his interests while he was inside. He knew what his contacts told him, but he couldn't always tell when they were speaking the truth. There were people out there who liked to take advantage when a man was away for a while. He soon realised that Ruby knew nothing. She was just a punter, someone whose money they took but with whom they didn't share their secrets. He lost interest and returned his gaze to Len.

The boy had certainly grown up to be good-looking, which was just as well because, to Norman's eyes, he didn't seem to have much else about him. He looked like he wanted to hide under the chair. Maybe, Norman thought, he would make a good husband for a rich, spoilt Jewish girl. It would be better than lying around under other people's cars for the rest of his life. He stared hard at him, trying to recall what he'd been like as a child. Being honest with himself he found it difficult to remember. His childhood was all a bit of a blur to him. He didn't know whether it was because he'd pushed it out of sight in some dark recess of his brain, or whether he'd simply been too busy at the time to take much in. His abiding memory of Len was of a child with a constantly runny nose and a whinging voice, always asking Norman to take him with him wherever he went.

But Norman had never wanted to take Len with him because he had always, from the age of seven or eight, wanted to operate alone. He had watched the other boys in the streets running around in gangs, and seen them nearly always getting caught sooner or later. It hadn't taken Norman long to work out the reason: it was because they were only ever as fast as their slowest member. If he took Len with him on a job and they had to leg it, chances were that Len would get caught, and that would lead them to him. It wasn't a difficult lesson to learn, but it had made Norman a great deal more successful than all the other kids in the area. No one had been able to pin anything on him until he was fourteen years old, and that had been his own fault. He'd got overconfident, believing he was invincible. It had been inevitable. He could see that now, all part of the game.

'Everyone has a favourite story they like to tell about you,' Ruby was saying. 'They call you the Mad Scouse.'

Len stiffened in his chair, unsure how Norman would take this piece of news. As a boy he remembered seeing his brother beat a man twice his size senseless for a lesser insult.

'Is that right?' Norman stared at her hard. 'Do I seem mad to you?'

Ruby took a long, thoughtful drag on her cigarette. 'You seem dangerous.'

'It doesn't seem to bother you,' Norman said.

'I like a bit of danger,' she smiled and Len prayed to God that Jack Rabitz never found out he had arranged this introduction. Jack was finding it hard enough to accept that his daughter was going to marry a no-hoper Scouse kid who was going to need bankrolling in some sort of business if he was ever going to make anything of his life. To find out that the same kid was allowing his wife to flirt with a convicted criminal would not improve their relationship.

'We should be going,' Len said, standing up to show he meant business.

'Yeah,' Norman nodded, keeping his eyes fixed on Ruby's. 'You probably should. Keep in touch. Let me know what's going on in the clubs. Tell them I'll be back soon.'

'How much longer do you reckon you'll be in here, then?' she asked, still not standing up or looking away from his gaze.

'About another couple of years should do it,' Norman said. He knew what her game was. If things were going badly for her at the poker table one night, she would casually mention that her friend Norman Dorset was going to be out soon. In an instant she would find them more than happy to grant her more credit, maybe even forget her debts for the evening. He could live with that. She might be useful to him. She was certainly going to be useful to Len.

Pretending to notice for the first time that Len had stood to leave, Ruby stubbed her cigarette out, snapped her bag shut and stood beside him, her eyes fixing themselves back on Norman's.

'I'll be in touch,' she said, speaking more with her lips than her voice. Then she turned and walked away. Len glanced back over his shoulder and saw Norman pull himself to his feet and walk off in the opposite direction with the guard. It reminded him of the times they had sat with their mother, watching their father walking out of the house.

Jarmina peered out of the limousine window at the passing city streets. It was the first time she had been to London, the first time to Europe even. In fact, the only other times she had been out of the Kingdom of Domai had been to visit relatives in other Middle-Eastern countries. It had taken a great deal of nagging to get herself included in this trip. She had finally managed to convince her father that she would be good company for her mother.

The Queen was sitting beside her on the back seat of the Daimler, paying less attention to the scenery than to the box of Black Magic chocolates that lay open on the seat between them. She made a great show of choosing exactly the one she wanted before popping it into her mouth, even though Jarmina knew she would have eaten them all by the time they reached the hotel. She worried about her mother. The Queen was now well over twenty stone and took no exercise beyond walking between her limousines and her bedrooms. All she seemed to do all day was eat chocolate and gossip with the coterie of attending women who travelled with her everywhere she went. The thought that her life might pan out to be equally pointless weighed heavily on Jarmina's mind. She glanced through the back window to see if the identical limousine carrying this entourage was still with them. It was. Behind it another car carried the rest of their luggage.

She went back to studying the people on the pavements. The clothes amazed her. Everyone looked like the pictures she had seen in the glossy magazines that were delivered to the palaces in Domai. There were women showing bare legs and bare shoulders, some even exposing the tops of their breasts. She pulled her scarf comfortingly around her head, feeling the warm protection of the many layers of brightly coloured silk that encased her from head to foot.

While she pitied her poor sisters and cousins who had married into other royal families like the Saudis, and had to cover their faces as well as their bodies in black every time they stepped outside their palaces, or when they were in the presence of men, she still couldn't understand how these

Western girls could bear to walk around practically naked with men staring at their exposed flesh. Sometimes she had a nightmare from which she would wake with a scream of panic, and in which she found herself walking down a street with no clothes on at all. It made her heart pound with excitement but the feelings of embarrassment and disgrace would stay with her for several hours after waking. She tried to imagine how she would feel to be in one of the miniskirts and low-cut tops that she could see all around. Even the thought made her shiver.

She wondered what it felt like to be able to walk along a street full of people on your own. She had never been anywhere without a convoy of cars and bodyguards. In her own country there would be armed guards in the car with her and the streets would be cleared to allow her to travel, uninterrupted by crowds or traffic, to her destination. If she wanted to shop then the stores would be emptied of people and she would be able to stroll, unhindered, with her troop of female relatives, friends, servants and bodyguards trailing along behind, laughing at every joke she made, rushing to put right anything that annoyed her. The shopkeepers would bow their heads and kiss her outstretched hand. She couldn't imagine what it must feel like to be alone in such a situation. It must seem dangerous and exciting. She sat back in her seat and helped herself to one of her mother's chocolates.

'That was my favourite!' the Queen complained, a troubled cloud passing temporarily over her usually sunny expression.

'You know the doctor has told you to eat less of these,' Jarmina replied petulantly. 'I'm just trying to improve your health, Mother.'

The Queen pushed another chocolate into her mouth quickly, before the Princess could steal it, and frowned. She sometimes worried about her daughter's impertinence. She would never have dared to speak to an elder in such tones when she was twenty-five. She blamed her husband and son. They both indulged Jarmina far too much. It was almost as if they feared the lash of her tongue. The Queen had been brought up amongst men who were afraid of nothing and she sometimes pined for those days. She also knew that there was truth in what her daughter said. She could see the back of her personal doctor's head in the front of the car, sitting between the driver and the bodyguard. She was well aware that he believed she should be losing weight and, she vowed to herself, she would – just as soon as she had finished this last box of chocolates.

The cars swept to a halt in front of Claridge's and were immediately surrounded by doormen, bellboys and reception staff as the ladies and their luggage were disembarked and ushered the few yards across the pavement into the calm security of the hotel. The Queen's entourage gathered around her, clucking and whispering, as she waddled towards the lift. The Princess stood back a few feet, allowing them to reinstate themselves around her mother. She wanted to take her time getting to the suite, knowing that once she was inside she would be virtually a prisoner again. She wanted to stare at the other people in the foyer, some of whom, she noticed, were already staring at them. She realised they must have been making a colourful spectacle in their long flowing skirts and scarves. She didn't imagine that London saw too many people like them.

Eventually they were all installed in the suite. The Queen was lying on her four-poster bed and one of her friends, a woman who was married to the King's younger brother, squatted beside her, breaking open a fresh box of Black Magic for her while another plumped up the pillows behind her. The Queen sank into them with a deep sigh, as if reaching the end of an arduous journey. She decided to have just one more box of chocolates to comfort herself before starting her diet.

Jarmina felt quite different. She felt as if she had just arrived somewhere so exciting that she couldn't wait to explore. She watched with mounting despair as the other women settled themselves down on the bed or rolled out mats on the floor around it, roosting like exotically plumed chickens. She could see they were not intending to go anywhere else that day. They made her want to scream with frustration.

Excusing herself with a badly acted yawn, she left the room and went to her own bedroom. Walking to the window she pulled back the net curtains and stared out. She struggled with the window catch and was on the point of giving up and calling for someone to do it for her, when she finally managed to work it out and throw open the window. She leant on the sill to look out. Below her the street was bustling with people. She knelt down, resting her chin on her hands, and stared at them for a while, as fascinated as a small child unearthing an ants' nest for the first time. After a few minutes she began to feel bored and unsatisfied with simply watching. She wanted to get in amongst them, stir up the ants in this adult nest. She was fed up with being a distant observer; she wanted to be part of the world around her.

Standing up she stamped across the room and threw herself down on the bed, burying her face in her pillow. She felt like screaming and beating her fists but she knew there was no one in the room to hear her. She would have liked to cry but somehow the tears wouldn't come. Sitting back up again she folded her arms and stared straight ahead with a furious frown, as if concentrating on the empty ache inside her would make it go away. But it didn't. She was going to have to take some action if she wanted to change her life.

Climbing off the bed she opened the bedroom door a crack and peered out. She could hear the other women's voices chattering and laughing in her mother's bedroom. The door to the suite was open and bellboys were wheeling in trolleys piled with matching luggage. She stepped out of her bedroom, pulling her scarf across her face to shield herself from the men's eyes. The staff had been well trained in how to deal with the Arab women who were starting to arrive in London, and they did not address her or look in her direction. They just continued with their work, waiting for her to speak to them. She walked quietly to the open door and went out into the corridor.

Her heart was thumping in her chest and she found she liked the sensation. She was tempted to run to the lifts, but forced herself to walk at a slow, discreet pace. She did not want to draw any attention to herself. Once in the lift she indicated that the bellboy should press the button for the ground floor, hardly able to breathe from the excitement as the floors passed and the doors opened out onto the sedate bustle of the lobby.

At any moment she expected to hear her name called out and some man to hurry her back up to the suite. But as she made for the door, the uniformed man who stepped forward simply opened the door for her with a broad smile and a faint nod of the head. Jarmina didn't respond. She had been taught never to smile at servants, or even to signify that they were there unless it was to issue an instruction or a reprimand. She walked through the door and out into the street.

'Taxi, your Highness?' the doorman enquired and she waved him away with an imperious gesture. If she climbed into a taxi she wouldn't know what to say to the driver, and she would have no idea how to pay him at the end of the journey. She didn't know where she wanted to go; she just knew she wanted to go somewhere.

Should she turn left or right? She chose right and walked briskly away, trying to look purposeful, and feeling suddenly exposed in her traditional flowing robes. Looking around she could see no one else dressed in anything remotely similar. She pulled her scarf more tightly across her face and kept on walking. She crossed a small street and then came to a crossroads. She turned right again, comforted by the sight of expensive shops lining both sides of the street. These were the sorts of shops she was used to seeing. She even had clothes from places like these, although she was never allowed to wear them in public. Some of the suitcases in the suite held expensive Western designs which none of the women had yet worn. She had also bought shoes and jewellery from stores like these in hotels back home. She glanced up at the street sign and recognised the words 'Bond Street' – she had heard the older women talking about this place.

Gaining confidence from the fact that no one had yet accosted her, she slowed her pace and began to look in the windows. Her heart rate was beginning to settle down and she felt a curious lightness and freedom. She grew used to the feel of people looking at her. She noticed they would nearly always look away if she caught their eye, embarrassed to have been caught staring. One or two of them smiled at her, but she merely pulled up her scarf and averted her gaze. She paused to look at a clock in a window of Asprey's and was suddenly aware of a man standing beside her.

'Hello, pretty lady,' he said, making her jump and look into his face before she had time to cover herself. Flustered, she grabbed at her headdress and tried to move round him, but he moved too, blocking her path.

'Has anyone ever told you, you have beautiful eyes?'

He was a handsome, swarthy young man with an accent she didn't recognise. She tried again to dodge round him, her heart thumping once more. No man in Domai had ever had the courage to talk to her in this familiar manner and she had no idea how to respond. Her English was good enough to grasp the gist of what he was saying, but not good enough to be able to produce an appropriate reply to get rid of him.

The man could tell that it didn't matter how many clichés he used, this woman would not have heard them before. He had learned long ago that, with enough confidence, his corny pick-up lines could be delivered to good effect, as most young women were too polite to laugh in his face.

'I come from Rome,' he said, 'so I have seen many beautiful women, but I have never seen anyone like you.'

She put her head down and tried again to pass him, unable to think of a single thing to say.

'Don't rush away, pretty one. Tell me your name at least, so that I can dream about you.'

She could see his shoes were expensive, his trousers neatly creased. Swivelling on her heel she found herself facing the doorway to Asprey's. She lunged towards it and a doorman appeared, as if by magic, on the other side, pulling it open and allowing her in. The man followed and she immediately felt trapped.

'Let me buy you a gift,' he was saying. 'Choose something and I will buy it for you. So you will think of me whenever you look at it.'

She tried to think of the right words to ask one of the shop assistants for help. They were all hovering back, unsure of the situation. Were these two lovers having a tiff? Was the man annoying her or courting her? They often saw these sorts of men with rich women. They knew what their game was, but then they too were involved in the same games of flattery and seduction, albeit with different goals in mind.

Finally losing her cool, Jarmina started flapping her hands at the man, making noises as if she were shooing away a persistent dog. As several staff members in black tails and pinstriped trousers moved forward to assist the lady, the young man held up his hands in mock surrender.

'Just remember,' he said, 'that a handsome Italian man once told you you had the most beautiful eyes in the world. Just think of me sometimes.' He blew her a kiss before turning and walking calmly from the premises.

An assistant led her to a chair and she sat down, fanning herself wildly with her fingers with a mannerism she had seen her mother use a thousand times and hated. A manager had been discreetly summoned from the back and appeared by her side. He knew who she was. It was his job to know such things.

'Is there anything we can do to help, your Highness?'

It didn't seem strange to her that this man who she had never seen before in her life should know who she was. In the shops in Domai, everyone would have recognised her instantly.

'Please,' she said, taking a deep breath and summoning her English. 'Ring for my car to come and collect me.'

'Certainly, your Highness. Whom should I ring?'

'Claridge's,' Jarmina said in a small voice. She knew now that she was going to be in trouble, but she wanted to get back to the safety of the suite more than anything else. She had had enough adventure for one day.

The King's suite was on the same floor as the Queen's, but sufficiently separate for him not to be disturbed by any dramas that might occur there. As Jarmina was being brought back to the hotel from Asprey's in the limousine, the King and his advisers were listening politely to what Sir Roderick Salisbury had to say.

'All we are saying, your Highness,' Sir Roderick repeated patiently, as if speaking to a small child, 'is that we would like to ensure that your borders are not encroached upon by any of your neighbours. We are simply extending a hand of friendship to someone we have known and enjoyed friendly relations with for a long time.'

He paused and tried to read the King's expression. It was impassive. The lines in his face were deeply etched and folds of tired skin hung down over his eyes, masking any thoughts he might have. Sir Roderick thought he looked not unlike one of the many camels his ancestors had traded so successfully for so many centuries. The advisers all waited with Sir Roderick in silence, not knowing what reaction their master expected from them. After what seemed like an age, and just as Sir Roderick was about to surrender the silence and start talking again, the King burst out laughing. It was a deep, gurgling roar of pleasure, bubbling up from his stomach in an uncontrollable explosion. Sir Roderick smiled uncomfortably, not aware he had said anything amusing, and feeling like a sober man amongst drunks as all the advisers joined in with their King.

When the King finally managed to control himself and wipe the tears from his eyes, he let out a deep sigh of satisfaction, as if the laughter had somehow cleansed his spirits and he now felt ready to carry on with the serious business of the meeting.

'Oh, Sir Roderick,' he said, 'how charmingly you express yourself.'

Sir Roderick inclined his head in thanks for the compliment, aware it was likely to carry a sting in the tail.

'I'm deeply touched that your government should have my welfare so much at heart. But I am puzzled as to why you should think I am in so much danger from my neighbours, many of whom are my friends and allies; some of whom are even married to my sisters and my daughters. One of my neighbours is my wife's brother. I'm surprised that you think they would want to invade my country.'

'That isn't what I said, your Highness.' Sir Roderick raised his hands in protest. 'We're well aware that you have excellent diplomatic relations with all your neighbours, but these are unstable times. It would only require one revolution and a change of leadership to alter the political geography of the whole area. Domai is an immensely rich country with only a small army. An opportunist coming suddenly to power might find your oil wells just too tempting to resist. We would simply like to offer you our protection.'

'We have so many friends,' the King laughed. 'You want to protect us, so do the Americans, so do the Russians. It amazes me how popular we are with you government people when, in the newspapers, I read how much the Arabs are disliked by the people of your country.'

'The newspapers are an inaccurate barometer of any country's true feelings,' Sir Roderick protested rather feebly.

'Oh, Sir Roderick,' the King said again, as if despairing of his old friend. 'You were not always like this. I remember when we first met. Do you remember that day?'

'Of course,' Sir Roderick nodded with a faint smile. He would never forget it. He'd been travelling across the deserts of Arabia, a young man in search of adventure. His father, a diplomat, had given him introductions to a number of local chieftains, including the King. He could clearly picture the tent in the middle of the sand, a bonfire burning beside it to keep off the chill of the night air, the smell of roasting meat and coffee mixing with camel dung and perfumes.

'You were a free man then,' the King said wistfully. 'We both were. Now I'm rich beyond anything my father could ever have dreamed of, and you are a powerful man and can no longer say what is truly on your mind.'

'I try to speak truthfully,' Sir Roderick blustered.

'Tell me truthfully why you want to move your troops into Domai?' the King said. 'No. I will tell you, to save you from telling more lies. You want to have a presence in the area. You want control of the oil. You want to keep the flag of the old empire flying over a bit of the world for a little longer. This is the truth. I am sure you are sincere when you say you want to protect Domai from invasion, but you do not mean that as an act of friendship. It is an act of self-interest.'

The King fell quiet again and Sir Roderick looked down at his hands for a moment, trying to arrange his thoughts. 'I'm very sorry if you believe that, your Highness,' he said, eventually, 'because I truly regard you as a friend. I hope that you and your advisers will consider what I have said and try to imagine what might happen to Domai should the area become unstable. It might be harder for our government to come to your aid once trouble has started than it would be for us to help you create a deterrent against any aggression.' He paused for a moment and then asked, 'How is your son? I trust he is well.'

'Najid is well,' the King nodded, his face inscrutable once more. 'As you know, he is commander-in-chief of our army, the army which you hold in such low esteem...'

'I didn't say that,' Sir Roderick protested, but the King held up his hand to silence him.

'But thank you for enquiring.'

'And your daughters?'

'All married now, except for the Princess Jarmina. In fact she is here in London now with her mother. I tell you, Sir Roderick, if you truly wish to show me the extent of your friendship, find me a man who will marry that girl.'

He smiled and the twinkle in his hooded eyes betrayed the affection which the old man felt for his eldest and prettiest daughter.

'I often think that if Jarmina had been a boy then the future of Domai would be more than secure,' he went on. 'She is the most fearsome of women. I have introduced her to any number of eligible princes and she has turned them all down flat. Even King Hussein came calling on her and was sent packing. Her mother and I despair.'

'I will put my mind to it, your Highness,' Sir Roderick replied, with a smile to indicate that he appreciated what the old man was saying. If Jarmina was to be the next ruler of Domai instead of Najid, things would indeed be very different. It was something he was already aware of. He thanked God there was no chance, even in the relatively Westernised country of Domai, that a woman could ascend the throne. Dealing with Jarmina would be every bit as difficult as dealing with her father, possibly even more so. Her brother, Najid, however, was already in Sir Roderick's sights.

When Jarmina was delivered back to the suite in Claridge's the women swarmed around her, telling her off for being so reckless with her precious life and wanting to know every detail of the adventure. They had all dreamed at one time or another of doing exactly as she had done, but none had ever had the courage. The Princess was a mystery to them. They could not understand how she had managed to hold out for so long against her father and brother's wishes that she be married. They didn't understand how she could have turned down marriage proposals from some of the wealthiest and most powerful men in the world. She frightened them with her imperious manner and sarcastic tongue, but at the same time they pitied her because they knew she was as trapped as they were. She might not have to submit herself to the attentions of a husband, but she was still not free to do as she wished.

They carried her along on a wave of chatter to the Queen's bedroom. The Queen had broken open another box of chocolates to soothe her nerves when she heard that her daughter had left the hotel unattended, and had almost finished it by the time the Princess arrived back in the suite.

'What am I going to tell your father and brother?' the Queen moaned. 'They will be so angry with me.'

'If they have to know,' Jarmina was calm now, back in control of her emotions, 'then I will tell them I escaped. That it was all my fault.'

'They'll say this is proof you should be married.' The Queen wagged a fat be-ringed finger at her daughter. 'You should have children and a household to look after by now. Then you wouldn't have the time or the inclination for such foolishness.'

Jarmina said nothing, waiting patiently for the storm to pass. She would never be disrespectful enough to argue properly with her mother. There was no point anyway; she would never be able to make her understand how she felt.

'You could have been murdered or kidnapped,' the Queen wailed on. 'What were you thinking of? You must never go out without guards. You have royal blood flowing in your veins. There are many people out there who would like to see it staining the street.'

Jarmina bowed her head. She had to admit that her mother had a point. She had felt horribly vulnerable outside the confines of the hotel. It had been exhilarating to start with, but the way in which the Italian man had approached her, with no respect for her royal blood, had unsettled her. He had also, she now realised, excited her in a way none of her formal suitors had been able to do. His well-practised words echoed in her head and she couldn't help but imagine what would have happened if she had succumbed to his charms. She blushed at the boldness of her own thoughts, and felt a shiver run through her as she remembered his handsome face. It was an unfamiliar feeling.

'You are right, Mother,' she said eventually, her eyes fixed to the floor for fear of what her mother would be able to read in them. 'I have learned my lesson. It was a foolish thing to do. I will not go anywhere without guards in future.'

With a respectful bow she returned to her own bedroom. She wanted to be alone with her thoughts, to replay everything that had happened in the previous couple of hours and to try to understand the feelings that were passing through her.

CHAPTER TWO

Captain Michael Beckett walked from the modest bachelor flat which had been rented for him in Baker Street to Berkeley Square. He was in evening dress. It was still early in the evening but he was not the only person dressed formally on the streets of Mayfair – others were on their way to parties or to jobs as waiters or musicians.

The Clermont casino was on the west side of the square in an elegant old town house. The basement of the house was given over to Annabel's, the favoured nightclub of the international establishment.

A great many high rollers frequented the Clermont. Michael couldn't afford to match them at the tables but he was still welcomed at the door because of his connections. That evening he had arranged to meet Crown Prince Najid at the club, and no self-respecting casino would turn away the young Najid.

The two men had met as schoolboys at Eton and had gone on to Sandhurst together to become soldiers and officers. When Michael's father first dropped his son off at Eton, he had told him that the greatest gift which the school would give him was contacts. He had been proved right. Michael was a model pupil; a good sportsman and a popular boy. He played in all the teams and bonded with a wide circle of other boys from influential families. He was well aware, however, that his greatest contact was the handsome and pleasure-loving Prince Najid. Newspapers frequently referred to the King of Domai as the richest man in the world, although admittedly there were several close contenders for the title, and Najid would one day inherit everything.

Michael's decision to go to Sandhurst had been founded on his childhood wish to become a soldier, but was confirmed when he managed to persuade Najid that he should do the same thing.

'That way you can be useful to your country,' he had told the doubtful prince as they battled it out on the school squash court. 'You'll be able to serve your father and protect him from his enemies.'

'My father doesn't have enemies,' Najid had replied. 'He is loved by his people.'

'He may be loved,' Michael said, 'but he also has powers which other people would dearly like to take from him. Not to mention riches.'

The arguments had gone on for some time, but eventually the peace-loving Prince, who would rather have been a concert violinist than a soldier, gave in and now he was Commander-in-Chief of all his father's forces; a title which filled him with horror whenever he saw it printed beneath his signature on a document ordering tanks or machine-guns, fighter planes or missiles. Even now, Najid still carried an air of shyness and reserve about him. He liked to have Michael around because the young Captain was so sure of himself, both mentally and physically, so confident in all the areas where Najid was still tentative.

It had not been long before other people noticed how close the two young men were and Michael found himself being invited to lunch in Whitehall. The first few discussions were with relatively junior civil servants who Michael assumed had been given the job of sounding him out, finding out if he was a reliable man and whether he might provide a route to getting Najid's signature on more order forms for British military hardware. Sir Roderick Salisbury had been the fourth, and most senior, civil servant who casually chatted to him about a number of things, including the delicate situation in Domai and the need for the British to maintain an influence within the area.

'We think the Prince will need a great deal of help when he comes to power,' Sir Roderick had said over the port, after a pleasant lunch. 'Military advice, back-up on the ground and so on. We hope he'll have some friends like you he can count on when he needs them.'

Michael had known better than to tell Najid about these meetings, and he had been surprised by how quickly his discretion was rewarded with promotion within the army and the use of the Baker Street flat in London when he needed it.

Najid had not arrived at the Clermont when Michael got there, so he went to the bar and ordered himself a large brandy. He received nods of recognition from many of the other visitors, most of them older men. One of them joined him without being invited. Michael knew he was one of the highest rollers in London, a financial entrepreneur who thought nothing of losing a hundred thousand pounds in a night.

'Your young friend, Najid, coming tonight?' he asked.

'I believe so,' Michael smiled non-committally. 'He said he might pop in.'

'Tell him there's going to be a private game upstairs later on if he's interested. High stakes.'

'I'll tell him.'

The other man took a few puffs on his large cigar and ran his hand over the surface of his smooth bald pate. Michael could see a reflection of the chandeliers in the highly polished skin.

'I hear the days of the Sultan are numbered,' he said.

'I wouldn't know,' Michael feigned indifference. 'I'm not what you'd call a political animal.'

'Hmmm,' his companion looked sceptical. 'If he was to fall from power, is your friend ready to take over? Think he's up to the job?'

'Not something I would have an opinion on,' Michael replied.

'There's a lot of money coming out of the ground over there,' the financier continued. 'If your friend ever needs help structuring the financing I would always be happy to chat to him.'

'At the moment I don't think Najid is thinking about taking over the country. He has the greatest respect for his father.'

'Absolutely,' the other man agreed. 'But things can change bloody quickly. Volatile part of the world, the Middle East. Hard to predict what'll happen in the next few years. It would be as well for him to be prepared.'

At that moment Najid appeared at the top of the stairs and Michael rose to meet him, not wanting Najid to come to him or he would find himself obliged to introduce him to the financier.

'Tell him about the game,' the man said as he walked away.

He and Najid embraced with genuine warmth. Najid looked immaculate in his evening clothes, with not a hair out of place or a fingernail unbuffed. They went through to the tables.

Michael did tell Najid about the private game but the prince waved the idea aside. 'They'd just let me win,' he said. 'They'd put their losses down to expenses for making a good contact.'

Michael was surprised by Najid's perceptiveness. Perhaps he was finally shedding some of his innocence.

'Maybe you should just take their money and buy yourself something nice,' he suggested. 'A villa somewhere. It would serve them right.'

'I don't need a villa anywhere,' Najid smiled. 'I have them everywhere.' He thought for a moment. 'Okay. I'll tell you what we'll do. We'll play and I'll use the winnings to buy you a villa somewhere.'

'I couldn't accept,' Michael laughed. 'Honestly, I couldn't.'

'I think you could, my friend. Come on, introduce me to these high rolling friends of yours.'

Three hours later they were back in the bar and Michael was fifty thousand pounds richer. The game had gone exactly as Najid had predicted. Two young women had joined them and were now sitting with them. There was a bottle of champagne open on the table in front of them.

'I feel like dancing,' Najid announced, sliding his hand around the waist of one of the girls. 'Shall we go downstairs to Annabel's?'

By the time they had found their way to a table in the nightclub, two other girls had joined their party and Michael settled back to enjoy himself for the night. Najid danced energetically for a while and then collapsed onto the seat beside him. The girls were talking amongst themselves, taking no notice of the two men, waiting to be told what was required of them.

'My father has arranged for me to marry,' Najid said. 'Will you be my best man?'

'Of course,' Michael replied, startled by the news. 'Who are you marrying? Do I know her?'

'Her name is Nabila. She's a member of the Saudi royal family. A princess of the blood! She'll have been well trained. She will not cause me any problems.'

'Is that what you want?'

'What do you mean?'

'Do you want an arranged marriage? Wouldn't you rather wait until you find someone who really interests you?'

'My dear Michael,' Najid threw his arm fondly around Michael's neck. 'You are such an innocent Englishman. I need to have a suitable queen so that I can produce suitable heirs to the throne. It doesn't need to make any difference to my life. If I meet someone else who "really interests me", I will still be able to have an affair. I could even marry her. Nabila looks very pretty – I have been shown photographs. What we really need to do is find someone to marry my eldest sister, Jarmina. She's proving very stubborn. Wouldn't you like to marry her, Michael?'

Michael knew this was the drink talking. There was no possibility that the King would ever allow his eldest daughter to marry an English soldier.

'I would be honoured,' he laughed. 'Your sister is a beautiful woman. But I think your father might not take to the idea.'

'She is a beautiful woman, isn't she,' Najid mused. 'And clever. Much cleverer than me. If she were a man she would make a great sultan. As she never ceases to remind me. But…' He banished the thought with a shrug and turned his attentions back to the women. 'Ladies, it's becoming boring here. Let's go back to the Dorchester and have our own party.'

The women giggled and were obviously pleased with the idea. They'd all heard about or experienced first hand the sort of tips that Arab men were renowned for giving their women. They stood to come away with decent bits of jewellery from tonight if nothing else.

'I thought you always stayed at Claridge's,' Michael said, as they walked out to the waiting limousine.

'My mother and father and Jarmina are staying there,' Najid confessed. 'I prefer to have a little independence.'

There was more champagne waiting for them in the suite at the Dorchester and Najid and Michael settled down to another bottle as the girls fussed over them, stroking their foreheads, loosening their ties and unbuttoning their shirts. Before long they were all naked on the king-size bed and Michael's well-honed powers of reasoning were leaving him.

'England is a wonderful country, Michael,' Najid said, as he sank himself into one of the girls who had crouched obediently on all fours in front of him, while another ran her fingers over his buttocks and down to the tight, sensitive bag hanging below. 'I think I should build a home here.'

The day after his visit from Len and Ruby, Norman was told he had more visitors. This time he was sure it would be one of the blokes from the clubs. He was beginning to feel uncomfortable about the lack of information he was receiving. He knew the Krays had been trying to muscle in on his territory while he was inside. That didn't worry Norman too much. He'd known the twins for years. They were men he could do business with if necessary. But Reggie and Ronnie had been put away now too, and that meant there was a vacuum. Norman worried that he didn't know who was likely to fill it.

When he saw Kathy and the girls waiting for him in the visiting room he felt a mixture of emotions. First there was lust. It had been a while since he had been close to a woman and Kathy still had the ability to make him salivate just from looking at her. That was what had got him into trouble in the first place. Norman had always been proud of the way he'd handled his women until he met Kathy. He'd always been able to get them interested, and he had never had any trouble getting rid of them once they started to become a nuisance and ask questions about what he was up to and why he was always late home. With Kathy it had been different. The moment he'd clapped eyes on her in the pub he'd known he was in trouble. He had been careful never to let her know just how strongly he felt about her, never allowed her to get the upper hand that way. No declarations of undying love or lavish gifts or anything like that. But women had instincts about these things and Kathy seemed to know he wouldn't be able to dump her as easily as he had the others. She even took the risk of getting pregnant without telling him. He'd been angry, but he hadn't hit her, and he hadn't given her her marching orders either.

Like all of them she had tried to pin him down. Once they were married she wanted to see more of him around the home, that sort of thing, and he'd never taken any notice of that. But he couldn't quite bring himself to tell her to get lost. The thought of never being able to touch her again was just a little too much for him to be able to contemplate.

Now there were three kids, all girls – Teresa, Rachel and Vicky – and he knew there was no chance he could ever dump them. He might not see them very much, but he would always be there for them, making sure they wanted for nothing, offering them protection. He didn't want them to have to suffer childhoods like his. There had never been any money in his family. When his father was away at sea his mother had always done her best, but she hadn't stood a chance. Whatever she was able to earn was swallowed up long before it reached the children, something Norman was never able to forgive his father for. No one could accuse him of not providing for his girls. He made sure they had more than enough. He knew from the feelings that he had for them, that he had never really loved Kathy, or any other woman apart from his own mother. It was possible that the three girls and his mother were the only human beings he'd ever loved.

When he saw the girls he felt a warm glow of pride and sadness. Kathy had dressed them nicely for the visit to their father. They looked well fed and healthy, their hair glossy and their teeth white. He wished Kathy hadn't brought them. He didn't want them to have to experience this side of life, and seeing them made it harder for him to settle into the dull routine of the days, made him more anxious to get out. Not that he fooled himself he would ever be able to spend more time with them than he had before he was sent down. He would have a lot of business to take care of when he got out. It was bound to occupy him full time.

'Hello, Norman,' Kathy said as he sat down opposite her. The girls squirmed closer to their mother, shy in front of a man they hardly knew, a man who never seemed able to make any open show of affection to them or their mother.

'You all right?' Norman asked gruffly. 'I wasn't expecting you.'

'We're all right,' Kathy replied. 'Aren't we girls? We're missing Daddy, though, aren't we?'

The girls all nodded solemnly, but did not leave their mother's side. Kathy made small talk for a while.

'It's hard, Norman,' she said eventually. 'There's a lot of bills for the house and the girls need new clothes...'

Norman looked at his daughters' dresses and thought they looked pretty good to him.

'You saying you need more money?' he demanded.

'It's hard, Norman,' she repeated in the whiny voice that had always annoyed him. 'The cost of living keeps going up...'

'Haven't they been bringing you payments?' he asked.

'Oh yes,' she said hurriedly, not wanting to cause any offence to the men who turned up at the house every now and then to check she was managing and to give her envelopes full of cash. They were not the sort of men who looked like they should be upset. 'They keep bringing the money like you arranged,' she said. 'But they don't know how the cost of things has gone up. They don't know the expense of running a family.'

None of Norman's friends looked to her as if they would have wives and children, or even homes. They looked like the sort of men who lived in rented rooms and spent most of their time hanging around in pubs and clubs or at the races. She suspected they came round more to check that there were no signs of any other men as much as anything else. Kathy was always meticulously careful to ensure that there were never any signs.

'I'll have a word,' Norman said. 'See if they can get a bit more to you.'

'Thank you, Norman.'

She seemed to hesitate, as if there was something else she wanted to bring up but didn't know how to put it.

'You got any more problems?' Norman asked. He was beginning to wish the visit would end. The girls were still staring at him as if he was a stranger and he wanted to get away from them. Half of him wanted to scoop them up in his arms, but the other half told him that if he did that it would be harder to let them go – just as half of him wanted to touch Kathy, remind himself what her lips tasted like, but the other half knew that if he did that he would have even more trouble getting to sleep that night. He had to protect himself.

'It's Pete,' she said. 'He doesn't seem to be able to get his life sorted out.'

Norman remembered Kathy's kid brother clearly. He was a nice enough lad but it was obvious he was a no-hoper. There just wasn't enough spark to get him going. He was still a teenager when Norman started his latest sentence, and was hanging around with a group of other good-for-nothings on the corners of the local high-rise blocks.

'He's been getting into a bit of trouble. He needs money and he can't seem to hold down a job.'

'Do you want me to see if I can organise something for him in the clubs?' Norman asked.

'Would you?' Kathy looked as if a weight had lifted off her shoulders. Norman liked the feeling of being able to solve family problems from behind prison walls. 'I'd be very grateful, Norman. He's not a bad boy. He just needs to be given a chance.'

'I'll see what I can do,' Norman said. He paused for a moment. 'Is there anything else?'

'That policeman keeps coming round,' Kathy said, trying to keep her tone light so as not to alarm the children. She saw her husband's fists clench in his lap.

'Moody?'

She nodded. 'He says you got away with murder. That you should have been put away for life, not seven years. He just keeps on coming back, asking more questions. He wants to know where I get the money to run the house from, with you in here. He says he intends to put you straight back inside on the day you come out.'

'He's sick in the head,' Norman snarled, aware that his daughters' eyes were fixed on his face, watching every twitch and flicker.

'He says you're one of the top six bad men in London and that you shouldn't be allowed to walk the streets.'

'He's no bloody angel. I could tell his bosses a few stories about him, but they're as bent as he is.'

Norman could feel his temper boiling up and he fought to control it. He needed to have someone to hit, but there was no one available. Once Kathy had gone he would go to the gym and take his anger out on the punch-bag. Or he would stir up trouble with another prisoner and punch him, imagining Moody's smug, smooth-skinned face as he drove his knuckles in. It would be worth going back into solitary to vent some of the rage he felt towards that man.

'Next time he comes round, tell him I want to talk to him,' he said eventually.

'Will he do that?' Kathy couldn't help but be impressed by her husband's self-confidence. It had been what first attracted her to him. While all the other lads were getting flashier and flashier in their attempts to impress her, Norman had always remained silent. When he did finally speak it had been with an authority way beyond his years. She didn't understand how her husband's world worked, but she knew that within it he was a man of influence. People did as he said and she could understand why.

'Is there anything else?' Norman asked, making it obvious he now wanted them to go.

'No, nothing else.'

Kathy stood up with the girls and the guard showed them out. There was no smile on Norman's face as he watched them leave. All the children turned for one last look at their father, their faces still solemn and puzzled.

Gerald came to see Norman the next day. The message had come to him that his partner was getting fretful and wanted a meeting. Gerald knew that one day Norman would be back on the outside and he didn't want to incur any bad feeling in the meantime. He felt overdressed in his sharp cream suit and thick knitted tie. His hair was long but beautifully cut at a salon off Grosvenor Square – the building it occupied was owned by his family.

Gerald's family did not approve of his association with Norman. Not because they had anything personal against Norman, but because they didn't think clubs turned a good enough profit. But Gerald had a bigger plan, something he did not bother to tell his family about. Clubs provided something more than turnover. They provided meeting places where he could do business and entertain potential partners for the future. Gerald understood the importance of motivation. People liked to be associated with him because he was a club-owner and a generous host. He could introduce them to the odd show business star and invite them to parties filled with beautiful and willing young women. Businessmen liked to do business with Gerald and the ambience of the clubs helped.

Gerald's club was very different to the clip joints that Norman was usually associated with. It occupied a large basement premises next to Madame Tussaud's in Baker Street and had had a lot of money spent on the decor. Norman's idea of decor was to stick a bar in the corner and make the lights so dim no one could see the state of the place, but Gerald had bolder plans. He had started by installing leather banquettes and strobe lighting – something which made Norman feel slightly queasy – and things had moved on even further since Norman had been inside. Gerald had employed the first topless waitresses in London, and put a disco floor in the corner of the restaurant. There were statues and fish ponds with fountains to give the impression that the basement was in fact a terrace overlooking the Mediterranean.

Norman was very necessary to Gerald's plan, because clubs needed security. They needed to have someone around who had a reputation, otherwise people started taking liberties. It might be customers getting drunk or deciding not to pay their bills, or rival companies trying to close the place down. Norman's reputation for fearless discipline was good for keeping all that sort of thing at bay. Even when he was out of circulation, the Mad Scouse's name gave Gerald's club a layer of protection – because everyone knew that one day Norman would be out again.

The Krays had been the only ones who had been willing to chance their luck against the absent Norman, but Detective Inspector "Nipper" Reid had taken care of them.

As his partner, Gerald felt an obligation to Norman, but that didn't mean he liked prison visiting. Gerald wasn't the only partner Norman had, but he was the richest. The other clubs that he had arrangements with were mostly small-time and temporary; seedy basement rooms in Soho where members and guests met to gamble and drink illegally or where foolish men from the straight world were fleeced of their money by hookers pretending to be hostesses with bottles of something fizzy that they said was champagne. Norman also kept in contact with his partners in these places, but it was Gerald whom he mainly relied upon to look after his interests while he was inside.

'I had a visit from Kathy and the children,' Norman said as soon as he sat down.

'That's nice,' Gerald said. 'Nice to see the family.'

Norman ignored the interruption and continued. 'Kathy says she needs more money. Inflation and all the rest.'

'More money?' Gerald felt alarmed. He didn't like the sound of this. Once a man's wife and children started asking for more money there was no end to the demands which might follow. 'I've been sending the lads round regularly…' he protested.

'I know,' Norman reassured him. 'I'm not complaining, but the kids are growing up. They need things. Try to bung her a few extra grand now and then, will you? I'll see you're sorted when I get out.'

'I don't doubt that,' Gerald said. 'But business hasn't been so good recently…' He saw that Norman was staring at him with the sort of blank expression he had once seen him use just before cracking a man's skull open on a concrete pillar. He knew Norman knew he was lying. 'Okay,' he said. 'I'll see to it.'

Norman nodded as if satisfied. 'You been getting visits from Moody?'

'The policeman?' Gerald thought for a moment. 'He comes in for a drink now and again. I make sure the girls give him a good time and that his bill gets mislaid. He never seems that grateful. I haven't seen him for a few weeks. Why?'

'Kathy says he's been sniffing around the house, making threats about finding something to put me away for good.'

'There's nothing for him to find is there?' Gerald asked.

'There's always things that can be found,' Norman said, 'if someone wants to find them badly enough.'

Gerald looked uncomfortable. 'I don't want them nosing around the club at the moment. I have a lot of good things going on.'

Norman nodded and they fell silent for a few moments. Gerald was used to Norman's silences. When he first met him he used to rattle on to try to fill them, ending up feeling stupid. Now he knew to wait them out.

'Kathy wanted something else,' Norman said eventually.

'What's that then?' Gerald's heart sank.

'She's got a kid brother. He needs a job. I think he's okay, just a bit useless. Could you find him something?'

'Sure.' Gerald heaved a sigh of relief. Giving a dead-end kid a job was no problem. There were always crates that needed to be lifted around, or messages to be taken or glasses to be polished or paintwork that needed sprucing up. 'Tell him to come round.'

'Ring Kathy, will you. She'll pass on the message. Tell her about the money as well.'

'Okay.'

Another silence.

'Know anything about a man called Jack Rabitz?'

'Absolutely. Goes back a long way with my father. They've done a lot of business together, financed the odd synagogue as well, I think. He's the genuine article. Why do you ask?'

'Just curious.' Norman never believed in giving out more information than was strictly necessary. It was personal anyway, family business.

Detective Constable Moody came to see him the following day. Norman could smell the stale sweat in the policeman's old tweed jacket the moment he walked into the room. Moody started by pretending to be friendly but Norman's glower soon demonstrated the futility of that approach.

'I hear you've been going to the house,' Norman said. 'Upsetting my wife and children.'

'I've paid them a couple of visits.' Moody settled back into the hard little chair with a self-satisfied smirk. Norman despised him. He knew that if men like Moody didn't have the weight of the force behind them they would be nothing. Strip them of their badges and put them in a place like this, he thought, and they wouldn't last five minutes. Send them out into the wide world to make a real living and they'd be starving within a week, or dead in a gutter somewhere. They were minnows swimming amongst sharks, but that didn't mean they weren't dangerous, because they did have badges and that gave them a lot of advantages.

Norman had often toyed with the idea of joining the force, but he knew his record was too long now. He should have made the decision right at the beginning. But then he wouldn't have had the right exams, not having been to school much after the age of seven.

'There's nothing for you to find there,' Norman said.

'Maybe there isn't,' Moody shrugged. 'But I want to know everything about you, Norman. The thought of you coming out of here in a few years and going back to your old ways makes me sick. I've decided I'm going to put you back in here for good next time. I'll do whatever's necessary.'

'You're talking through your fucking arse,' Norman growled. 'You've been watching too many American TV shows. You're a poxy little bent copper, a fucking Plod. If there was anything for you to find, do you think I'd leave it lying around the house?'

'Who knows what mistakes you've made, Norman,' Moody said, ignoring the accusations. 'But I intend to find out.'

'I'm fucking warning you for the last time, Moody.' Norman leaned forward so that his face was inches away from the policeman's. He could see the dandruff in Moody's hair waiting to fall. The guard took a step forward, ready to separate them if necessary. Moody didn't flinch, which surprised Norman. 'If you don't leave my family alone I'll come looking for you the day I get out.'

'I won't be hard to find, Norman,' Moody replied, his voice steadier than he expected it to be, 'because I'll be right behind you.'

CHAPTER THREE

1972

The wedding took place in a traditional tent, modelled on the kind of structure the King and his ancestors had spent most of their lives in before the oil came bubbling to the surface of their desert and swept their lifestyle away on a tide of money. This wedding tent, however, was bigger than anything any Bedouin ever slept in. It was big enough to hold two thousand guests for a banquet and it was lined with silk the colour of the night sky, sewn with sequins which sparkled like the stars the King remembered seeing as a child when he went riding with his father and grandfather. An army of waiters, with trays lifted high, glided amongst the lavishly laid Western-style tables, and a roar of high spirits filled the air.

Michael could see the old man was happy with the match. The bride, Nabila, was every bit as beautiful as her pictures had promised and seemed suitably shy without the veil that had covered her in public every day since she first turned from a girl into a woman. She blushed prettily whenever any man, including her handsome new husband, talked to her.

'Stop staring at my wife,' Najid whispered in Michael's ear, surprising him.

'I'm sorry,' Michael stammered, caught unawares, 'I wasn't...'

He turned and found Najid laughing at him. 'Come on,' Najid said, 'Let's get out of here.'

'It's your wedding feast,' Michael protested. 'Shouldn't you stay?'

'It'll go on for days. No one will notice.'

He led the way out of the vast tent, past the fires where whole carcasses were being slowly turned over the flames by an army of cooks. They walked round the palace which seemed strangely peaceful compared to the heat and noise of the festivities.

'So, what do you think of my new wife?' Najid asked.

'She's very beautiful. You're a lucky man.'

'I doubt there are many luckier in this world.'

They came to a swimming pool. The lights in the water were on, making it glow and attracting insects which were flitting across the calm surface.

'Shall we swim?' Najid asked.

'I don't have a costume,' Michael protested.

'Michael,' Najid laughed, 'you never used to be so coy.'

Michael watched as his friend stripped off and dived in, the waves trapping some of the slower insects and making others dart up into the darkness. He followed Najid's example. The water felt softer and cooler on his skin than it did during the day. They swam a couple of vigorous lengths and then came to a stop. Treading water, their bodies made liquid shadows in the underwater illuminations.

'Don't you think all this is worth protecting?' Michael asked. 'Especially now you're a married man, maybe soon a father.'

'Protecting from whom?' Najid asked.

'You know from whom,' Michael replied. 'We've had this conversation a thousand times. Let us help you strengthen your army. Let us train them and equip them.'

'I don't like the idea of fighting with anyone about land. We were a Bedouin people. It seems undignified to be squabbling about boundaries.'

'Hopefully you never will have to fight. If you're strong then no one will attack you. You're more likely to have to fight if your enemies can see you're weak.'

'Why don't you come and run the army for me yourself?' Najid asked.

'That's what I've been suggesting.'

'I don't think so. I think you have been suggesting bringing a British force out and stationing them here. I don't want that. I don't want to be a colony for your Queen to visit every few years. You're a good soldier, Michael, take a job with us.'

'What will your father say?'

'He's handed over the running of the army to me. Besides, he likes you. He told me so.'

'Let me think about it,' Michael said. 'I'm flattered to be asked.'

'Say yes, Michael,' Najid said. 'We could have a lot of fun.'

He pushed Michael's head under the water and swam quickly and cleanly away. Michael rose to the surface, choking and spluttering, and set off in pursuit.

Norman took his belongings from the guard and checked through them with a studied slowness. He didn't want it to look as though he were in a hurry to get out. In a way he was and in a way he wasn't. There were one or two screws he wouldn't miss. They were little more than animals, always shouting and screaming. He wouldn't miss them. But life was simple when you were inside. There was plenty of time to relax and think your own thoughts. As soon as he stepped back into the outside world he would have to start making decisions and exerting authority again. And he just knew that his ulcers would start playing up.

There would be benefits of course, the freedom to spend all night in the clubs and restaurants, the occasional fights which he enjoyed, and the little things that money could buy, like pretty girls and the odd beer. He ostentatiously counted the money the guard handed back to him before signing for it. Even after seven years of inflation it was still more cash than a prison guard saw in a month and it was just the wad he had been carrying in his pocket when he was brought in.

He had an urge to run his finger around the inside of his shirt collar. It felt a great deal tighter than he remembered. He resisted the temptation. Little mannerisms could give a man away. You had to be still and quiet if you wanted to impress people. He'd learnt that years ago, and it had always stood him in good stead. If he remained silent and immobile, other people would become nervous and start to make fools of themselves.

The guard busied himself with the next released prisoner and pretended not to notice Norman's presence. He was a man who liked a quiet life. He didn't want to get on the wrong side of Norman Dorset on the day the man was released. Norman had a reputation for settling grudges quickly and effectively.

It felt good to be out of prison uniform again. Norman liked wearing good suits. He'd had this one made in Savile Row just before he was sent down. It was pinstriped and had a bit of a sheen to it. He'd been watching the suits that his visitors had been coming in wearing and he knew that fashions had changed a lot since he'd been away. It was the seventies and men about town were sporting great wide lapels, pinched waists and baggy trousers. Norman thought they looked stupid. He liked the classic look. He didn't believe it would ever die. Who would show respect to anyone wearing flares and a kipper tie?

Carefully packing everything into the holdall he had arrived with seven years earlier, he strolled towards the door as if he didn't have a care in the world. He had told Gerald to arrange for a driver to be waiting outside for him. There were several cars parked up in the street as the doors were opened and he stepped through. Two of them were Jaguars. The black one, with tinted windows, he knew belonged to Gerald because he recognised the number plate. The other one, a gold one, he didn't recognise. The driver in the black car climbed out to greet him. Norman extended a hand. He remembered the man. He was a sound boy – at least he had been a boy when Norman had last seen him.

'Norman!' A woman's voice interrupted the handshake and he realised it came from the gold Jaguar. The woman at the wheel had wound down the window and lifted her dark glasses. He knew he knew her but he couldn't place the face. 'Ruby Rabitz,' she said helpfully. 'I thought you might like a lift.'

Norman turned to the driver. 'Thanks for turning out,' he said. 'She's family. Have a drink before you go back.' He slipped a five-pound note into the man's hand. 'Give Gerald my regards. Tell him I'll be in to see him tonight.'

'Okay, Norman.' The man pocketed the money and climbed back into the car. It was no bother to him that his journey had been wasted. It was good to see Norman Dorset back on the streets again. Things had been dull without him.

As the black Jaguar accelerated away, Norman walked over to Ruby's window. 'I believe we're related now,' he said with no sign of a smile.

'Sorry you missed the wedding,' she said. 'It was a good do. Cost Jack a fortune. Tony Bennett sang.'

'I heard.'

'Want a lift?'

'I'll drive.' Norman indicated she should move over into the passenger seat, and watched as her skirt rode up her thighs. She had amazing legs for her age. Skinny, but well muscled. After seven years Norman felt a sudden urgency in his loins. He climbed into the driver's seat. 'Where to?' he asked.

'Jack's away up north, watching some talent show,' she said. 'There's no one at the house. I gave the staff the day off.'

'Where's the house?'

'Highgate.'

Norman nodded and accelerated away. The car was as smooth as silk. He smiled involuntarily. It was good to be on the outside. He felt her hand running up his thigh and kept his eyes on the road. It was important never to let them know how much you wanted them, but his crutch was betraying him.

The house was just as flash as he had expected it to be. There were polished floors and the living room boasted a grand piano covered in pictures of the family with stars and royalty. In the pink, white and gold bedroom was a wedding picture of Len and Babs.

'How's Len?' he asked.

'He's okay,' Ruby shrugged. 'Jack got him a job with a limo company, driving some of his VIPs around. If he does good Jack says he'll set him up in business. Jack says there's a big future in security and chauffeurs.'

'There was always money to be made in security,' Norman said and tried hard to imagine his little brother attempting to protect anyone.

While Ruby went downstairs to fix them a drink, Norman took his jacket off and placed it neatly on a hanger on the door of a wardrobe. He didn't want to crease it. He did the same with the trousers. By the time Ruby got back to the room with the ice clinking around the champagne bottle, he was naked.

'Jesus,' she said, putting the tray down on the bedside table. 'You are an eager boy!'

Norman pressed her down onto the bed, pushed her skirt up and pulled down her tights. He tore her knickers apart with both hands. She protested at the roughness of his approach and tried to kiss him. Norman turned his head aside and immediately penetrated her. After a few quick thrusts it was all over. He rolled aside and closed his eyes as Ruby sat up irritably to light a cigarette and pour herself a flute of champagne. Had he remained awake long enough he would have realised she was more than a little annoyed, not that he would have cared.

He woke up an hour later to find her with her mouth round his dick. He liked the feeling and pushed her head hard onto him. She coughed and gagged but after a few moments it was all over and she was crawling to the edge of the bed spitting and spluttering.

'Christ,' she spat, 'your techniques could do with a bit of polishing.'

'If you don't like them perhaps you should stick to your husband,' he said, climbing off the bed and walking to the bathroom. Once he had cleaned himself up, he dressed and left the house, borrowing the car and leaving Ruby thinking things over.

'He's offered to make me a colonel,' Michael said, and neither man spoke for a moment, continuing with their eating in silence. Then both broke into laughter at the same time. A few disapproving heads turned in the heavy stillness of Sir Roderick's club dining-room and they controlled themselves.

'I don't suppose that's all he's offered, is it?' Sir Roderick said.

'The financial package would be very good,' Michael admitted.

'I dare say it would make you a rich man within five years. You would never have to work again.'

Michael said nothing. He was quite willing to help Sir Roderick out in any way he could, but he did not feel particularly comfortable discussing his private financial situation.

'Quite right,' Sir Roderick said, taking a sip of claret. 'None of my business. Well, from our point of view it's a good second-best. If we can't have forces on the ground over there, at least we can have one of our own people running his forces for him.'

'I would be working for him primarily,' Michael warned. 'He's already my friend and he would then be my boss. My first loyalty would be to him.'

'Of course.' Sir Roderick spread his hands in a gesture of innocence. 'We would never expect you to do anything that would not be in the Prince's best interests. What I mean is, it's comforting to know he has someone there who'll be giving him the sort of advice we would be giving him were we in a position to do so.'

'Hmm.' Michael went back to his food. Someone on the far side of the room let out a loud cough but otherwise the sound of other members' knives and forks was the only thing breaking the silence.

'We'd like you to take the post, Michael,' Sir Roderick said eventually. 'If you did so, I could safely guarantee that you would be rewarded for your services once your contract was up and you were back in England.'

'Rewarded?' Michael felt a mischievous urge to make Sir Roderick speak plainly for once. 'Rewarded how?'

'Well...' Sir Roderick looked uncomfortable. 'You know.'

Michael raised his eyebrows and waited for the older man to continue.

'The Palace would be very grateful...' Sir Roderick left the suggestion hanging in the air and Michael knew that that was as far as he was likely to be able to push him.

'Ah,' he said with a trace of mockery, 'the Palace.'

'Quite,' Sir Roderick said. 'Shall we have pudding?'

When Norman arrived at the club, Gerald was waiting for him, and another bottle of champagne was opened. Norman ignored this one too and asked the barman to draw him a pint. He didn't want to aggravate his ulcers before he had to.

'You have no idea how good it is to see you back here,' Gerald gushed. He was wearing a purple suit with matching tie and shirt – Norman had trouble keeping his eyes off it and Gerald was visibly uncomfortable under his gaze. 'We're going to have to get you some new togs, Norman,' he said. 'There've been a lot of changes since you went away.'

'So I see,' Norman said, sipping on the beer and looking around at the scantily clad girls walking amongst the fish ponds and fountains. Two go-go dancers were gyrating in a cage hanging from the ceiling. 'Do the punters like all this, then?'

'They love it, especially the businessmen. Hefner has changed everything in London with the Bunny Club.'

'I heard about that,' Norman nodded.

'Brilliant concept,' Gerald said, putting his arm around the waist of a waitress as she bent down to replenish his bowl of peanuts, his eyes on her firm young breasts. 'But I think we can take it a stage further.'

'Right.' Norman was beginning to lose interest. Gerald could turn this spiel on all he liked for the backers, but it didn't cut any ice with Norman. As long as he had somewhere to sit when he felt like it, eat when he was hungry, and enjoy a bit of company, he didn't care what the 'concept' was behind it. Norman just liked a peaceful life. He liked to be left alone.

'Have you noticed much else changed?' Gerald asked him.

'Yeah,' Norman nodded. 'A lot. Thought I might stroll over to Soho later and go round a few clubs; see what's happening. Want to come?'

Gerald knew it wasn't a genuine invitation. Norman liked to move about London on his own. He didn't want to be having to watch Gerald's back as well as his own. Anyway, he knew he was an embarrassment in the sort of places Norman liked to go, with his purple suits and permed hair. Norman had only made the offer because he knew Gerald wouldn't take it up. Gerald never liked to be away from the business for long. He wasn't one for just hanging out places, he always had to be making money.

'Can you let me have some cash?' Norman asked.

'Sure.' Gerald went to the till at the bar and returned with a wad of notes which Norman slipped into his pocket without a word.

'See you later,' he said and walked out.

He drove Ruby's car down Baker Street and across Oxford Street. The traffic jams were as bad as he remembered. Eventually he lost his patience, turned into a side street and abandoned the car on a pavement. It was growing dark and the neon lights of Soho were bright against the gloom of the old buildings. Norman felt a warm glow of familiarity as he made his way through the traffic-congested streets and alleys and dived down a staircase to a basement club.

The young man on the door obviously didn't know who Norman was, and made as if to stop him and ask for an entry fee. Norman pretended not to hear and walked straight in. Things had changed inside. He remembered a comfortable, dingy room full of gambling tables, with a few hostesses at the bar waiting to talk punters into buying them drinks.

Someone had given the place a make-over. There was a lot of glitter everywhere and a girl in nothing but a G-string was winding herself around a pole in the middle of a cramped stage. Was every club in London being turned into a strip joint, he wondered.

The man from the door had come in behind him and signalled to the barman to help him evict this potential troublemaker. The barman, also young, came out from behind the bar.

'I'm afraid it's members only, sir,' the bouncer said. 'You could become a member if you like.'

Norman turned and looked at him. His face had no expression at all. It just rested on his neck like granite, with two pale eyes staring out.

'I am a member,' he said.

'We've never seen you here, mate,' the barman said. He was more confident than his colleague and looked as if he might be able to handle himself. Norman decided he should start with him. It was disappointingly easy. As Norman's mighty fist slammed into his face, blood spurted from the young man's nose and lip. A small piece of tooth flew across the room. The man reeled backwards, clutching his face and Norman wiped the blood off his suit. The doorman backed away.

'Norman Dorset,' a woman's voice cut in over the music. 'Nice to have you back.'

'Oh fuck,' muttered the barman through broken teeth.

'Hello, Doris,' Norman said as the woman appeared out of the shadows. He remembered her as being young. She used to have a body like the one cavorting on the stage but time had been unkind to her. 'You managing the place now then?'

'I am, Norman. Too old for all that now,' she said, gesturing at the girl who was still making love to the pole, apparently oblivious to the action in her audience.

'What's all this, then?' Norman asked. 'Are we a strip joint now?'

'We have to move with the times, Norman. It's what the punters want. Do you want a drink?'

As the barman had disappeared out the back to try to repair his damaged face, Doris fetched Norman a beer herself.

'I don't like it, Doris,' he said after a while. 'It's not the way a club should be.'

'The twins changed everything around here,' she said.

'I've got nothing against the twins,' Norman said. 'They've done me a few favours over the years. But they're not here any more. So now we can go back to doing things the way they should be done.'

'Times have changed, Norman,' she repeated. 'I don't like it any more than you. People want entertainment.' She gestured at the handful of men sitting around the tables staring at the girl on the stage.

'I'm telling you,' he looked at her coldly. 'Things are going to change.'

'You're the boss, Norman,' she said. 'Whatever you want to happen will happen. But the partners may not like it.'

'I'll talk to the partners,' Norman growled.

At every club he went to that night the story was the same. The sex industry had arrived and pushed out the gamblers. Contacts told him that the good games had moved to other places at more private addresses. Later that night he went to Paddington, to a new club that someone had told him about, and won a few pounds. For a moment it felt like the good old days, but not for long. He left the place in the small hours of the morning feeling despondent and lost. Life had moved on and he was going to have to think again about finding himself a place in it.

At three in the morning he drove the Jaguar back to Highgate and let himself into the house with the front-door key on the keyring. The house was silent. He got halfway up the stairs when the alarm went off, making his heart miss a beat. He ran up to the bedroom, looking for Ruby. The last thing he wanted was to have the police coming round. She looked relieved to see that the intruder was only Norman as she fumbled to pull her dressing gown around her. She looked rough without any make-up. He looked away.

'How do you turn the fucking thing off?' he asked her.

'Jesus Christ,' she muttered. 'You could have rung to say you were coming back.'

'We're not fucking married,' he snapped, following her back downstairs to the control box. She punched some buttons and the sirens fell silent. The ring of the phone made them both jump.

'That'll be the police to check I'm okay,' she said.

As she picked up the phone and assured them the alarm had been triggered by accident, Norman made his way into the kitchen in search of a beer.

'Everything's different,' he said when she came in. 'It's not the same.'

'What do you expect?' she said. 'The whole world can't wait for you to come out. There are different clubs now. You have to adapt.'

'It's all strippers.'

'People want entertainment,' she said, just as Doris had done. 'Jack has an interest in some of the new places coming up. He's got one that's packing them in down in Streatham. People want to see the famous faces, Shirley Bassey, Tom Jones, Engelbert Humperdinck. It's them that bring in the punters these days. And it's bigger money than it ever used to be. People have more to spend than in the old days. You don't have to exist by skimming a few card games and taking protection money out of the till, you can make real money now in the club game. You ask your friend, Gerald. He's doing all the right things.'

'You know Gerald?' Norman had forgotten that connection.

'We know the family.'

Norman went through into the living-room and studied the photographs on the piano more carefully. Maybe she was right. Maybe this was the way forward. Maybe he should go into show business.

'What's the name of this club of Jack's in Streatham?'

'The Country Club.'

'In Streatham? Hardly my idea of the countryside.'

'They started out playing country music, then they went more middle of the road, but they kept the name because everyone knew it. Why?'

'Just curious.'

Norman turned the lights out and screwed Ruby once more for good measure on the furry carpet.

Norman could see what Kathy meant. The marital home looked shabby as he drew up there the following afternoon. The windows needed repainting and the garden was overgrown. It needed a man's touch. He rang the doorbell and Teresa answered it. She was still in her school uniform.

'Hello darling,' he said, wanting to bend down and hug her but not knowing how to do it. 'It's Daddy.'

'Hello, Norman,' Kathy said, coming out of the kitchen. 'I heard you were out. What took you so long?'

'I had business to attend to.' He hovered on the doorstep, uncomfortable beneath the piercing gaze of his daughter.

'Of course.' Kathy gave a wry smile, glancing at the gold Jaguar parked in the road. 'Want a cup of tea?'

'Ta.'

He followed her through to the kitchen where Rachel and Vicky were eating fish fingers and baked beans. They kept eating, their eyes fixed on their father as he leant uncomfortably against one of the work surfaces. Kathy didn't suggest he sat down. It didn't feel like being at home.

'I need to get something going so I can get you some money to do this place up.'

'That would be nice,' Kathy said, busying herself with the kettle.

'It shouldn't take long. I've got a few ideas, made a few enquiries.'

'Okay,' Kathy nodded, indicating that she didn't want to hear any more details in front of the children. 'Nice car,' she said, gesturing at the Jaguar outside the window.

'Borrowed it from a friend. He wants it back now. I'll have to get myself sorted out with something else.'

Norman drank the tea and felt his ulcers stirring for the first time in seven years.

'Nice of you to drop by,' Kathy said sarcastically. 'How long have you been out?'

Norman ignored the jibe. 'There have been a lot of changes up West. I'm going to have to re-establish myself. It'll take a bit of time. You may not be seeing too much of me for the next few months.'

'That'll make a change,' Kathy muttered and Norman wondered if there was any chance he could persuade her to go to bed with him quickly before he went. Feeling the eyes of his daughters on him he decided that was unlikely. He felt a twinge of regret and his ulcers stirred again.

Major Cox was riding alongside the Sultan of Domai as they trotted at a steady pace out of the palace and towards the desert. The keeper of the royal birds was following behind with his assistant and two of the King's finest hunting hawks. Major Cox was looking forward to the day. Being in charge of the Sultan's security was not an arduous job and he felt himself to be extremely well rewarded. He earned twice the salary he had finished on in the British army and there were all the perks of travelling the world with one of its richest men. When the King stayed in a five-star hotel, Major Cox was never far away. He ate in the same restaurants and attended the same functions.

One of the reasons he was pleased to be out of the palace for a few hours was Michael Beckett. Major Cox greatly resented the fact that the younger man had been made into a colonel and virtually put in charge of Domai's army. It wasn't that Cox had expected a job like that himself – he knew his limitations all too clearly and this was why he had left the British army when he had, knowing that he was unlikely to be promoted any further. What he resented was that Beckett had been given overall responsibility for the security of the Royal Family. That made Beckett into Cox's boss and the older man did not like it one bit.

Today, however, he could forget about all that. It would be like the old days, just him and the Sultan out for a day's hunting. If there was one thing Cox was confident about, it was his horsemanship, and the King's stables boasted the finest collection of Arab horses in the world. He could feel the power of the bay he was riding that day – one of his favourites – as she tried to enter into a gallop. He liked the feeling of holding her back, reserving her power for later. He knew the King would want to race after they had finished with the birds and before they returned to the palace.

All the horses reared up in fright as the small helicopter rose from the other side of a sand dune like a giant, angry insect, buzzing up as if from nowhere to pester them. Cox found himself facing away from the King as his bay reared and pirouetted, and he fought to bring her back down to earth.

In the few seconds it took him to regain control of his mount, the helicopter was almost upon them. He could see the Sultan was also struggling to bring his horse under control, and the hawks were flapping their wings angrily as their handlers' horses gyrated around in the sand. At the same moment Cox saw that one of the men in the helicopter was taking aim with a rifle.

With the sheer force of his horsemanship, the Major pushed the bay forward into a gallop, placing himself between the King and the helicopter. He drew his own gun from inside his robe and fired a wild shot towards the cabin of the little aircraft. But the helicopter kept coming and he heard a series of retorts from the rifle. He fired off another shot, and saw the rifle falling from the man's hands at the same time as he realised there was a terrible pain in his own right shoulder.

The pilot of the helicopter, unable now to continue his mission, pulled the craft into a steep climb and disappeared back across the desert as quickly as he had appeared. Confused by the messages coming from the man on her back, who was now in considerable pain, the bay reared again and threw the Major to the ground. He was still conscious, and was aware of the giant animal's body flailing above him. As her front legs came down, one of the hooves landed hard on the shoulder that held the bullet. The pain swept over him and he succumbed to unconsciousness.

CHAPTER FOUR

1974

Upton Park was unrecognisable to Sir Roderick as he made his way up the winding gravel drive. There were workmen and lorries everywhere. He drew his car up and sat for a moment, staring at the gigantic pink stone edifice and trying to picture how it had looked in his childhood.

If he stood with his back to the house he could just make out some familiar bits of scenery in the distance, but close up, the bulldozers and utilities workers had ripped up the stately old gardens beyond recognition. It was no more than a muddy quarry. He went to the boot of his car and changed his polished black shoes for a pair of green wellingtons, pulling on a waterproof jacket to try to protect his suit a little from the mud.

'Sir Roderick,' a voice called out from behind him, and he turned to see Michael Beckett striding towards him with his hand outstretched.

'Colonel,' Sir Roderick responded, returning the firm handshake. 'This all looks a little chaotic.'

'There's method in it,' Michael laughed. 'Let me show you around.'

'This place holds childhood memories for me, you know,' Sir Roderick said as he slammed the car boot shut and followed the younger man.

'Is that right?'

'A friend of mine from school used to live here. I often came for weekends and holidays when I didn't go home to my own parents. They were abroad a lot – diplomatic service.'

'Ah, well you'll see a lot of changes.'

'I can see that already.'

'It was pretty run down. I think the last owners had run out of money at least twenty years before they finally sold up. Nothing much had been done to it. I should think it still had the same wiring as when you were here.'

'It was pretty shabby even then,' Sir Roderick admitted as they stepped over a trench of pipes and wires. 'What's all this?'

'Security,' Michael explained. 'Did you see the gatehouse as you came in?'

'I saw it, but there was no one there.'

'Well, we have no one to protect yet. It'll be manned permanently with two men twenty-four hours a day. They'll have surveillance cameras all around the perimeter fences and around the house and stables. We're enclosing an area of ten acres with high security.'

'How many acres are there in all on the estate?'

'A couple of thousand, mostly tenanted farms. A couple of small villages.'

'We're very anxious that nothing should befall this family while they're living on our soil,' Sir Roderick said, as they made their way past a half-finished swimming pool which was being linked up to a waterfall and fountain. 'Is this gold leaf?' he asked, gesturing to the decorations which were being applied to the bottom of the pool.

'I believe so.'

'Good God.'

'Quite.'

'So, who'll be in charge of security when you aren't here?'

'A man called John Cox,' Michael said. 'I'll introduce you. He's been with the family a long time. He lost an arm protecting the King from that attack in the desert a couple of years ago.'

'Ah, the gallant Major. I read the reports. He stopped a bullet and then his horse smashed his arm to pieces.'

'That's the one. He has jurisdiction over the grounds but the house will be protected by a separate security company. We haven't employed them yet. Once the family's in residence we'll start thinking about that.'

'So when will it all be finished?'

'About another six months. The stables are already up and running. Cox lives up there. His other job is looking after the horses. The King wanted them to have a home as quickly as possible, to settle them. He has some very expensive bloodstock. I'll take you over there. It's bloody impressive.'

They walked across a bare expanse of mud. Piles of rolled turf stood at one side waiting to be laid out into immaculate lawns. The stable complex was shielded behind a line of poplars which shimmered silver and green in the breeze. Michael led the way in.

It certainly smelled like a stable but it looked more like a hotel as they made their way down the corridor past the stalls, each one containing its own heating and air-conditioning system. The feed was laid out in a room more like a giant commercial kitchen than a stable – all stainless steel and spotlights.

At the end of the corridor they came through some double swing-doors into an indoor sand school. Michael led the way up a sweeping staircase to a balcony which ran all the way around the arena, with rows of comfortable seats for spectators.

A man was riding a pale grey horse around the ring below them, so deep in concentration that he appeared not to have noticed their entrance. The horse was the most beautiful creature Sir Roderick had ever seen. The rider was in complete control, despite the obvious high spirits of his mount, and despite the fact that he was doing it all one-handed. His immaculately pressed, but empty, right sleeve was pinned up neatly out of the way.

After a few minutes Major Cox looked up and saw them watching. Michael raised his hand in a greeting. The Major continued with the exercise he was doing as if he had not seen them and then drew the horse to a halt, petting him with extravagant praise, making it obvious he was in no hurry to come over.

Michael led Sir Roderick back down the stairs to wait for the rider to come out of the ring.

'John,' Michael said as he approached, aware that the Major preferred to be addressed by his title, but would never say as much to a senior officer. 'This is Sir Roderick Salisbury from the Foreign Office. He's just checking that we're doing a good job of the security.'

'You won't find anything to complain of here, sir,' Cox said, dismounting smartly and shaking Sir Roderick's left hand. 'This place is going to be the most secure house in England. Better than Buckingham Palace. No expense spared.'

'I can see that,' Sir Roderick replied, looking around at the palatial stables.

'His Majesty is very fond of his horses,' Cox said. 'Nothing is too good for them.'

His mount gave an arrogant snort, as if to confirm the fact, and the Major patted it affectionately on the neck. It was obvious he preferred the company of the animal to that of the two men.

'We heard about what you did for the King,' Sir Roderick said, gesturing towards the missing arm. 'It was a brave act.'

'It was my job, sir,' Cox replied. 'Couldn't have done anything else in the circumstances.'

'Quite.' Sir Roderick gave a thin smile. 'Well, don't let us keep you. I'm sure we'll meet again once the house is finished.'

'Yes sir,' Cox said, and led his horse away without a backward glance.

'Bit of a prickly character,' Sir Roderick said once he was out of earshot.

'Thinks I was brought in over his head. Loyalty can't be questioned though. He thinks he's been farmed out here because of the arm, which is partly true. He's no good to His Majesty as a personal bodyguard with his shooting arm gone.'

'No, quite.'

'Would you like to see inside the house?'

The two men strolled back across the gardens to the house and Michael led the way from room to room, pointing out the electronic shutters, the cameras and detector systems. In every room there were people at work laying floors, installing kitchens and bathrooms, painting or tinkering with electrical wires and water pipes.

'These are going to be the private quarters,' he explained as they climbed the grand staircase. 'At night, or in the case of an attack, they can be sealed off from the rest of the house. The staff will have access from the ground floor to their quarters at the top of the house by other staircases.'

'Do they expect attacks?' Sir Roderick asked.

'The Prince knows there is always a danger,' Michael said. 'I don't know what the King believes.'

'I saw His Majesty the other day,' Sir Roderick said. 'He seems to fear nothing. I don't think he really grasps the delicacy of his position in the world. He's a good man but I don't think he fully understands that not everyone feels as well-disposed towards him as he is towards them.'

'I don't know how much he intends to use this house himself,' Michael said. 'I suspect it's more for the Prince and for the women.'

'I think you may be right. His Majesty has always been very fond of Park Lane.'

'This is the guardroom.' Michael threw open the door to a room where every wall was a mass of cables waiting to be plastered over. 'All the telephones and in-house cameras will be routed through here. There is direct contact with the guardhouse at the gate. The main safe for the house will be built in under the floor.' He gestured to a gaping hole in the boards.

'I remember these rooms,' Sir Roderick said, wistfully. 'They were all part of the kitchens. I think this was the dairy.'

'Game larder, I think you'll find,' Michael corrected him.

'Game larder? Is that right?' He thought for a moment. 'Yes, I think I can remember being brought in here after a shoot one day and seeing rows and rows of pheasants hanging from the ceiling.'

For a moment Sir Roderick appeared to be lost in his memories, but he quickly snapped back to the present day. 'It all looks very efficient, Michael. I'm sure they're in good hands. I'd like to have a longer talk with you some time before you fly back to Domai. There are some manufacturers who are keen to meet you, a new sort of jet fighter which I think you'll be interested in, particularly good in desert conditions. They'd like you to come for lunch one day.'

'Of course,' Michael smiled. He always liked these lunches since they usually ended up with him earning another handsome commission. 'Call my secretary.'

No one at The Country Club in Streatham could quite remember how Norman Dorset had become such an accepted part of the establishment. He had just arrived one night, a couple of years earlier, giving everyone the impression that he was a representative of Jack Rabitz, although he had never actually said as much. No one felt, when looking into Norman's eyes, that he was a man who would welcome too many questions. Rabitz himself, on the few occasions he did come to the club, assumed Norman had been hired by the on-site management and never queried the decision. There was no reason to. Jack was not interested in the mundane, day-to-day details of the running of the club. For him it was a useful venue, somewhere where he could showcase new acts and where he could bring friends and business contacts for a good night out. If it also turned in a profit at the end of the year, then so much the better. So far The Country Club had never failed to turn in a healthy profit.

Whenever Jack was there it was always with a crowd of people he wanted to impress. There would be a big table set up close to the stage and all the attention of the staff would be focused on giving Mr Rabitz whatever he wanted. So why would he have any reason to question the apparently discreet presence of a man who appeared to be more than in control of the security of the place? Jack never noticed the discomfort of his wife, Ruby, when Norman was around, he was too busy ordering more champagne.

After a few weeks of dropping in at the club each evening, Norman had found a way to prove himself indispensable. Danny La Rue, at the time the undisputed Queen of the British drag scene, had been booked to appear as the after-dinner cabaret. A table close to the stage had been reserved for a stag party. When the revellers arrived, they made it clear they thought it was a strip club. The manager, Sidney Rose, politely informed them that Mr La Rue was the main act and that there were no strippers involved. They seemed to take the news in their stride, until the drink began to exert its influence.

'We've got trouble brewing,' Sidney said, as he watched the mood of the table developing from backstage.

'I can see,' Norman said, his narrowed eyes focussing on the young men who were shouting queer jokes at the star and laughing uproariously at their own wit.

'Do you think Danny will be able to deal with them?'

'I've seen him work before,' Norman said. 'He's pretty good with hecklers, but these ones seem a bit far gone. Maybe they need a little slap to sober them up.'

Sidney glanced across at the other man and said nothing. Norman seemed to be talking more to himself than anyone else. He continued to stare at the table, working out which ones were the ringleaders. The mood of the rest of the audience of four hundred or so diners was rising against the troublemakers. They wanted to at least be able to hear what Danny was saying, and they were embarrassed by the crudity of the comments flying up at him.

Sidney was about to say something else when he realised Norman had gone and a few seconds later he saw his dinner-jacketed form slipping discreetly across the back of the auditorium, skirting round to the troublesome table. Sidney watched as Norman bent down and whispered something in the ear of one of the men. The man put the flat of his hand into Norman's face and arrogantly pushed him away, hurling more abuse at the stage as he did so. None of the other members of the party seemed to notice as Norman's hands closed around the man's neck and he was lifted out of his chair in one clean movement. They both vanished from sight and a few moments later Norman reappeared beside the chair of another member of the party who was so absorbed in his own catcalls he hadn't noticed the sudden flailing departure of his friend. Sidney watched in open-mouthed amazement.

Once again Norman bent down and whispered, again he was brushed off, and once more the man disappeared from sight without anyone else in the audience being disturbed. The rest of the party, although they hadn't seen their leaders disappearing, were aware that some of the steam was going out of their heckling performance. Looking around, they noticed the two empty chairs and assumed their friends had gone out to the Gents. One of them tried another shout, and Norman was suddenly beside him, bent low and murmuring politely. The man nodded and apologised. The spirit of the table had been broken and the act on stage was able to progress undisturbed.

Sidney was amazed. In all his years in the business, and there had been many, he had never seen an unruly table quietened with such deadly effectiveness. He only hoped this wasn't going to lead to the club being landed with a writ for physical assault. As Danny La Rue burst into song, swishing from side to side of the stage, and as the audience waved and sang along jubilantly, Sidney walked round to the reception area to see if he could soothe any ruffled feathers. The two men from the table were both sitting on chairs, looking remarkably docile, both with identical bruises rising on their foreheads, as if they had had their heads banged together like naughty schoolboys. Norman appeared behind them.

'Ah,' Norman said with the utmost politeness. 'This is Mr Rose, our manager. Mr Rose, these two gentlemen are a little the worse for wear and have decided to sit the rest of the show out here, nearer to the fresh air.'

'Fine,' Sidney nodded his approval. 'Please let the staff know if you would like a glass of water or an aspirin.'

The two men nodded mournfully and Sidney gestured for Norman to follow him into the office.

'How did you manage to make them so quiet all of a sudden?' he asked.

'They were carrying these.' Norman dropped two small foil-wrapped packages onto the table. 'Nothing like the offer of an introduction to the drugs squad to make some people co-operative.'

'So you didn't have to smack them too hard?' Sidney asked, relieved.

'Not at all.' Norman sank into a chair and rolled himself a cigarette. Neither man was planning to mention the bruises.

'I'll let you into a secret, Sidney,' Norman said. 'If you can convince someone that you are quite willing to give them a smack, you almost never have to actually do it.'

'No,' Sidney nodded thoughtfully as he took in the information. 'I suppose you're right.'

He sat down on the other side of the desk and took out a large cigar which he lit with exaggerated care. Up till that moment he had been uneasy with Norman's presence in the club, believing him to be some sort of plant by the owners. There were things that went on behind the scenes which he wouldn't necessarily have wanted Jack Rabitz and the other owners to know about. He would be a lot more comfortable if he felt that Norman's first loyalty was towards him rather than the owners. Being a South London man himself, he had no idea who Norman Dorset was, but he was beginning to get the idea that he might be someone to be reckoned with, more than just a management stooge.

'You know, Norman,' he said, puffing contentedly on the cigar. 'We really ought to do something about formalising your arrangement with the club in some way, ensure that you are being suitably recompensed for your contribution to the management process.'

'That would be very generous of you, Sidney,' Norman said, as his loosely packed cigarette crackled hot and dangerous. He watched as Sidney relaxed in front of him and knew that the man's days were numbered.

The staff at Claridge's were in a panic. It seemed the two princesses were at war and the manager had no idea which side he should be taking. Nothing in his training had ever taught him who should have precedence when there was a dispute between a future queen and her sister-in-law, a woman who had been a good customer for several years. He took half-a-dozen deep breaths as he made his way up in the lift. Nothing in his calm, immaculate demeanour would have given away the fact that his heart was pounding uncomfortably in his chest. He had heard tales of Princess Jarmina's unpredictable temper and he did not like the idea that he might be about to be the next on the receiving end of it. So far he was proud of the hotel's record in not upsetting anyone from the royal family. Four years earlier, when he had just joined the hotel, there had been a potential incident when the Princess, on her first visit to London, had slipped out of the hotel unescorted. After she had returned, the staff were told that on no account were they to allow such a thing to happen again. The manager had no idea how he would be able to stop the Princess doing whatever she wanted, but fortunately she had never put him in such a position again, always behaving with the perfect decorum suitable for one of her position.

This new crisis had started when Princess Nabila, the wife of the future King of Domai, had requested the suite which Princess Jarmina and her mother traditionally stayed in. There had seemed to be no problem until Princess Jarmina made it known, a few days later, that she wanted her usual suite and would be arriving in London at the same time as her sister-in-law, albeit on a different flight. Her mother would not be accompanying her on this particular trip. It seemed to the manager almost as if Jarmina had discovered that Nabila had booked the suite and had decided, out of sheer bloody-mindedness, to evict her from it.

Both sides had been informed by the hotel of the clash of interests and highly suitable alternatives had been suggested. Neither had responded to the suggestions. They had arrived at the hotel within a few hours of each another, both adamant that they were going to be the one to occupy the coveted set of rooms. Both had insisted on being taken up and both were now *in situ*: Jarmina in the main bedroom, with her ladies-in-waiting insisting that she was asleep after her arduous journey; and Nabila in the sitting-room, insisting that her sister-in-law be removed so that she too might rest. Suggestions that one or other of them might occupy one of the secondary bedrooms in the suite had been met with furious indignation by all the women in both parties. It would be an unthinkable insult for either of them to have to put up with a secondary room, and anyway, they both had to have their own attendants close at hand should they need anything, and the attendants therefore needed the other bedrooms.

In fact, Jarmina was far from being asleep behind the locked bedroom door. She was instead on the phone to her mother, who was still in the Austrian spa hotel which Jarmina had just vacated, and was jabbering angrily about the high-handed way in which her sister-in-law was treating her.

'Of course to Najid she is nothing but a demur little kitten,' Jarmina ranted. 'He does not see the way she treats us, as if she was already our Queen and we were nothing at all. He cannot believe that we are telling the truth when we describe the way she tries to rule over us.'

'Men!' The Queen heaved a deep sigh of despair. 'So innocent. Your father is just the same, always thinking the best of everyone, never believing that just because a woman is young and pretty she can't be a scheming monster.'

'Exactly,' Jarmina agreed, although she felt a murmur of discomfort at hearing her mother criticise her beloved father. It was, after all, his constant good humour and tolerance of all around him that had allowed her to win far more freedom than most women in other royal families in the Middle East. She was well aware of that, and also aware that her mother had probably behaved as badly towards him over the years as Nabila was now behaving towards her.

'She must not be allowed to take advantage of Najid's good nature,' she insisted.

She would have liked to have said 'weakness' but knew that would have jarred on her mother's ear. Nothing her brother did could ever be criticised to their mother. As far as she was concerned, Najid was perfect. She might occasionally offer a little gentle criticism herself, partly by way of motherly guidance, but she would never tolerate others, even Jarmina, openly putting him down. Najid was her son and the future King, and as such, she would not tolerate direct personal attacks on him.

There was a polite knocking at the bedroom door. Jarmina dropped the receiver on the bed and went to open it, expecting to see one of Nabila's companions bearing a message of some sort. She was slightly disappointed to find herself confronted with the charming smile of the hotel manager. Jarmina was looking forward to a fight and for that she needed an equal.

'Your Highness,' the manager beamed, 'I am so sorry to disturb your rest. Her Highness the Princess Nabila has now arrived at the hotel...'

'Oh yes?' Jarmina feigned a mild surprise. 'How nice.'

'We still don't seem to have resolved the problem of which suites both your royal highnesses would like to occupy.'

'Oh, I'm quite happy here,' Jarmina smiled sweetly. 'I'm sure you can find something suitable for Princess Nabila. So, if you will excuse me, I need to rest.'

She shooed him away with her hand and closed the door smartly, returning to the bed and the telephone line to her mother. The manager took a second to compose himself and returned to the sitting-room.

'I wonder, your Highness, if we could show you another suite comparable to this,' he purred. 'So that we can make you comfortable as quickly as possible.'

'No,' one of the women beside the Princess spoke for her. 'Her Highness would like to stay here. Perhaps you could arrange for tea to be served for us while we wait for Princess Jarmina to vacate the bedroom.'

'Certainly,' the manager bowed his head, unable to see any way forward without breaching some invisible law of etiquette – like getting the Princess by the scruff of the neck and shaking some sense into her. He withdrew, issuing instructions for waiters and menus to go in.

'Get the Domai Ambassador on the phone,' he snapped as soon as he was back in his office. 'This is their problem. I'm a hotelier, not a diplomat.'

Najid was in his suite at the Dorchester when the call came through from the Ambassador. He was aware that his wife was in London, but he had other things on his mind at that moment. There was a young man waiting in his bed who had travelled as part of the royal party and with whom the Prince was eager to become better acquainted. He was not in the mood to have to go out and settle a dispute between two women. Women were beginning to bore Najid. The entourage which travelled everywhere with his mother and sister had always proved to be the perfect way to obtain sexual relief whenever he needed it. But, over the years, he had come to find that the passivity of the women, and their easy acquiescence to anything he demanded, had become monotonous. They reminded him too much of his wife who would turn her beautiful face away from him when he was on top of her, lying with her hands resting either side of her head on the pillow, waiting for him to finish. The more muscular delights of the young men who travelled in his own entourage now proved a more tempting diversion to the tedium of his days. They also provided the added advantage of not causing foolish scenes over things like hotel suites.

The Ambassador, however, pointed out that the longer the situation between the princesses was allowed to go on, the higher the chances of someone in the British media finding out and informing the wider world of their childish behaviour. This would simply confirm the great British public's prejudices about the spoilt ways of the rich Arabs they saw increasingly cluttering the streets of London.

'It will look, your Highness, as if you are unable to control the women in your own family,' he said, in the most respectful voice he could muster.

Najid took a deep breath. He was aware he was seen by many to be a weak man, and that it was necessary for him to reverse that impression in the interests of his country. 'Very well,' he said, realising he was going to have to postpone the pleasures awaiting him in the bed for a little longer. 'Tell them to have a car ready downstairs.'

The car, with diplomatic plates, was waiting outside the hotel by the time the Prince reached the front door and a few minutes later he was striding through the foyer at Claridge's, heading up towards the suite with the manager attempting to keep up whilst remaining a respectful few paces behind.

'Please,' the Prince instructed the room in general as he entered, 'ask Jarmina to come out for a moment.'

He stood, tight-lipped and silent, as his wife sat with her eyes to the floor, waiting for his sister to emerge. Jarmina came into the room yawning and giving an unconvincing performance of someone who had been roused from a deep sleep.

'Can both of you stay in this suite together?' the Prince asked.

Both women protested at once that the very idea was monstrous.

'Then!' He held up his hand for silence. 'One of you will have to move to another suite. Which is it to be?'

Both women started to jabber at him again. He looked from one to the other, his face impassive compared to their anger. When he looked at his sister he remembered the many rows they had had throughout their childhood – how hard he had tried to educate her in the natural laws of male supremacy and how constantly she had humiliated him and mocked him, sometimes in front of his friends and assistants. He knew that many people believed she would make a better king than he would. But there was nothing he could do about that, unless he was willing to have her removed from the scene permanently, and he was too fond of her to countenance anything like that at present. There was always a chance, of course, that they would manage to find someone to marry her and take her off his hands.

His young wife, on the other hand, had been brought up in a stricter atmosphere, never indulged by her father and brothers in the way Jarmina had been. She might bore him but she was hardly a challenge to his authority. This little display was more like a child testing its strength against the adults of the family. There was still every chance he could retain the upper hand in this relationship, whereas there was little chance he would ever be able to make Jarmina do anything against her will. His father's indulgence of her had set the pattern of a lifetime.

He beckoned the manager close to him. 'Is there another suite suitable for my wife and her attendants?' he asked, loudly enough for all the women in the room to hear.

'Yes, your Highness,' the manager replied. 'We could move them there immediately.'

'Then please do so.' The Prince saw his wife open her mouth to protest anew. 'Indulge me, my dear wife,' he said in a voice devoid of affection. 'My family have been using this suite for many years, my sister feels comfortable here. I am sure the hotel will be able to make you equally comfortable elsewhere. If you will excuse me I have a number of important matters of state to see to.'

As he left the room he saw the looks the two women exchanged and knew that this was by no means the end of the war. He wondered if he had made the right choice. Then he remembered the 'appointment' which was awaiting him at the Dorchester and put his family irritations to the back of his mind.

CHAPTER FIVE

'Take a look at this, Len,' Jack Rabitz said, dropping a folder of papers into his son-in-law's lap. The two of them were relaxing at Jack's golf club. They had completed a round with some of Jack's best clients and were now alone in the clubhouse, wondering about staying to eat in the restaurant. The others had gone home for their evening meals.

'What is it?' Len asked. He liked the time he spent with his father-in-law. The older man always treated him as an equal, something Len knew he never would be, but he respected Jack for pretending. He knew it must have been disappointing for Jack and Ruby that their daughter hadn't married someone who would add to the family fortunes, either financially or with business opportunities. But Jack never seemed to hold a grudge against Len personally.

'It's a company a friend of mine owns,' Jack said, taking a sip of lager and leaning back in the armchair. 'He's getting on a bit now and fancies spending more time out on the golf course. He's putting it up for sale. He gave me the prospectus. Thought I might be interested.'

'Are you?' Len asked, flicking open the folder and glancing at the pages inside.

'I might be,' Jack said. 'If I can find the right partner.'

'What sort of partner do you need?'

'I would need an active partner, someone who could take a day-to-day interest in the running of the business. Someone I could trust.'

'So, it's a limo company, then?' Len said, trying to make sense of the words in front of him without fully concentrating on reading the dense type.

'That's part of it. They do cars and drivers, but they also do a bit of security for their clients as well. Someone visiting England for a few weeks needs picking up from the airport and driving around and wants a bit of looking after at the same time – that sort of thing. Could be an American singer or film star needing looking after and protecting from the fans, or some visiting foreign dignitary. You know the sort of thing.'

'Do the sums add up?' Len asked, gazing blankly at the columns of figures.

'Yeah, I think so. I've had the accountants look at them. I've known the company for years, used them a lot for some of my own clients. I think it's a sound business. Interested?'

'Interested in what?'

'In being my active partner?'

'Me?' Len was startled. 'I haven't got any money, Jack. You know that.'

'You don't need to have. I'll put up the money; you do the work. You've already got some experience in the business. What do you think?'

'If you think the business is sound, that's good enough for me.' Len couldn't stop himself from grinning. He was flattered that Jack wanted to go into business with him, even though he knew it was only because of Babs.

'Good man,' Jack patted his son-in-law approvingly on the knee. 'You won't regret it. There's a lot of scope for a young man to develop a company like this. I'll start the ball rolling and introduce you to a few of the people involved.'

Sidney Rose lived a quiet life when he was away from the club. He lived, with his wife and handicapped adult daughter, in a suburban villa in Sheen. He was always careful to ensure that no one at work knew his address. He wanted to keep his private life and his working life completely separate. His daughter had a wasting disease which meant that each year she lived she became a greater burden on her mother. Sidney felt it was his responsibility to shelter them both from the harsher realities of life, to keep all the stress of his working life off the shoulders of his wife, so that she could concentrate on the daily struggle for survival that child-rearing had become.

He had been very successful at providing a tranquil and safe home, and so was not on his guard in the early hours of that Sunday morning when he was returning from work. He had parked the car in the drive, as usual, and was making his way across the grass in order to avoid making a noise on the gravel and waking them up. He noticed that the light in the porch, which his wife always left on for him to see where to put his key, had gone out. He made a mental note to change the bulb when he got up. He was looking forward to a leisurely day at home with the family.

As he fumbled for his keys he sensed a movement in the shrubbery behind him and turned to see what it was. He didn't hear the single shot that went into his heart, nor did he feel it. He died instantly. No one else heard it either and his body was not discovered until a fourteen-year-old boy came by a few hours later to deliver the morning newspaper.

The old King of Domai smiled benevolently at Aran, the young King of Syran. 'It is so good to see you,' he beamed. 'You have grown up to be so strong and handsome. Do you know, the first time I saw you was just after you were born. Your father was holding you in his arms like you were made of gold dust and might dissolve like sand in the wind if he didn't protect you with all his concentration. And now you are such a fine young man.'

The old King was being only partly honest. Aran did indeed have a handsome face, but it was resting on top of an unusually small body, a fact that the young King was obviously self-conscious about.

'I still miss your father, even today,' the King said wistfully.

'As do I,' Aran agreed, nodding solemnly. 'He was a great leader and a great man. It has been hard to even contemplate filling his shoes.'

'You have done a fine job,' the King assured the younger man. 'Your wisdom and strength are talked about everywhere I go. Your father would be proud of the way you are leading your people.'

'Thank you.' Aran bowed his head in acknowledgement of the compliment. There was a pause as he prepared to change the subject. 'I have come to see you on a personal matter.'

'Ah, yes,' the King nodded and smiled, encouraging the younger man to speak what was in his heart.

'I have felt for some time that I should marry. The death of my father and the subsequent political problems have made it inappropriate until now to take a decision on the subject. I did not want to commit myself to such a serious step until I was sure I could offer my Queen a stable throne.'

'Quite so, very wise.' The old King could see what was coming now, but he said nothing, allowing the younger man to finish his speech.

'I have for many years admired the beauty and spirit of your daughter, Jarmina, and have frequently prayed to Allah that no one else would come along and carry her away into the desert before I was in a fit position to ask your permission for her hand in marriage.'

'Ah, Jarmina,' the old King exclaimed, as if surprised by the news. 'My dearest daughter, as I'm sure you know, but a wilful creature.'

'One of her finest qualities in my eyes.'

'Quite so. You are a modern man, Aran, and Jarmina is certainly a modern woman. I would be proud to call you my son-in-law and ally our two countries more closely with such a judicious marriage. Sadly, the final answer is not mine to give. As I'm sure you have heard, others have come asking Jarmina for her hand and have been sent away. I do not know where her true affections lie – they may lie with you. If you can persuade her to accept your offer, you will certainly have my blessing.'

'Thank you.' Aran lent forward and kissed the older King's hand. 'I hope that soon you will be able to call me son and look upon my achievements with the same pride you might look upon those of Najid.'

'I hope so too. I will arrange for a meeting between you and Jarmina.'

'Could you not go to her as my emissary? She might be more willing to listen to you, the man she loves and respects above all others.'

'I'm flattered by the description, but I know my daughter and I think her reply to me would be, "Why does the man not ask me himself?" No, you would do better to grasp the bull by the horns.' There was a twinkle in the old man's eyes as he lent his head closer to Aran's: 'One word of advice. Don't let her see that you're afraid of her. If she sees fear she may well tear your heart out.'

Aran drew back, unsure whether or not to be affronted by the suggestion that he, a king, could ever be intimidated by a mere woman, and then he saw that the old King was laughing.

'Do you think he has any chance at all?' Sir Roderick asked.

'God knows.' Michael squatted down beside his fellow Englishman on the cushions which he had had scattered around his swimming pool. Both men were sipping at glasses of iced tea under the heat of the Domai sun.

Sir Roderick sighed deeply. He was getting too old for all this. There were things that needed doing in the garden at home and here he was chasing around the world trying to marry some woman off for diplomatic purposes – hardly a noble profession for a man of his stature.

'If she turns him down,' Michael said, sinking back into the cushions, 'is there anyone else?'

'To be honest, this is her last chance of anyone from any of the other royal families showing an interest. Most of them are looking for girls under twenty and she'll be thirty soon. It seems strange to me that a woman of her intelligence wouldn't want to escape from her mother. It must be appallingly boring following that woman around the world from one hotel suite to another, watching her slowly killing herself with chocolate.'

'Probably no worse than being married to someone who still views wives as being somewhere just above ploughs in the household pecking order,' Michael suggested. 'Maybe she's waiting for her parents to die and then she'll spread her wings and live a more Westernised life.'

'That's what everyone's afraid of,' Sir Roderick replied. 'What if she goes off and marries some American billionaire? It would make Domai very unpopular in the Islamic world. We need to be winning allies in the area, not losing them. A link with Syran would be highly beneficial for both countries.'

'Have you spoken to the King about it?'

'He just laughs and shrugs, as if he were some helpless Western father, unable to do anything about a wilful offspring. What about Najid?'

'The same, although he doesn't laugh much. He has the added problem of the feud between his sister and his wife. He would dearly love to see Jarmina married off and turned into someone else's headache. No doubt he can envisage all sorts of problems once the old man has gone.'

Both of them fell silent for a few minutes, lost in thought.

'We're really very unhappy about the way things are going generally out here,' Sir Roderick said at last.

'You're not the only ones,' Michael replied, his voice automatically becoming quieter for fear there might be servants listening. 'The top brass in the army are getting very fidgety indeed. None of them know what the old man is likely to do next, or which of his neighbours he is going to declare is his ally when everyone else can see they are a dangerous enemy. They all want Najid to take over as soon as possible. They feel that with him they would all know exactly where they were and they would also know they had the backing of the British.'

'Quite.' Sir Roderick sipped his tea again. 'Well, perhaps it will soon be time to think about making some changes.'

'Still a constable, Moody?' Norman enquired with a straight face as the detective came into his office at the club. He held out his hand but Moody didn't respond. Norman did not retract his hand, wanting to make the point that he was willing to let bygones be bygones. Moody glanced at the large, well-manicured paw with its shiny gold rings and identity bracelet, and moved away to lean against the suede-upholstered wall.

'Landed on your feet again then, Norman,' he said, looking around sulkily at the heavy, polished mahogany furnishings.

Norman finally retracted his hand and sat down behind the desk. 'I work hard, Constable, and I find that the rewards follow on.'

'A few lucky breaks too, Norman. Even you have to admit that.'

'I don't call seven years inside a lucky break.' Norman's voice was amiable although his eyes were cold.

'Considering the things you've got away with over the years, Norman,' Moody allowed himself a smile, 'I would say that seven years was bloody lucky. One day you may even get what you really deserve.'

'You have an obsession, Constable, did you know that?' Norman smiled and his eyes did not move, like a lizard watching a particularly juicy fly settling before him. 'You need to step back and look at the broader picture.'

'I was surprised to find out you were here,' Moody changed the subject. 'A bit of a change in style from the spielers I associate you with.'

'We all have to move on in this world. Well, most of us.'

Moody ignored the reference to his lack of promotion.

'This is Jack Rabitz's place, isn't it?'

'Not any more. He sold his share to the new partners.'

'To you?'

'I'm one of the new partners.'

'Who might the others be?'

'All sleeping at the moment, Constable, leaving the running of the place up to me.'

'That's what I thought.'

Norman said nothing, and concentrated on rolling himself a cigarette. There was a box of Sidney Rose's cigars still on the desk but he never bothered with them. He gestured to the box with his head, inviting Moody to help himself. The policeman ignored the invitation.

'So, is this a social visit then?' Norman enquired.

'Not entirely. I'm tying up a few loose ends regarding the death of a Sidney Rose.'

'I thought that had all been sorted. Case closed.' Norman licked the cigarette paper and rolled it shut, igniting it with a gold Dunhill lighter. 'Some mystery killer attacked him on his own doorstep, didn't they? No witnesses, no clues, just several hundred policemen chasing their own tails.'

'It was,' Moody said. 'Until I happened to come across the file and noticed your name in it.'

'There you go,' Norman said evenly. 'It's an obsession. All your colleagues think there's nothing to investigate, and just because you see my name you decide there must be something to dig up.'

Moody said nothing.

'Look,' Norman spread his hands, as if trying to demonstrate there was nothing up his sleeve. 'You said it yourself; I've come on in the world. This isn't some basement joint in Greek Street, this is a big business.'

'Which you are suddenly in control of, after the manager dies in a mystery shooting and half the existing partners simultaneously decide to sell out their shares.'

'Exactly. A bit of good luck for me, as you said yourself.'

'Not for Sidney Rose.'

'It's not my fault if the man made an enemy along the line.'

'So, who do you think did it, Norman?'

Norman spread his hands again. 'Like I told the officers who investigated the case to start with, I hardly knew the man. He was a South Londoner. Never came across him before I came to this place. But he'd been in the clubs business for donkey's years. He was good at his job. He'd probably made dozens of enemies. It might have been someone he upset twenty years ago, or someone who's just finished serving time on his behalf. Or maybe he was screwing someone's wife on the quiet and the guy found out. Maybe it was the woman herself? You lot are supposed to be the fucking detectives, you work it out.'

'Just asking, Norman,' Moody said with a thin smile. 'No need to get in a state.'

'I'm not in any state,' Norman hissed. 'Listen. If you turned my body up on a doorstep somewhere with a bullet in it, would you have any idea where to start looking?' He didn't wait for Moody to reply. 'Of course not. There're probably a hundred people who'd like to see me out of the way and they'd all have alibis for that night. There're some cases which don't need to be solved, Constable, and this is one of them.'

'Tell that to his wife and crippled daughter.'

'Stop it, you're breaking my heart,' Norman snapped. His conscience was clear there. He had personally made sure that the man's family was okay, that they were adequately recompensed for their bereavement.

'So, why have Rabitz and the other partners decided to pull out of the club and leave you in charge?' Moody asked, changing the subject.

'I made them offers,' Norman said, 'and they chose to accept. They were all interviewed by the police. It's all on the record.'

'Offers they couldn't refuse?'

'You watch too many fucking movies, Moody. Sidney's death unnerved them. They're all businessmen, not professionals in this game. They were glad to have someone take their shares off them at a fair price.'

'I wonder if the Inland Revenue has any records of them receiving a fair price from you?'

'Whether they fiddle their tax returns is up to them,' Norman said with a grin. He could see that Moody was losing the impetus he had come in with. 'I paid them what I paid them and they were happy to take it. Now, if that's all you need to know for the moment, I would thank you to piss off and let me get on with my job.'

Moody didn't move for a moment. 'I know you did it,' he said eventually. 'I know you killed him. The job has your fingerprints all over it.'

'If there were any fingerprints your colleagues would have had me in months ago,' Norman said.

'You know what I mean.'

'I don't have the faintest idea. Now piss off.'

Moody finally moved towards the door. 'I'm going to get you, Norman, one way or another.'

Norman said nothing, keeping his eyes on the policeman as he opened the door.

'I'm not going to let this one go, Norman,' Moody warned, his body already halfway out of the room. 'You shouldn't be out on the streets. You're a bleeding menace to society.'

'You need to calm down, mate,' Norman growled. 'You're starting to take it all too personally. You think you'll get a promotion just by chasing me from here to hell and back? If you're worried about your pension you should start looking around for other ways to supplement your income. We need security consultancy work here. You should think about it. There's more to life than chasing me, you know.'

'Are you offering me money?' Moody asked, knowing as he said it he would never catch Norman that way. Norman merely raised his eyebrows at him. 'It's not the fucking sixties any more, Norman, you know, and you're not in fucking Soho. You can't just buy coppers any time you please.' Norman's expression gave away nothing of what he was thinking.

Jarmina sat, quiet and composed, waiting for Aran to be brought to her. Her friends had finally finished fussing over her hair and her dress, twittering excitedly as they made the last few unnecessary adjustments to the picture they were creating. They wanted the King of Syran to walk into the room and have his breath taken away by the sight that met his eyes. They had chosen the material in which to cover her head, confident that its purples and golds would show off her thickly lashed black eyes. Her mouth was painted bright red with lipstick bulk-bought from Selfridges on their last trip to London.

Aran was announced and entered the room. The effect on him was just as the women had planned. Any doubts which he might have had about taking a bride who was a little mature and who had a reputation for not knowing her place, were swept away. He felt as if the breath had been knocked from his chest as he made his way across the bare, polished parquet floor towards the chair where she waited for him.

Jarmina gave away nothing in her expression. She had given away nothing to the women as they prepared her, either. As the King walked across the room, the women huddled in the antechamber and whispered amongst themselves. Their predictions varied from the belief that their friend and patroness was desperately in love with the handsome young King, to a certainty that she intended to spurn his advances just as she had all the others. All of them were certain they could read their mistress' mind.

The Queen had heard Aran was coming to call on her daughter, but saw no reason to meet him herself. She felt more and more tired these days, even getting off the bed for a meal was an exertion she found tedious. She lay, with her entourage sitting around her, in another part of the palace and waited to hear what her daughter's response would be. When the suitors had first started to arrive, the Queen had expended a great deal of energy on advising her daughter as to the best response to each proposal. All of them had been highly desirable matches – they would not have been allowed to get near to the Princess had they not had the blessing of her father – and the Queen had started out instructing her daughter to accept.

The first time Jarmina had disobeyed her and sent the royal suitor packing, her mother had been furious. The second and third times she was equally angry. But, as the years passed and her health became progressively worse, the Queen began to see the advantage of having a daughter who stayed with her family. It wasn't that the old woman was short of travelling companions, there were always plenty of them available for every shopping trip she suggested, but there was no one else who was ever willing to answer her back. Grudgingly, the Queen had to admit she enjoyed her daughter's company and no longer anticipated her leaving with any relish.

Despite her personal reservations, she could see, however, that Aran would be a fine match and such a marriage would bring credit to both Jarmina and her parents. So, as her friends whispered and giggled amongst themselves, she picked half-heartedly at an immense box of chocolates which Aran had had sent to her, and contemplated losing her daughter's company.

Jarmina lifted her eyes briefly from the polished floor as Aran came closer and was impressed by just how handsome he was. The fact that he was only about the same height as herself was disguised by the imperious way in which he held himself, his robes flying behind him.

A chair had been set beside hers and he sat himself down in it.

'I'm honoured that you agreed to see me,' he said, bowing his head.

'The honour is mine, your Highness,' she replied politely, also bowing her head and then looking straight at him.

'You are even more beautiful than I remember,' he said, disquieted by the way in which she stared into his eyes, almost as if she believed herself to be his equal.

'Thank you,' she replied, and he thought he noted the smallest clink of ice in her tone. He waited for her to respond with a similar compliment but none came.

'I have spoken with your father,' he said, aware that he was becoming nervous in her presence. 'I asked him if he would agree to my being your husband. He suggested I should ask you myself. I don't believe he has any personal objection.'

'My father is a very forward-thinking man. He would not simply give away his daughter to the first man who asked for her.'

'I doubt very much if I am the first who has asked. I would like to believe I may be the last.'

She allowed herself a small smile. 'I am deeply honoured by your offer, but I fear I would not make a good wife for you.'

'I think, if you will forgive me, you should allow me to be the judge of that.'

'Why? Because you are a man, or because you are a king?'

'Neither,' he said, flustered by her directness but enjoying it at the same time. 'Simply because I am the best judge of what would be best for me.'

She laughed. 'You don't know me well enough. I am a wilful woman. I would be disobedient. I would upset your friends and advisers.'

'I think it would be worth the pain.' He fell silent and thoughtful for a moment. 'But perhaps you are afraid of marriage.'

Jarmina's back straightened and her eyes flashed dangerously. 'I don't believe, your Highness, that I am afraid of anything.'

'Then marry me.'

She opened her mouth and thought better of whatever she was about to say. 'The truth is, I value my freedom.'

'I will allow you your freedom.'

'You are a king, you would not be able to fulfil such a promise, however much you might wish to.'

Aran's fingers were tapping irritably on the arms of the chair. He was used to getting his own way and the more she evaded him the more he wanted to force her to bend to his will.

'There would be many political advantages for your father,' he said, changing his tack. 'An alliance with my country would mean he would be in a better position to resist pressures from the British.'

'I don't think my father needs my help in dealing with the British,' she snapped.

'I think your father will soon need all the friends he can find,' Aran said, immediately realising he had gone too far and had lost all chance of winning Jarmina's hand.

'Please excuse me,' she said, rising from her chair and bowing her head respectfully. 'I must get back to my mother. She becomes fretful if I am away from her for too long.'

She walked from the room, leaving the young King sitting, alone and fuming, in the centre of the polished floor. But as she walked away, Jarmina was far from sure that she was doing the right thing. Did she really want to spend the rest of her life surrounded by women who agreed with everything she said? Wouldn't any man, especially one as fine as Aran, be better than a lonely old age? There were parts of her intellect which told her she would never find anyone better than the King of Syran, but something stronger told her that she couldn't link the rest of her life with anyone who didn't make her heart race and fill her with excitement. She remembered the Italian hustler in Bond Street and sighed at her own foolishness.

CHAPTER SIX

1977

Pete Chappell had made an appointment with Norman. Norman was surprised, and impressed, by the respect which this demonstrated. He had never been a great one for keeping diaries and appointments himself. He always believed it was better to take people by surprise, wrong-foot them and give them no time to think up excuses for whatever they might have done. If you gave them warning you were coming, he found, they tended to disappear – although this could sometimes be useful too. He wondered if he should get himself a diary if this sort of thing was going to happen regularly. He decided against it.

He had no idea what his young brother-in-law wanted. He'd seen him around Gerald's club a few times but had never talked to him about anything. As long as the boy had a job and Kathy wasn't on his back about it, Norman never saw reason to give him another thought.

The second surprise was the way Pete looked as he walked into the office. He wasn't really a boy any more. The years had passed quicker than Norman had realised. The man who came in through the door was obviously someone of some substance. His suit was smart, looked as if it had been made to measure, and his tie was discreet, not the usual King's Road flash which most of the young men seemed to like to sport around London at that time. The handshake was firm. Norman had to admit that Pete did not seem like the no-hoper he had had him down as.

'How's Kathy?' Norman asked when they had sat down. Pete showed no surprise at the fact that Norman was asking after his own wife. He knew the score. When you were in the club business you tended not to get home that much.

'She's not too bad, Norman, and the girls are growing up to be lovely. You must be very proud.'

'Yeah, right,' Norman grinned a little sheepishly. 'I should get to see them more. It's the pressures of the job, you know, Pete. Running a place like this takes up twenty-four hours out of every day. Take your eye off the ball and people are up to no good behind your back. You gotta stay on top of it. Maybe in a few years I'll have built it up and I'll be able to sell it and retire somewhere, spend a bit more time with the family, and on the golf course.'

They both laughed congenially, two men of the world, at ease with one another.

'This place is a credit to you, Norman,' Pete said, gesturing around him. 'You hear people talking about it all over London. Everyone's been here at some time or another.'

Norman nodded as he rolled himself a cigarette. He was used to hearing the club praised. He knew it was a success. He could tell that from the receipts alone. Most nights of the week they were turning people away, and they'd been able to mark up the prices on the wine list to match anything in the West End.

'That's why I wanted to talk to you, Norman.'

'Oh yeah?' Norman licked the cigarette paper, and watched the younger man.

'I've been working with Gerald for seven years now.'

'Nice little operation Gerald has going. I wish I could have spent more time up there in recent years.'

'It's a good operation,' Pete agreed, 'and I love working there, but I don't think I can go any further in the organisation.'

'How do you mean, "go further"?' Norman lit his cigarette. 'Where do you want to go?'

'Gerald is hardly ever there now either, always off on some business deal or other. I'm practically running it most days, but Gerald still sees me as the kid he took on as a favour to you.'

Norman nodded. 'You want me to lean on him a little? Give you a partnership?'

'I don't think it would work. I mean, if he has to do it to please you he's never going to trust me. And I'm not sure that this topless waitress thing is going to last much longer. People can see tits whenever they want to these days. Why would they want to go paying inflated prices, specially when they're told they can look but not touch?'

Norman shrugged. 'You'd have to make yourself indispensable, and then start instigating changes to keep up with the times.'

'I've already done that, but he doesn't realise it.'

'So, what do you want to do?'

'I want to work for you.'

'What makes you think I'd be any better to work for than Gerald?'

'You said yourself you're working all the time. You could use someone you could trust. Maybe together we could expand the business, open other clubs...'

'Whoa!' Norman held up his hand and laughed. 'Too fast, Pete, too fast.'

'Okay,' Pete grinned. 'I know, I'm sorry. But I'm anxious to work for the top man.'

Norman had been around long enough to know that flattery didn't mean a thing, but it was still nice to hear. He thought for a few minutes, drawing hard on his cigarette and making the tobacco crackle and glow with the heat. Pete knew better than to interrupt his thoughts.

'I'll tell you what I would do if I was you,' Norman said eventually. 'Keep working for Gerald, just drop in there each evening to check things are going okay, and pick up your wages for as long as he's willing to pay them. But start hanging around here, getting to know the place and how it runs. We'll see how things pan out.'

'Can't ask for more than that.' Pete sprang to his feet with his hand outstretched. 'It's a deal.'

The two men shook and went down to the bar for lunch.

'I can't hold them back any longer.' Michael was speaking into the phone. He didn't want to give any more details, being uncertain who might be listening in. He knew that Najid would understand what he was saying. The subject had been at the front of both their minds for several months. Both knew that this day had become inevitable.

'Does my father know?' Najid asked, his voice quiet.

'Not officially. I'll have to go to see him later today.'

'No,' Najid spoke sharply. 'I'll go to him.'

'It would be wisest if you persuaded him to go to London until everything's settled. It'd help calm things.'

'I understand. Does Sir Roderick know?'

'He will.'

'Very well.'

Najid hung up without saying goodbye. He felt as if there were a lead weight lying in his chest. He had dreaded this day for so long, and now it had arrived. The generals had finally grown tired of waiting. They wanted to consolidate the security of the country. They wanted to move forward and become a major military and political power in the area. They knew they could never do that with a king who still believed he ruled over a desert tribe. Najid was also aware that the British were behind it, and that Michael was the instrument they had used. But he could see no way that his country could prosper in the future without an alliance with one of the Western powers. The oil needed more protection than the army could provide without assistance. And at a personal level, Najid was also unsure how he would manage without Michael to advise him.

Jarmina was woken by a frantic knocking on her bedroom door. She shouted to indicate that she was awake and the door opened and three agitated women came into the room. Jarmina would normally have shooed them away with an imperious flicking of the fingers so that she could return to her dreams, but she could see something was seriously wrong. This wasn't just a deputation to bring her some juicy bit of palace gossip.

'Your Highness,' all three were talking at once. 'There are soldiers downstairs. You must dress at once. They're threatening to come up.'

'What soldiers?'

'They say they're seizing power and that we're under arrest!'

'Arrest?' Jarmina pulled off the sheets and started to dress. 'Have my breakfast sent up and then I'll talk to them.'

'They've taken over the kitchens,' one of the women cried. 'They're taking everything.'

'Are they indeed?'

Jarmina sat down at her dressing-table and started selecting herself some appropriate jewellery while one of the women automatically brushed her hair. Even in the midst of a revolution a princess could not descend among her people without the appropriate preparation. Ten minutes later she was dressed and ready to meet the invaders. The other women fell into a twittering group behind her as she regally descended the stairs. Two soldiers who had been lounging on chairs in the main courtyard sprang to their feet as they saw her appear. Her step was deliberately slow, her eyes straight ahead. She ignored them and walked on towards the kitchens. Several more soldiers were sitting around, eating and drinking. The kitchen staff were skulking in corners of the room, obviously intimidated and unsure what was happening.

Jarmina's entrance transformed the room. The soldiers jumped to their feet, saluting, and the kitchen staff, emboldened by the sight of their employer in full flight, started to busy themselves as if it were a normal day at work.

'Where is my breakfast?' she demanded, ignoring the presence of the soldiers. 'I want it served in the main dining-room now.' She was determined to put on a show of power – these people had to know that their royal family was still in control.

'Where is your commanding officer?' she demanded of the nearest soldier.

'The General is in the library, your Highness,' he replied, his body stiff with respect.

'Inform him that I will receive him in the dining-room when I have finished my breakfast.'

She swept from the room with her now silent entourage following on behind.

'Has my mother been woken?' she asked, once she was seated at the end of the mighty Italian dining-table and the food was being laid out before her.

'She has been woken but she has asked to have her breakfast in bed,' one of the women informed her.

The Princess gave an impatient sigh.

'Very well,' she grumbled. 'Ensure that she's left undisturbed by the soldiers. Inform me if there's any danger of her privacy being invaded.'

'What will become of us, your Highness?' another woman squeaked.

'Nothing will become of us,' she snapped. 'But something will become of these upstarts once I find out who's behind this outrage.'

Half an hour later she had finished her breakfast and the General entered the room with several of his staff. He was putting on a brave show of confidence but it was obvious he was newly promoted and unsure how to behave in the presence of royalty. The Princess sensed she still had the upper hand.

'What is the meaning of this invasion, General?' Jarmina asked, staring at him in a manner she was sure no woman in his family ever would.

'It's purely for your own protection, your Highness,' he replied. 'And for the protection of your mother and family members.'

'Why do you feel we need this protection? It seems to me that your soldiers are the only ones threatening our privacy.'

'There are political matters under way in the city, your Highness, which might make the people restless. It was thought prudent that you should be protected.'

'Thought by whom?' The Princess was becoming increasingly annoyed at not being told what was happening.

'By His Highness Prince Najid and by General Beckett.'

This was the first time she had heard that Michael had been promoted to general.

'They're behind this outrage are they?' Jarmina slammed her fists down hard, making the gold table decorations jump and rattle. The General kept his eyes on the wall behind her and said nothing.

'Where is my father?' she demanded.

'I'm sorry, your Highness, I do not know.'

'Then find out and come back and tell me!'

The man swivelled on his heel and left the room with a smart salute, relieved to have been given an excuse to escape the wrath of his new King's sister.

The old King was already sitting at his desk when he was informed that his son was there to see him. His informants had told him exactly what was happening amongst his generals and he knew it was now just a matter of hours before he had his powers removed. He was in no hurry to allow Najid to break the news to him officially.

'Najid,' he beamed as the Prince came in. 'How splendid to see you, and looking so well.'

He rose from the desk and embraced his son as if he had nothing on his mind beyond the beauty of the morning that was still breaking outside the windows. He could feel Najid stiffen, every muscle tensed in preparation for the treachery he was about to perform. Najid noticed that two of his father's most trusted bodyguards were standing behind him, their normally impassive faces nervous and ready to pounce on anyone who posed a threat to their beloved master. Normally he would have taken their presence for granted, not even registered their existence.

'I have been sent to see you by the generals, Father,' he said.

'Generals are sending princes on their errands?' The King shook his head, tut-tutting. 'You must make sure they realise their place, Najid. Can you imagine any of them daring to send your sister anywhere?' He let out a deep laugh and his son allowed himself a small, dry smile. He was becoming increasingly tired of hearing how much more frightening than him his eldest sister was. All his life she had taunted him with the fact that she would have been the sultan of Domai instead of him, had she been born a different gender. The older he became the more impatient he felt with women who did not know their place. He believed his father had allowed Jarmina far too much freedom and now it might well be too late to curb her reckless ways. She was not an asset to the family any more.

'The army is taking over the country, Father,' Najid announced. 'They fear for the security of the area and they want things to change.'

'They have always wanted things to change,' the old man said, sitting back down in his chair, leaving his son standing like a naughty schoolboy before him. 'Haven't they seen enough changes in the last few years? Can they not be content that they live in what is now one of the richest countries in the world where once it was one of the poorest?'

'The rich have to be strong, Father,' Najid said. 'They have to protect themselves from predators.'

'And you think I am not strong?' The King raised an eyebrow and both men knew without a shadow of a doubt which was the stronger character.

'I doubt there is a stronger man in all Arabia,' Najid said, truthfully. 'But you are growing old, Father, and the world has moved on. You were brought up to be a desert Bedouin – that training is no longer enough to run a modern state.'

'This is all decided, is it?' the King asked quietly.

'It is.'

'And have they offered you the throne?'

'They have asked me, yes.'

'And you have agreed to overthrow your father?'

'I have agreed to serve my country in any way the people see fit,' Najid corrected him.

'You even talk like an Englishman.' The old King showed a spark of irritation for the first time. 'I sometimes regret that I sent you there to be educated. Perhaps if you had never met Colonel Beckett you would be more of a man today.'

Najid drew himself up to his full height and, for a moment, he looked every bit as much the desert warrior as his father.

'General Beckett is a good soldier who has served this country well. We should be grateful to him for our military strength.'

The old King raised an eyebrow at the news of Michael's promotion. '*General* Beckett is a mercenary and an adventurer and he has talked you into handing your heritage over to the British.'

Najid's nostrils flared as he took in a deep breath to stop himself saying something deeply disrespectful he would regret forever.

'The RAF have prepared a plane for take-off. It would be advisable if you were to go to London for a few weeks, until the country has settled down once more.'

'If I leave this country I will not be returning,' his father said. 'You know it would be impossible.'

'The British Government has agreed that you can stay there for as long as you wish.'

'I do not intend to live the rest of my life in a hotel suite.'

'The house is almost ready in the country,' Najid said. 'You will be able to live there.'

'I will find somewhere in London. The house is designed for women.'

'Whatever you desire you can have,' Najid assured him.

'Except my throne.'

'You have been a great king. You have led your people from the desert to the cities. You have turned them from nomads into citizens of the world. But now it is time for changes and for you to rest.'

The old man opened his mouth as if to speak and thought better of it.

There was a hammering on the door and a platoon of soldiers barged in. Both royal men swung round to glare at them.

'King's escort reporting, Sir!' the Captain in charge barked, saluting.

'My father will make his own way to the airport,' Najid said.

'We have orders to escort him,' the Captain insisted.

'I am countermanding your orders.' Najid raised his voice and the two bodyguards stepped forward from behind the old Sultan's throne, pulling pistols from inside their robes.

It was hard to see what happened next. A flurry of panic filled the room. There was shouting and shots were fired. Najid's father and one of the bodyguards both fell to the floor. The other bodyguard dropped to his knees to cradle his master's head in his hands.

'Stop shooting, you idiots!' Najid screamed, and the Captain ordered his men to fall back. His face was ashen. Najid ran to his father.

'Where are you hit?' he asked.

'In the leg, I think,' his father replied.

'Get the doctor and call an ambulance. My father needs to be taken to a hospital.'

Two hours later, with his leg temporarily bandaged and his personal physician at this side, the ex-King of Domai was taken to the plane which had been prepared for him and was flown to England, where a floor of a private hospital overlooking Regent's Park was being cleared in preparation for his arrival.

It was the first major piece of new business that Len Dorset had gone after since Jack Rabitz had bought the company. He felt distinctly nervous. Nothing in his background or his nature had ever prepared him to be a salesman. He had always been a man who had trouble speaking anything but the truth.

Beneath the nerves, however, he felt confident as he headed for the Dorchester and his appointment with the man who had telephoned the office the day before. He felt confident because he knew he had a good product. When Jack had first suggested the idea of buying the company and putting him in charge he had thought it would be just another of his father-in-law's plans to keep him busy and stop him spending his wife's money, but as soon as he saw the offices and met the staff he realised he was being given a genuine opportunity to make something of his life. The company was in the best possible shape. The fleet of cars was in good condition and the drivers were all highly trained in the skills needed for chauffeuring the rich and famous. They knew how to react to assassination attempts and high-speed car chases. More often than not they only got to try their skills out against the paparazzi as they sped film stars between airports and hotels, but they were still amongst the best in their business.

The man on the phone had not given his name, just a room number at the Dorchester and a time. It had crossed Len's mind that it might be a hoax, but it was worth following up anyway.

'Please ring room 142,' he asked the receptionist, 'and tell them that Mr Dorset is here for his four o'clock appointment.'

The receptionist did as requested and then directed Len to the lifts. When he got out on the first floor, a young man in a suit and tie met him and walked with him to the door of room 142. The man's hair was short and his demeanour suggested he was a soldier by training. The door stood open and Len was ushered in.

Inside, another man was waiting, sitting in an armchair reading a newspaper.

'Mr Dorset, General,' the young soldier announced.

Michael put down the paper and stood up to shake hands. Len was surprised to hear a man who looked the same age as himself being referred to as 'General'. He was also surprised to find that a military man could afford to stay at the Dorchester.

'Take a seat, Mr Dorset,' said Michael, indicating another armchair. 'Thank you for coming at such short notice. Would you care for tea?'

For twenty minutes they took tea together and chatted like casual acquaintances. Finally, Michael decided to come to the point. 'I'm employed by one of the Middle-Eastern royal families,' he explained. 'Several members of the family are going to be spending time in England over the next few years and I need to find a reliable security company to handle the transport and some of the domestic security at their properties over here. In the short run I need someone to drive me around, but in the long term it could prove to be a major royal contract for a company.'

A small knot of excitement formed in the pit of Len's stomach. For the first time in his life he was bringing in some business, and, more importantly, was justifying Jack's faith in him. He was going to be able to hold his head up at the golf club now as an active business partner and no longer just the kept son-in-law. He was in the running for a royal appointment.

'I think we can handle all that for you,' he said.

'I'd like you to be my driver for the next few weeks,' Michael said.

'All our drivers are highly qualified,' Len assured him. 'Most of them better than me.'

'I would still like you to drive me.' Michael's voice was quiet but it was obvious he did not intend to argue about it. This, it seemed, was a non-negotiable condition for getting the contract. 'I always like to get to know the bosses of companies I plan to do a lot of business with.'

Len thought for a second. It wasn't how he had seen his future role with the company. He had seen himself more in a management position than as a driver, but he liked this man. There was an air of authority about Michael which he felt comfortable with. He decided it was something worth doing.

'I don't think that would be a problem,' he said. 'I would be pleased to be your driver for as long as you need me.'

'Excellent. It's a deal then.' Michael held out his hand and Len took it eagerly. Both men felt good about the way the meeting had turned out.

Over the next few weeks Len didn't regret his decision. He found it easy to be the quiet, reliable man in the background escorting the dynamic young general from meeting to meeting. The trips were always interesting. There were visits to high security army and naval bases, and to arms factories. There were lunches and dinners at top hotels and penthouse suites around the City. Michael made sure that Len was never left out. There was always somewhere for him to go to eat or rest and, whenever it was allowed, he would join the group viewing whatever products were on sale, introduced by Michael as 'my colleague'. He learnt more about the workings of the latest tanks and fighter aircraft than he would ever have thought possible. Being with a general who appeared to have an unlimited budget for the purchasing of arms seemed to open every door for him.

When Michael visited Whitehall, however, Len was not included in the meeting.

Sir Roderick looked pleased with himself and with Michael. Lunch had been laid on for the two of them in a private room and they made small-talk until the butler had served them and left.

'I saw the King yesterday,' Sir Roderick said.

'The ex-King,' Michael corrected him.

'Quite, quite. I can't get used to the idea of Najid being on the throne. I've been working with His Majesty for a long time. Najid still seems like a boy to me.'

'How is he taking it, the old man? He's not planning on trying to win the throne back is he?'

'Always hard to tell with foxes as old and wily as that,' Sir Roderick said, sipping his wine thoughtfully. 'But I don't think so. To be honest he seems tired to me. He looked at least ten years older than the last time I saw him. The operation on his leg took a lot out of him. Had they taken the bullet out in Domai instead of flying him all the way to London, he would not have lost so much blood. Whose decision was that?'

'Najid was there at the scene of the shooting.'

'Did the doctor not advise him?'

'I believe the doctor did advise him to have the bullet removed there but Najid decided that in the climate of instability it would be better to get his father out of the country as quickly as possible.'

'Oh, the treachery of children,' Sir Roderick mused, more to himself than to Michael. Knowing Najid as he did, he doubted Michael was being entirely truthful about who had made the decision.

'Is he happy with the apartment?' Michael changed the subject – there were certain aspects of the recent coup he preferred not to dwell on.

'He didn't say. It's one of the best in Park Lane, so he should be. I doubt he's taking much notice of his surroundings. He's worried about his wife and daughter.'

'Is he planning to send for them?' Michael enquired.

'Oh no, I don't think he's travelled with them for a long time. But he's very fond of his daughter and he worries she'll not fare well under her brother's rule.'

'She's a powerful woman,' Michael agreed.

'Does Najid see her as any sort of threat?' Sir Roderick asked.

'No woman is that powerful in Domai. He sees her more as a nuisance. He would rather she was married off and someone else's problem. He would like to find a way of containing her a little.'

'The mother won't live for ever, of course, not carrying all that weight.' Sir Roderick gave a thin, apologetic smile. 'What do you suppose Jarmina will do once she's gone?'

'It's not something I've given too much thought to. I've been concentrating on other things.'

'You may have to give this a little more attention,' Sir Roderick warned gently. 'The old man wants the women to spend more time in England.'

'At the apartment?'

'No, at Upton Park.'

'Ah,' Michael sighed. Having them in England would make them the British Government's responsibility as well as the Domai security services. That made him doubly responsible in his role as the bridge between the two. 'I see.'

'We wouldn't want anything to happen to them while they were over here. I don't need to tell you what an enormous embarrassment that would be. It would jeopardise our relationship with Najid. They'll need to be very well protected.'

'The Princess is not always the most co-operative of people.'

'I'm sure you can find a way of charming her. You'll need to select her people with great care.'

'I will. I have a good man on the payroll – Len Dorset. I've been using him as my personal driver to get to know him. He seems very reliable.'

'Good.' Sir Roderick filled their glasses up and they ate in silence for a few moments. Michael hadn't been lying; he had been extremely busy with the Domai Army procurement plan. It was work he was happy to do, mainly because the percentage of each deal which found its way into his private bank account was very substantial. He was relieved he had found Len, a man he could trust to take some of the weight off his shoulders.

'We're going to take a drive down to the country, Len,' Michael announced the next morning when Len picked him up from the hotel. 'There's something I want you to see.'

Michael was reading papers all the way to the house and said nothing during the journey beyond giving the odd direction, until they reached the electronic gates. Through the bars Len could see the immaculate gardens and house gleaming in the sun. The guards in the gatehouse recognised Michael and allowed them through. Fountains were gushing water all around the parking area and Len drew up in front of the main doors. A butler was opening the front door before they had even stepped out of the car.

'The ex-King bought this place a few years ago,' Michael explained as they walked into the cool, cream-marbled hall. 'But they've hardly ever used it. At one time I thought the old man would retire here, but he prefers Park Lane and the delights of the City. God knows why, he hardly ever steps outside the apartment.'

'It just stays like this?' Len looked around at the huge, pristine rooms opening off the main hall in every direction. 'It must take an army of staff just to keep it going.'

'It does,' Michael said, ruefully. 'But it looks as if it might be coming into its own soon. The King's mother and sister are planning to spend more time in England and they'll be using this as their base.'

He led the way through to the kitchens and down a corridor to a room with a secure-looking door. Michael tapped and it was opened from the inside by a uniformed security guard. Another sat at a desk watching a variety of screens, each showing changing views of the grounds outside and the doors to the house.

'This is the security centre.' Michael nodded to the men to continue with whatever they were doing while he and Len strolled around the room looking at the equipment. Len said nothing. He was too amazed. All this security and the King didn't even come here?

A few minutes later they were sitting in one of the drawing-rooms, looking out through the windows at the grounds beyond. Someone from the kitchen had brought them coffee. Michael seemed totally at ease, but Len couldn't help feeling he was trespassing. He sat uncomfortably on the edge of his seat.

'The guards here are from one of the big security firms,' Michael said. 'I don't think that's good enough. I want to put my own people in here. People I can trust. Would you be able to handle that?'

'All the security for this place?' Len had a feeling he was moving out of his depth and felt a twinge of nerves.

'No, I'm willing to let the existing staff handle the grounds and the entrance. There's a good man, a Major Cox, who oversees the estate. He's very loyal to the family and runs the place like the army.'

'Why doesn't he handle the house as well?' Len asked.

'His loyalty is mostly with the father and not the son. It would be better if I had my own people inside the house. Could you handle that?'

'Sure.' Len swallowed hard. He wanted the business and he also wanted to please the General, a man he had come to think of as a friend.

CHAPTER SEVEN

1979

Norman lowered himself into the swimming pool with a sigh of satisfaction. Upstairs, the young lady he had met a few days before, whose name, Lorraine, he was having difficulty remembering, was showering and dressing to go out on the town for the evening. Norman was pleased to be alone for a while. When you've spent as many years in solitary confinement as Norman, you sometimes need to escape from everyone and spend a little time inside your own head without the distraction of other people.

The late afternoon Spanish sun was still hot and Norman felt good after a long afternoon sleep. In fact he had been asleep most of the day, having been out in the clubs all the previous night, drinking, meeting people and doing business. He'd been in Spain a fortnight and he was still as white as when he arrived. Even without the sunbathing, however, he liked the lifestyle.

Maybe, he mused to himself, he should give up the rat race and retire down to Marbella permanently. The villa was all paid for, he would only need enough money for food and drink and a few light clothes. There were plenty of young women hanging around the bars who were more than happy to keep him company in exchange for a chance to stay in town and access to a private pool. What did he need with all the aggro of London at his age? He was nearly forty now, perhaps it was time to retire and enjoy the fruits of his labours.

The club would run without him, at least for a while. It was a legitimate business, well almost, and people wouldn't dip their fingers into the till as long as they thought there was some chance he would be coming back to check the takings. Perhaps he could spend his summers at the villa and pop back to Streatham for a month or two in the winter to keep an eye on things.

'Normie!' the girl's voice rang out from the balcony above. 'Telephone.'

Norman considered ignoring the call, but changed his mind. She would only keep shouting until he responded. He might as well find out who it was. Pulling himself out of the pool he padded in through the French doors and picked up the sitting-room extension.

'Yeah?'

'Norman?'

There was a click as the girl hung up in the bedroom.

'Yeah.'

'It's Pete.'

He knew Pete wouldn't ring him unless it was something important. The man had proved himself to be just as good as he'd promised. Norman wasn't sure what Gerald felt about losing him, but he was pleased Pete had come to him. He wouldn't have been able to leave the club and come down to Marbella if he hadn't known Pete was there to look after things.

'I've had a detective constable nosing around,' Pete said.

'Moody?'

'Yeah. He wants to bring you in for questioning.'

'Did he say what for?'

'No, but he was persistent. He asked a whole lot more questions about Sidney Rose as well. I thought I was never going to get rid of him.'

'Where did you tell him I was?'

'Up north, doing some business.'

'Good. You're not calling from the club are you?'

'No.'

'Anything else happening?'

'Everything's fine. I just thought I'd warn you.'

'Thanks.' Norman hung up. This was exactly the sort of thing he was tired of. Moody's obsession had gone beyond a joke. How could he possibly still be trying to get him after all these years? The man seriously needed to get a life. But the fact that he was asking about Sidney Rose meant that Norman was going to have to be a bit more careful in future. Maybe he had teased the policeman a little too much, made it too personal. There had to be a way round this, but it would take him time to think it through.

'You all right, Normie?' Lorraine was clopping down the wooden stairs in perilously high heels and the sight of her, in the skimpy little white dress, with her long blonde hair and perfect suntan, knocked all thoughts of Moody clean out of his head.

'I'm fine,' he grinned. 'I'll just pop into the shower and pull on some clothes and we'll go out and paint the town. Yeah?'

'Yeah.'

An hour later they were in a bar and Norman was huddled over a corner table with two Moroccans he had arranged a meeting with. The blonde danced alone, but apparently happily, on a tiny dance floor beneath a revolving light. He talked with the two men for nearly an hour and then they left after the customary ritual of embraces. Norman felt pleased with himself. If he could arrange a few decent-sized shipments of cannabis into England he would be able to retire from the club game for good. He could sell up his interests in The Country Club and stay in Marbella all year round, away from Moody and his endless questions.

Seeing the men leave, the blonde came back to Norman's side and they left to find a restaurant, and preferably one which would serve them a well-cooked lobster. That wasn't hard to find. The head waiter knew Norman and immediately led him to a table outside, which was almost completely surrounded by foliage and palm trees, and so private from the ogling eyes of passers-by.

The lobster was good and the wine drew the two of them closer together as the sky grew dark and the street lights came on. Norman felt a glow of well-being spread through him in the warm evening air. This was how life should be.

'Do you want to go on to a club?' he asked as the waiter brought their bill.

'Sure.' Lorraine smiled tipsily and stroked his face with dainty, long-nailed fingers.

Norman put down a wad of notes and they stood to leave. As they made their way towards the exit in the palm trees, weaving their way through the closely packed tables, Norman knocked into the elbow of a man who was just raising his wineglass to his lips. There was an expletive and the man turned to abuse Norman.

The two of them stared at one another for a few seconds and the onlookers were convinced there was about to be a fight.

'Norman!'

'Len!'

After a few seconds of awkwardness, in which the brothers both grappled for an appropriate response to the meeting, Len stood up from the table and they embraced one another. For a moment Norman felt a surge of warmth for the kid brother he hadn't seen for several years. He was shocked by how broad Len's shoulders had become and by the power of his grip. It seemed his kid brother was no longer a kid.

'You staying down here?' Len asked.

'Yeah,' Norman replied. 'Got a villa just up the road.'

'Very nice.'

'Where are you staying? You must come and stay with us.' Norman had a sudden urge to spend some time with someone who was family. For over twenty years he had done everything possible to try to stay away from them, but in his present hazy glow of contentment he felt the need to talk to someone he shared a past with. And Len seemed to have turned into the sort of man he would like to spend time with.

'I'm staying at a friend's place, just outside the town,' Len said. 'Why don't you come over tomorrow, about lunch-time. We can sink a few pints and talk a bit.'

For the first time Norman noticed the others at Len's table. They were all men and it looked as though they were having a business meeting. 'Sure,' he said. 'That would be great. Give me the address.'

Len ripped a page from his pocket diary and jotted down an address and drew a scrawled map of how to get there.

'I'll see you tomorrow then,' Norman said. 'About midday.'

'I'll be there.'

'You didn't introduce me,' the blonde grumbled as they came out into the street and joined the other evening strollers.

'You wouldn't be interested,' Norman replied, only half concentrating, his thoughts elsewhere. 'It was just my kid brother. He's a driver or something.'

'He looked kind of cute to me.'

'Yeah?' Norman looked at her in surprise. 'You think so?'

'Not as cute as his big brother though,' she whispered, rubbing her hand against his crutch and stretching up to wiggle her tongue in his ear.

'Cut that out,' Norman snapped, pushing her away. He had never been comfortable with public displays of affection. The girl looked crestfallen and stayed a few paces behind him as they made their way to a club a couple of streets away.

That night Norman found himself dreaming about his childhood for the first time in years. The images were as clear as if he was still there. He saw the back of his father leaving the kitchen with his greatcoat on and a haversack over his shoulder and knew he would be gone for months. His mother was shouting at the disappearing man, pleading with him to leave her some money, and there were other children all fighting for the bread that was on the table.

Norman was shouting after him too. 'I'm gonna kill you, baldie,' he yelled. His father swung round and stared hard at him, but Norman didn't flinch, even though he knew how hard the man could hit. His father said nothing, just turned again and walked away. Norman stood up and tried to run out of the room after him. He had a knife in his hand. He was having difficulty moving his feet in the heavy wooden clogs that he had always worn until they became too much trouble and he resorted to running barefoot everywhere. The faster he ran in the dream the heavier the clogs became, making it almost impossible to lift his feet in the end. His father was growing fainter and more distant and he knew he would never catch up with him. He woke to find the girl lying with her head on his bare chest, her hair wet from his sweat.

'Why can't I come?' Lorraine wanted to know as Norman got ready to go out later in the morning. 'I don't want to hang around here all day on my own. It's boring.'

'Do some shopping,' Norman said, feeling his irritation at the girl building. 'You wouldn't like it. We'll just be talking about the past, you'd be bored. Find someone your own age to play with.'

'I'd like to find out about your past.' She changed her tone to a purr and stroked his hair in the hope of lightening his mood.

'I'm off,' Norman announced, shrugging her away as if he wasn't even aware she was touching him. 'I'll see you this evening. We'll go somewhere nice for dinner. Buy yourself something new to wear.' He handed her some notes and walked out without looking back. He half hoped she'd have found herself another man by the time he came home, but only half. Women were a mystery to Norman and part of the mystery was why he felt he needed them as much as he did. Even now he still found Kathy slipping into his thoughts unbidden. Whenever that happened he had to make an effort to think of other things.

Len's scrawled map was deceptive. It had looked as if the place he was staying at was just on the edge of the town, but a road which was only an inch on the page turned out to be several miles. As he drove on along the coast, Norman began to wonder if he had misread the directions completely. Then he saw a sign at a gate which was the same as the village Len had marked on the map. Except it wasn't a village, it seemed to be a private gate in a wall. A guard in a small hut was lounging just the other side of the gate. Norman climbed out of the car and walked over, waving his piece of paper.

'I'm looking for Len Dorset,' he said, loudly, to ensure the man could understand.

'Okay.' The guard grinned and set about opening the gates so that Norman could drive through. 'Go straight to the house. Mr Len is expecting you,' he said, and waved him through.

Norman was confused. He seemed to have come on to a private golf course. As far as the eye could see there were immaculate greens with sprinklers whirring and hissing to keep them fresh in the baking midday sun. Lines of palm trees stretched along either side of the drive, but he couldn't see any house. He drove on, past groundsmen working in lushly coloured flower beds and shrubberies. After driving for what seemed like half a mile, he turned a corner and there was the house. It looked more like a large hotel, perched on the side of the hill, the colour of clotted cream with dark green awnings over every window. Norman decided he must have misunderstood. Surely Len must have said he was staying at a friend's hotel, or maybe he had an apartment in the house.

As he drew up in front of the main steps Len appeared at the top of them and waved cheerfully. Norman parked and got out, making his way up to embrace his brother.

'This is a beautiful place, Len,' he said, gesturing around at the views out over the grounds to the sea beyond.

'Isn't it great? Belongs to a friend of mine.'

'The whole place?'

'Every inch of it.'

'Who the hell is your friend and what's his line of business?'

'He's the Sultan of Domai and his business is oil.'

For a moment Norman stared at his brother with his eyes narrowed and his mouth a thin line. Unsure if he was being sent up or not, he decided to say nothing. Len put his arm around his big brother's shoulders and steered him into the house. Cool tiled floors stretched away in every direction through double doors which all stood open to show more shiny floors dotted with ornate pieces of furniture, through to vistas of the grounds beyond.

'So you're staying here?' Norman said as they settled down near to a bar in one of the rooms.

'Got the whole place to myself,' Len grinned happily as he brought them both drinks and settled on the sofa beside his brother. 'Apart from the staff, of course.'

'What about Babs?' Norman asked. 'She out here?' He wondered if Ruby might be staying, but didn't think it diplomatic to ask outright.

'No.' Len shook his head. 'I needed a break from all the rabbit. So when I was offered this I jumped at it. Told Babs it was work.'

Norman sipped at his drink and said nothing for a few moments. In his experience, when he stayed silent people tended to tell him everything that was on their minds, saving him the trouble of asking any questions.

Sure enough, after a few seconds, Len started to burble happily. 'I've been doing a bit of work for the Sultan. Mostly for a friend of his, a general who seems to be in charge of security for the royal family. We've become pretty friendly since I've been driving him around. He's a good bloke. No side to him. If he's hungry we eat together, you know the sort of thing. Not like most of my clients. Anyway, he's like that,' Len held up a pair of crossed fingers, 'with the Sultan. So whenever he's in the country I drive him too, and I provide a few security services for them.'

'So business is good?' Norman asked.

'Business is bleeding incredible. Once you get a name for being reliable and discreet they come flocking in. To be honest we're working at full stretch. We couldn't take on any new business at the moment, not without going in for some heavy recruiting.'

'My brother the tycoon,' Norman teased.

'Too bloody right,' Len said. 'You can get used to this sort of thing, you know.' He gestured around the room.

'I bet you can,' Norman nodded.

Len chatted on with all the news of what he had been doing since he last saw Norman. It felt good to be able to report that he had achieved something in life. He could see that Norman, for all his inscrutability, was impressed by the mansion and surprised to find Len there. That felt good to Len. All his life he had been trying to impress Norman.

'Can you actually pin it on Norman Dorset?' the Inspector wanted to know.

'I know he did it,' Moody said, staring at his hands and noticing his cuffs had become remarkably frayed. He glanced up at his superior's wrists – just as he had expected, they were pristine. He was going to have to get his act together. He would never get promotion if he didn't smarten himself up a bit. He kidded himself that he dressed down in order to blend into the crowd and not be noticed. He told colleagues it was an advantage not to look too much like a policeman when you were chasing crooks, but he knew it was nothing that deliberate. He had simply let himself go. It had taken several years to reach the stage he had got to now and he wasn't sure he knew how to pull himself out of the decline.

'But can you prove it?' The Inspector was being patient because he knew Moody had some strong points as a policeman. He was dogged and had a good nose for a guilty man. There had been one or two arrests in the past which had been purely down to Moody's instincts, and each had proved him right. But none of the cases had been high profile and the man hadn't managed to create any sort of reputation for himself within the force. In fact, his colleagues saw him as something of a joke, but the Inspector was always willing to listen to what he had to say, particularly if it meant they might get to someone like Norman Dorset.

'I can't prove it right now,' Moody admitted, 'but if I could bring him in for some questioning and see what sort of alibis he has, I think there's a good chance I could pin it on him. Several people have said they're certain Sidney Rose was standing in Norman's way and that Norman wouldn't have hired anyone else for a job that important. He would have handled it himself.'

'What sort of people are saying that?'

'Informants, people who know what's going on.'

'People who might have a grudge against Dorset?'

'A lot of people have grudges against him. He's thrown a lot of people out of a lot of clubs in his time. He's broken a lot of noses.'

'And slept with a few people's wives, I dare say, too.'

'I dare say,' Moody shrugged. 'But this story came from several sources. And when I went to see him four or five years ago, when he first took over the club in Streatham, he couldn't offer any explanation as to what might have happened to Rose.'

'Four or five years ago?' The Inspector was startled. Even by Moody's standards this was showing extraordinary persistence.

'Something like that.' Moody shifted in his chair uncomfortably, aware that it sounded bizarre to still be worrying such an old bone.

'You're that sure?' The Inspector was inclined to think that if the man had been chasing Dorset for this long, he must have a very strong gut feeling.

'I'm sure. He's done a lot more, but this is the one I think we could pin on him to put him away for good. There's something else…'

'What's that, then?'

Moody took a deep breath. 'I've been asking some questions around the area of Sidney Rose's house.'

'In Sheen? Where he was bumped off?'

Moody nodded.

'Do the officers who handled that case know you've been sticking your nose in?'

'No,' Moody shook his head. 'I thought it better not to say anything until I'd found something. No point upsetting anyone if it wasn't going to lead anywhere.'

'And have you found something?'

'I think so.'

'What?'

'Two people have said they're pretty sure, from looking at pictures, that they saw someone answering Dorset's description hanging around the area that night.'

'They've got bloody long memories, haven't they?'

'That's what worries me. Dorset's defence is bound to say they couldn't possibly remember that far back.'

'And if they're so sure, why didn't they come forward at the time?' the Inspector asked.

'One of them lived a few streets away and had never heard about the killing. He remembered seeing Norman Dorset because he nearly tripped over his dog.'

'Dorset had a dog with him?'

'No, Norman tripped over this bloke's dog, or at least over the lead, as it was taking a crap. Apparently Norman was a bit hostile. That would be something that would stick in the mind of most people. He's pretty scary when he's angry. The other one had heard about the murder and said she did come forward at the time, but the officers on the case weren't interested.'

'Weren't interested?' The Inspector didn't like the sound of this. He didn't want Moody to pull this off if it made the rest of the force look like idiots.

'She's an old girl,' Moody explained. 'A bit batty. I think she'd been ringing the police rather a lot with her suspicions. She may have cried wolf once too often. They were polite to her and said they would note down her evidence, but I couldn't find any reference to it in the case notes. If I could get him off the street and check his alibis and search all his premises, I'm sure I could put him away this time.'

'I would like to see that happen,' the Inspector admitted. 'He's one of the ones I would like to see permanently off the streets. So where is he now? Can you pull him in easily?'

'I'm not too sure where he is,' Moody admitted, staring hard at his bony fingers again. 'His people say he's up north somewhere, on business, but they won't say where or when he'll be back.'

'Well, we can't afford a full-scale manhunt,' the Inspector said, 'and after this long I can't honestly make a case for any urgency about the whole thing. But I think you should bring him in and see if you can make it stick. Keep an eye on the club and any other haunts where he might turn up, but don't use up too many man-hours.'

Len was asleep when the call came through. He fumbled for the phone and put it to his ear without opening his eyes. He and Norman had gone on drinking until late into the night, digging up memories which neither had thought they would ever see again. They'd emptied a good few bottles between them, too many for Norman to be able to drive back to his villa. Since there was no shortage of guest suites at the mansion, Len had suggested he sleep it off there and go back the following day.

'Len?' Michael's voice sounded wide awake.

'Yes, General.'

'Several members of the family are going to be arriving at Upton the day after tomorrow. Can you make sure there's a full security staff and two permanent drivers available?'

'Yes, sir.'

Michael had hung up before Len could ask any more questions. He sat up too fast and his head felt like it was going to split open. Len let out a small cry of pain and groped his way to the bathroom and the shower cubicle. A quarter of an hour later, with his head still pumping, he was eating breakfast in the kitchen and making phone calls. The first was to Upton Park.

'It's Len here,' he announced. 'Is that you, Ron?'

'Ron gone,' a foreign voice announced.

'Gone where?' Len asked.

'Ron gone three days ago. Had big fight with Major Cox. Major ordered him to go. So Ron gone.'

'Shit! So who's taking care of the house?'

'We take care.'

Len realised he was talking to one of the Filipino house staff. 'That's great,' he said. 'Keep up the good work.'

The next number he dialled was Ron's home. Ron answered immediately. 'Ron, it's Len. What the fuck happened? Why aren't you at Upton?'

'That fucking idiot Major ordered me off the premises. He said he had the authority of the Sultan.'

'He doesn't have the authority of Jack Shit. Get back there and mind the shop. I'll be sending someone else to help you. The royal family are on their way over.'

'I can't.'

'Can't what?'

'Go back. I've got another job, a nice one. I'm not going anywhere near that mad bastard.'

'I'll take care of the Major,' Len assured him. 'He shouldn't be allowed to step inside the house, that's our territory, he's only responsible for the grounds. You don't have to have anything to do with him.'

'I'm not doing it, Len, I've had enough of that place. Anyway, I've heard what that Princess is like from the other staff. I don't want to be around when she arrives.'

'I don't know if she's going to be there,' Len protested. 'You can't let me down, Ron. You owe me.'

'Sorry, Len.' The line went dead and Len hung up with a stream of invective. The English-speaking cook gave him a dirty look.

'This Princess Jarmina,' Len said, 'is she as scary as everyone says?'

'The Princess?' The cook raised her eyes to the ceiling. 'She's a holy terror. She was always difficult, but since that Princess Nabila became Queen she's been like a bear with a sore head.'

'Shit,' Len said again and found another number to call. 'Gerry? It's Len. I need you to work this week.'

'Can't do it, Len, sorry, broken my leg in a bit of an incident.'

By the time Norman came into the kitchen, looking showered and sharp and ready for action, Len had spoken to a dozen of his best men and none of them was available to work at short notice. His self-esteem had plummeted. Yesterday he had felt like a successful young businessman, riding the crest of a wave. Today he felt ill and humiliated.

'You look rough, Len,' Norman said, slapping his baby brother playfully on the shoulder, sending an electrical storm of pain up into the front of his head. 'You need coffee.'

Len, unable to form words for a moment, gestured to the coffee-pot which the cook had prepared for him and which was already half empty. Norman helped himself to a cup and asked for a cooked breakfast. The cook looked as if she was going to tut, but saw a glint in Norman's eyes which made her think better of it. She started cooking.

As the smell of frying sausage and bacon infiltrated Len's nostrils, making his stomach shift uneasily, he sank his head into his hands.

'What's up?' Norman asked, swallowing a glass of orange juice.

'The royal family are about to arrive at the house in England and I can't find any staff.'

'Staff problems,' Norman nodded understandingly. 'You don't have to tell me anything about that. Manager's nightmare. And when you can get them they're fucking useless, or they try to dip their fingers in the till. You've gotta take a firm line with them, Len.'

'Not my men,' Len retorted, suddenly defensive. 'We have a very tight vetting procedure. It's just hard to find enough of them to meet the demand.'

Norman was about to say that was what he was saying, but thought better of it. He felt sorry for the kid, who was obviously seeing his dreams of impressing his big brother with his business empire withering before his eyes.

'Can't you do the job yourself?' Norman asked, as the cook placed the plate of fried food in front of him.

Len let out an involuntary groan. 'I'm not free,' he said. 'I have to be driving the General around. I don't want him to think I'm running a one-man band here.'

'No, I s'pose not.'

Norman tired of the subject and concentrated on his breakfast as Len continued to make calls to England. He wondered if he should go back to the villa, but decided to put off facing the blonde for a few more hours. For some reason he found he had had enough of her and preferred Len's male company. He decided to hang around until lunch-time and then make a decision. Maybe the blonde would grow tired of waiting and go off with someone else. Len was still on the phone, shouting frustrated abuse at some poor bloke in England, as Norman finished eating and made his way out to the pool. He picked up a newspaper from the pile in the hall and settled himself down for a doze in the sun.

He had no idea how long he had slept when he was woken by Len flopping down in the chair beside him.

'How's it going?' Norman enquired, not really interested in the answer.

'Hopeless,' Len said. 'I've been thinking, how would you like to earn a few quid for a few days' work?'

'I don't need a few quid, Len,' Norman laughed.

'Everyone needs a few quid,' Len protested.

'Not me. I've got more than I need. If I needed money I'd get myself a job.'

'Well, just to do me a favour then?' Len looked as appealing as he could manage.

'Are you asking me to pose as one of your poxy little security guards?' Norman asked, chuckling at the very thought of it.

'You'd be fine. You know how to handle yourself. You'd get a comfortable billet for a few days, just while I sort out some new staff. How hard can it be to keep a house secure when there's an army of security people guarding the grounds outside? There can be good perks in working for these people. Look at this place...' Len gestured around them at the beauty of the house and grounds.

Norman chuckled. 'And end up in the same state you're in? My ulcers have only just started to ease up after being down here a few weeks. To be honest, I'm trying to keep a low profile in England at the moment,' Norman confessed. 'There's this copper who's got it into his head that I bumped off some bloke and he's determined to make my life uncomfortable.'

'Perfect,' Len shouted happily. 'What better place to hide than in a respectable job in a royal household. Who would ever think of looking for you there?'

'I'm not much good at all that bowing and scraping and touching my forelock to people. You know that. Look at the fights I used to have with the old man when we were kids. I was never able to let him get away with anything.'

Len grinned at the memory of some of the rows he had witnessed between Norman and their father. His brother had always been too nimble on his feet for the old man to get hold of him. Then he remembered his problem and frowned.

'You don't have to have anything to do with them. You can stay in the control room or the kitchen most of the time. You hardly have to see them if you don't want to.'

'I'd have to use another passport to get back into the country, in case the Customs and Excise have been tipped off to watch for me.' Norman was still doubtful about the idea of working for someone, although he could see there might be advantages.

'Oh.' Len looked crestfallen as yet another stumbling-block appeared in his path.

'But that's not a problem,' Norman continued. 'I always carry a couple of spare passports, just in case I need them.'

'So, you'll do it?' Len perked up again.

'As long as you promise me it's only for a few days.'

'No problem, Norman, on my honour. I'll have you out of there the moment I manage to recruit someone new.'

'All right, then.' Norman gave his kid brother a comforting pat on the shoulder. 'Just till you're sorted out, then.'

Moody had been sitting for three days at an upstairs window opposite The Country Club, watching for Norman to make an appearance. He didn't mind the waiting. It was something he was good at. Moody had been born with endless patience for the more tedious elements of police work. As a child he'd been good at all the hobbies which required hours spent hanging around waiting for something to happen. He'd spent several years as an avid bird-watcher, crouched in damp bushes with binoculars, and then there was his train-spotting phase, watching the engines coming and going and jotting down the minutiae of their movements. Moody liked the sense of order, coupled with the frisson of expectation, involved in watching.

On the third day he saw a face he thought he recognised going into the club early in the day, at a time when the only other callers were cleaners and tradesmen delivering stock. The man had long, thick hair and dressed like a hippy from ten years before.

By the time the man came back out again, half an hour later, Moody had managed to search through his memory and pinpoint where he'd seen him before. His name, if Moody remembered correctly, was John Parsons and he was an ex-public school purveyor of drugs who had never quite managed to grow up. Moody remembered using him in the past as an informant. The man was acutely keen to stay out of prison and more than willing to talk to anyone in authority who could help him do so. Moody decided to pay him a call.

Early the following morning, armed with a search warrant and backed up by a young constable who was happy to get out of the station for a few hours, Moody was knocking on John Parsons' door. Parsons himself was still asleep, but a young girl with heavily dilated pupils and a permanent simpering smile, let them in and led them upstairs to the bedroom where Parsons lay sprawled on a mattress on the floor. The room was dotted with abandoned take-away containers which had doubled as ashtrays, and the air was stale with the mixed aromas of perfumed smoke and beer-soaked ash. Moody wrinkled his nose in disgust.

Parsons, woken by the sound of men's footsteps on the stairs, pulled a T-shirt and jeans onto his tall skinny body as the constable read him his rights.

'I have a search warrant for these premises,' Moody told him, waving the piece of paper in his face. He hated public schoolboys. He hated the condescension he sensed in their plummy accents whenever he had to deal with them, the supercilious way they looked at him when they knew they were going to end up with a fine they could pay without a flicker of discomfort. He always enjoyed encounters like this where he knew he could make one of them squirm. 'But I might be dissuaded from using it.'

'Okay,' Parsons nodded, his face white and his hands shaking as he lit himself a cigarette.

'The Streatham Country Club, what's your connection?'

'No connection. It's an address where one of my customers hangs out. I meet him there sometimes. I've never been there during opening hours.'

'Is your customer Norman Dorset?'

'Norman Dorset?' His shaking seemed to get worse. 'I don't know anything about him. I've never had any dealings with him.'

'Any idea where he is, then?'

'He's never been at the club when I've been there.'

'So, who's your customer then?'

Parsons let out a high, whining sound, as if begging to be let off from having to sneak on someone who might take it out on him later.

'Don't worry,' Moody assured him. 'They'll never know you've talked to me. You can go on with your business for a bit longer.'

'Chappell, Pete Chappell. I've known him a long time.'

'Dorset's brother-in-law?' Moody felt a twinge of excitement. It seemed he was edging closer to his prey.

'Yeah. But I've never had anything to do with Dorset himself. He'd never have anything to do with someone like me. Chappell only lets me come to the club when Dorset's away.'

'Away where?' Moody tried again.

'I told you, I don't know.'

'Is Chappell a big user?'

'He's a good customer. I don't know how much he uses himself.'

'Do you think he might be dealing?'

'I didn't say that!'

'But do you think it's possible? Does he buy in big enough quantities for that?'

'Yeah, I guess so.'

'Okay.' Moody held up the search warrant in both hands and symbolically tore it in half, allowing both halves to flutter to the floor. 'You live to trade another day, John.'

'Thanks.' Parsons sounded genuinely grateful, which only increased Moody's contempt for him.

'But if you get the slightest whisper as to where Dorset might be, I want you to ring me. Do you understand? That way you might buy yourself even more time on the outside.'

'I swear I'll ring the moment I hear something.' Parsons took the card which Moody was holding out, and slipped it into a small beaded bag which lay beside the mattress with his cigarettes and lighter.

'And there's something else I want you to do for me.'

CHAPTER EIGHT

The passport-control officer at Heathrow stared hard at Norman's face. Norman held the stare without a flicker of self-doubt. The man's eyes dropped back down to the photograph in the passport in his hands, and then back up to Norman's impassive face. Len watched from a few yards behind in the queue. To him the silence between the two men seemed to last forever, although no one else appeared to have noticed anything.

'Thank you, Mr Foster,' the official said eventually, and Norman walked through towards the baggage reclaim area.

One of Len's drivers was waiting for them at the exit from customs and led them to a Mercedes with darkened windows, parked in the short-term car park.

'Anything you need to do before we go to the house?' Len asked.

'Nothing,' Norman replied, settling into the seat.

'Upton Park,' Len instructed the driver and they headed west, away from London.

After a few minutes of silence, Len spoke: 'I've managed to find another guy to work with you – a man called Mark. He's just a kid really, so you'll be in charge, but you can send him on any errands that need doing. He's a good lad, used to be in the army but got into a few too many fights in bars.'

Norman raised a quizzical eyebrow.

'You have no idea how hard it is to find good people,' Len shrugged. 'All you need to do is open the house up each morning and close it again at night. Any calls that come in will go through the security room, so one of you needs to be there to re-route them or take messages. You need to vet any visitors or tradesmen, liaising with the men on the gate. The guy in charge of the outside security is a man called Major Cox. He's a major pain, but good at his job. He thinks he should be in charge of the house as well, so don't let him take any liberties or he'll be all over the place. You have total authority over everything that happens inside those doors. But if you want to get Mark to handle all the face-to-face stuff, there's no reason why you should ever leave the security room.'

A trace of a smile passed over Norman's expressionless face. Len was right, this would be the perfect place to lie low until Moody had let up on the pressure – or until he had managed to ensure that his alibis for the night Sidney Rose died were cast-iron.

The car drew up at the gates to Upton Park and the window purred down. 'Good afternoon,' Len called out to the guard who came out to see them. 'This is Norman Dorset. He's going to be in charge of the house with a lad called Mark for the next few days.'

The man leant in through the window and shook Norman's hand. He looked old to Norman, but his grip was hard.

'I gather the family are arriving tomorrow,' Len went on.

'So I heard,' the old man nodded. 'The old lady and the Princess, apparently. Not the Sultan himself.' The old man waved to someone inside the guardhouse and the gates swung open. He gave them a last nod and the driver took them through into the front courtyard.

'Oh God,' Len muttered. 'The Princess!'

'What's the problem with the Princess?' Norman asked.

'I've never met her myself,' Len said. 'But anyone who has tells me she's something of a monster. The old lady's okay though. Stays in her room the whole time. You won't even know she's there.'

'What kind of monster?' Norman wanted to know.

'A royal one,' Len grinned. 'I'm sure you can handle it. Just be polite and show respect.'

Norman remained noticeably quiet as Len led the way round to the side of the house and let them in through the security door. Norman spotted a camera that was pointed down in the eaves at the doorway. As they walked through, a young man with a holstered gun hanging loosely around his shoulder came out to meet them.

'Hi, Mark,' Len said. 'Everything all right?'

'Sure.'

Norman noticed Mark was pulling himself up in front of Len, as if addressing a superior officer. His qualms about doing the job increased. Norman had never been very good at showing respect for authority.

'This is Norman,' Len said. 'He'll be in charge for the next few days. The royal family is arriving tomorrow so you'll need to smarten up, wear a jacket over that for a start.'

'Yes, of course, Mr Dorset.' At this, Mark became even more ramrod straight.

Len gave him a reassuring pat on the shoulder and led Norman into the security room where all the screens showed pictures of various doors and rooms. Len unlocked a cupboard and pulled out a .38 revolver and holster and chucked it across to Norman.

'You need to wear this at all times downstairs,' he said, 'and have it with you when you go upstairs to bed. You're allowed to use it if at any time you feel the lives of any of the royal family are in danger.'

He tossed over a round of ammunition which Norman caught before flicking open the box.

'Dumdums?' he said.

'When you're guarding royalty you don't want anyone coming back for a second shot,' Len said. 'You have to make sure they're taken out from the start. Don't worry. We haven't had a single incident here yet. Keep the holster covered with a jacket when the family are around.'

Norman raised an eyebrow at what sounded like an order from his baby brother. Len realised he had overstepped the mark and held up his hands in mock surrender.

'Come on,' he said. 'I'll show you where you sleep.'

A modest staff staircase snaked upwards from behind the kitchen. On the first-floor landing there was a discreet panelled door amongst a wall of linen cupboards.

'That leads through to the family's quarters. At night it's locked and only you will have a key,' Len explained. 'Once they're upstairs the whole floor can be sealed so no one can come in or out, up or down, without triggering the alarms.'

'Let's see the rooms,' Norman said.

Len hesitated for a second and then went to the door. They came out into a wide, thickly carpeted landing area with doors leading off in all directions.

'You'll find floor maps down in the security room,' Len said as he led Norman from one palatial bedroom to the next. 'They give details of who sleeps where, where everything is; all the alarm wires, telephone wires, heating pipes, anything and everything that could possibly go wrong.'

'They certainly know how to live,' Norman said, impressed despite himself at the lavishness of the furnishings and decorations.

'Yeah.' Len paused for a second to look around at the room they were in. 'I guess I've got used to it.'

'Right.' Norman looked closely at one of the pictures on the wall. 'Are all these pictures original?'

'Every one of them. Most are gifts from various governments grateful to Domai for doing business with them.'

'Bloody hell!'

Once they'd seen all the family's rooms, Len led him back through the panelled door and on up the staircase to the staff bedrooms above. They were basic but comfortable, each with their own wash-basin, almost like superior student accommodation, or, as Norman thought, a very sophisticated prison cell.

'This one's yours,' Len said, indicating one of the larger rooms at the top of the stairs. 'The staff will bring your bags up later.'

'I don't know if I can do this, Len,' Norman said. 'I'm no good at all this bowing and scraping and knowing my place.'

'Don't worry.' Len waved his brother's fears aside. He was too dependent on Norman staying to be able to contemplate any alternative. 'Just be your usual charming self. They'll love you. And it'll only be for a couple of days at the most.'

'Make sure it is, Len,' Norman growled. 'Make bloody sure it is.'

The following morning, having breakfasted well, waited on by a cheerful staff of Filipinos, Norman went through to the security room to read his newspaper. Mark, who had already been on a run round the grounds, made a few attempts at conversation, but received only grunts in response and so gave up trying. Norman was just getting into the sports section when Mark noticed some action on the monitor covering the gate area.

'They're here, Norman,' he announced.

Norman lowered his newspaper and watched the screen covering the approach to the front door as three of Len's Daimler limousines moved slowly forward from the gates and came to a halt at the door.

'Looks like a bleedin' funeral procession,' he muttered.

On another screen he saw the front door being opened by the German housekeeper, a woman he had noticed in the kitchen remonstrating with the chef in a way that had instantly told Norman they had been married for a good many years.

After they had come to a final halt, the drivers climbed out of the first two cars and went round to open the doors, placing small footstools on the ground for the passengers to step out onto. Women in flowing robes and scarves seemed to pour out. Norman counted eight of them as they eddied around the third car, clucking over the mountains of suitcases that were being unloaded. Some of them then returned to the first vehicle where the driver was still holding the door open, apparently waiting, like some guard of honour, for someone else to appear. After a few moments another woman stepped out and it was obvious from their actions that she was senior to the women already milling around the car. They appeared to be nervous of her. This woman also waited by the car door and Norman put down his paper to watch more carefully what might happen next.

They all seemed to be talking to someone still inside the car, as if encouraging whoever it was in some way, until finally, mighty piece by mighty piece, the mother of the Sultan of Domai emerged into the light, her bulk so enormous she barely fitted through the door of the limousine. She came slowly, as if every movement was an effort. Her face beamed happily at those around her as her cheeks puffed up with the air needed to keep herself going.

'Bloody hell,' Norman said out loud. 'What the hell is that?'

'I think that's the Queen Mother,' Mark said. 'Len told me she was pretty big.'

'Jesus Christ,' Norman muttered. 'You'd better pray there isn't a fire or you'll be the one carrying her out.'

Mark let out a guffaw of laughter and then realised he was being disrespectful to his employers and immediately silenced it.

'It's all right, lad,' Norman said, his face showing no trace of a smile. 'You're allowed a sense of humour in this job.' This boy reminded him of some of the younger, more eager screws he had come across in his time.

'Right you are, Norman,' Mark agreed and Norman shook his head sadly.

The cameras followed the progress of the enormous woman and her entourage through the front door and across the hall to the lift. The other women loaded her into it and then scampered up the stairs, holding up their long skirts as they went, in order to be at the top in time to meet her. The other important woman, who Norman assumed was Princess Jarmina, had already taken the staircase and was making her way to her bedroom. Once through the bedroom doors they were out of sight of any cameras and Norman went back to reading his paper.

For the rest of the day neither of the royal ladies emerged, although some of their court could be seen scurrying from one room to another. The kitchen buzzed with activity as the cook tried to keep up with the various demands for meals. Norman and Mark took it in turns to go upstairs to their rooms to get some sleep in the afternoon. To Norman it seemed a bit like he was still on holiday – but without the annoyance of the blonde's nagging.

He gave a small smile as he remembered her. She had still been at the villa when Norman went back to pack after spending the night with Len, and had been extremely unamused by his attitude.

'You could have phoned for Christ's sake,' she'd wailed. 'All night I was sitting here wondering what could have happened to you. You could have been dead in a ditch somewhere, or lying in a hospital bed. All you had to do was give me a call and I could have put my mind at rest.'

'Give your tongue a bloody rest, woman,' Norman had growled.

'Don't "woman" me,' she'd screeched. 'Who do you think you are? You can't treat people like pieces of dirt and just get away with it.'

Her voice had ground on and on in his brain, until he couldn't take it any more. His hand came up with a speed he had first perfected in the boxing ring in Liverpool – he had even gone professional for a few years although, latterly, he'd had to use his skills in other ways. The blonde wasn't ready for it and he caught her face in his fingers, pinching the open mouth that was still halfway through a word until it was frozen and the eyes suddenly fearful. The strength in his fingers could have crushed the bones, at least that was how it felt to her. She flailed at him with her arms, one extended nail grazing his neck, but he only increased the strength of the grip and she allowed her arms to fall loosely to her sides.

'You're giving me a headache,' he said very quietly, and very close to her face. 'If you don't shut your mouth now, I'm going to have to shut it for you. I've never hit a woman in my life, but I'm willing to make an exception in your case if you don't stop the nagging right now.'

He opened his fingers and she staggered backwards, rubbing her jaw. For a moment it looked as if she was about to start shouting again, but Norman raised a finger in warning and she turned and ran upstairs, her heels clacking in the sudden silence of the villa.

In the end Norman had gone upstairs and found her lying on the bed, sobbing. She looked so young with all her make-up gone he was reminded for a moment of his own daughters.

'Here,' he said, tossing a pile of money onto the bed. 'Find yourself a hotel room for a few days while you work out what you want to do. Now pack your bag and get out.'

Norman smiled to himself at the memory of her sprawled on the bed. The image made him feel uncomfortable in the crutch of his trousers and he readjusted himself.

That evening, when it looked as if the Princess and Queen Mother were not going to come out of their rooms again, Norman rang Pete Chappell at the club to tell him he was back in the country and to check everything was okay.

'Give us your phone number then, Norman,' Pete said, 'just in case I need to get hold of you.'

'Nah,' Norman replied. 'I'll call in from time to time.' He hung up, knowing that Moody could well be trying to trace the call.

The next morning nothing had changed. The royal women were still in their rooms and the household staff were rushing back and forth with trolleys and trays. At twelve o'clock, as Mark and Norman were in the middle of a game of cards in the security room, the screen covering the landing showed the Princess emerging from her room and making her way downstairs. Norman kept one eye on his hand and one on her progress as she appeared on the next screen, crossing the hall.

'She's heading this way,' Mark said, folding his hand.

'Don't you bloody dare,' Norman said. 'Not when I'm just about to relieve you of a week's wages.'

Mark forced himself to look back at his cards, although Norman could see it made him nervous. He saw the Princess disappear off the screen through the door to the kitchen area. He could hear raised voices outside the security room door. Someone was remonstrating with the cook in an angry voice. He kept playing, aware that Mark was now far too disconcerted to stand a chance of beating him.

The door burst open and Mark sprang to his feet, struggling to get his jacket on and bow at the same time as the Princess swept into the room. Norman kept staring at his cards, his cigarette smouldering in the corner of his mouth. The Princess appeared to be lost for words as she glowered at him. A puzzled look flitted across her face at the sight of an employee who seemed not to notice that she was in the room at all. Unable to think of anything to say, she turned to Mark instead, who was behaving as she expected.

'Your name?'

'Mark, your Highness,' he barked back, like a soldier on parade. Norman looked up with an amused expression and caught the Princess' eye. He didn't avert his eyes, or remove the cigarette from his lips, or make any attempt to stand. She opened her mouth as if to say something to him but thought better of it and swept from the room.

Norman followed her progress on the screens, back across the hall at speed and through one of the drawing-room doors. Norman pressed a button on one of the other screens that covered the outside of the house and could see her moving around inside the drawing-room through the window.

'Sit down and play,' he told Mark.

'Bloody hell, Norman,' Mark said as he sank back into his chair.

'What?'

'She's a Princess for God's sake. Doesn't that mean anything to you?'

Norman looked puzzled. 'How long were you in the army then, lad?'

'Ten years.'

'Too bloody long, obviously. They're no different from us, apart from having more money. They have to shit, just like the rest of us.'

Mark went back to the game but Norman could see his heart wasn't in it. The poor boy obviously hadn't met anyone quite like Norman before.

'Not a bad-looker, though, do you think?' Norman said after a few minutes.

'Who?' Mark asked, assuming Norman was referring to some picture in the paper.

'Her Highness, the Queen of Sheba.' He gestured towards the screens with his head.

'No, not bad,' Mark agreed. 'If you like that sort of thing.'

Norman said no more.

Lunch was served to the Princess in the dining-room, and to her mother in her bedroom. Norman and Mark took it in turns to eat in the kitchen. After eating, Norman went back to the security room and settled himself down for a nap with his feet on the desk. He was still asleep when the Princess emerged from the dining-room and swept back across the hall. The first he knew of it was when the door of the security room flew open and she was standing over him. Norman, startled awake, blinked at her for a few moments.

'Can I help you?' he enquired, without moving from the position he'd been sleeping in.

'I want to see the horses. You come with me.'

'No thanks,' Norman retorted. 'Not interested in them, unless I'm betting on them. There're plenty of people up the stables who'll show you around.'

Jarmina felt herself beginning to shake. She had never met an employee who dared take such an attitude with her. 'No,' she snapped, 'I want you to escort me.'

'He'll take you.' Norman gestured towards Mark, who was coming out of the kitchen behind her.

'I am ordering you to escort me to the stables,' she shouted.

Norman waited for a couple of beats before lifting his feet off the desk. 'Follow me, then,' he said wearily, pulling his jacket on over his holster and making his way to the back door. It wasn't until he was outside that he realised Jarmina wasn't with him.

'Where's she bloody gone?' he called through to Mark.

'Through to the front door,' Mark replied.

Norman let out of whistle of irritation and walked around the house, finding the Princess standing on the front doorstep, apparently unable to work out what to do next.

'I thought you were following me,' he said.

'I don't go through servants' doors,' she retorted.

'Oh, is that right?'

He could see the other women huddled in the hallway behind her, their mouths hanging open in disbelief at the way their mistress was being treated.

'You coming, then?' he asked.

Jarmina opened and closed her mouth and then nodded, bustling to keep up with Norman's stride as they headed for the stables. The other women rushed to the door to watch them go and Norman could hear their suppressed giggles. Neither of them spoke on the way over. As they came close to the buildings Norman saw Major Cox emerging from the indoor school, brushing himself down and smoothing his hair in preparation for receiving a royal visit. He gave a smart bow as the Princess drew close. She ignored him and walked into the building with Norman. The Major fell into step behind them, burbling sycophantically.

The Princess made her way through to the loose boxes where a number of horses were poking their magnificent heads out in search of company.

'Feed them,' she said to Norman, gesturing towards a barrel filled with what looked to Norman like shrivelled dog-biscuits.

'No thanks,' he replied. 'You want to feed them you do it yourself. Horses and me don't get on.'

He heard a muted sound as the Major appeared to implode behind him. The Princess glared at him and then stalked over to the barrel, scooped out a handful of the pellets and made her way along the row of horses, pointedly making conversation with each one and ignoring the two men behind her.

'Show the woman some respect, man,' the Major hissed in Norman's ear.

Norman gave him a cold glare and said nothing. Pulling out his pouch he rolled himself a cigarette with steady hands.

'No smoking in the stables,' the Major said. 'Too much straw.'

Norman didn't even look at him before lighting up. Small flakes of burning tobacco escaped and drifted towards the ground. The Major jumped forward and stamped them out angrily as Norman gazed thoughtfully after the Princess.

When she had finally reached the end of the line of animals, Jarmina strode back towards the door. 'Take me back to the house now,' she ordered, without looking at Norman or breaking her stride.

'Right then,' Norman suppressed a grin. 'I'll do that, then.'

They walked in silence for a few moments.

'So,' she said, 'you are afraid of horses?'

'No question about it,' Norman agreed. 'Bloody terrified.'

'And you are supposed to be the brave man who is guarding us?'

'If the house comes under attack by a highly trained gang of Shetland ponies, you can count me out,' Norman replied without a smile.

'Who are Shetland ponies?' she asked, puzzlement in her dark eyes.

'Never mind,' Norman said, opening the front door for her and then walking in behind her.

The women were still there, waiting for the return of their Princess, and they immediately gathered around her as Norman made his way across the hall and through the door to the security room without a backward glance.

'I think she was expecting you to go round to the back door again,' Mark said as Norman came in, having observed the whole scene on the screens.

'Have you met the Major up the stables?' Norman enquired.

'Yeah, why?'

'Because you two make a right pair. Now go and ask cook to make us a cup of tea.'

He glanced at the screen, watching the Princess crossing the landing towards her bedroom door, dismissing the other women, who scuttled back towards the Queen Mother's room. She seemed to Norman to pause on the threshold as if trying to decide whether to come back downstairs and say something else. For a second Norman hoped that she would. He rather relished the idea of another skirmish. The woman was interesting. The Princess changed her mind and went into the room, slamming the door behind her.

The following morning Norman was on the phone to Len. 'How's your recruitment programme going then?' he asked.

'What?'

'Have you found anyone to take over this bloody job?'

'Oh yeah, right!' Len was obviously trying to muster his thoughts. 'No problem. I'm working on it. I'm pretty sure I can get you out of there in a couple of days.'

'I want to get out now, Len,' Norman warned. 'Don't mess me about.'

'I'm not messing you about, Norman, honest. Just give me a couple more days. Relax, enjoy yourself.'

'Relax?' Norman thundered. 'Have you met this woman? It's like working for Hitler in a headscarf.'

'I bet you're charming the pants off her,' Len laughed. 'Don't worry Norman, I'm sorting it.'

'Just make sure you are,' Norman growled and hung up.

Breakfast went upstairs to the ladies in their rooms. Just before lunch there was a flurry of activity on the screens again and the Princess arrived in the security room. She seemed slightly ill at ease, as if uncertain what sort of response she would get from Norman.

'This afternoon,' she announced, looking directly at him, 'we will go shopping to Harrods. Please order the car and the doctor and be ready to leave at two o'clock.'

'Mark will go with you,' Norman said. He didn't fancy being responsible for someone as unpredictable as this on the street and he was trying to keep a low profile after all.

'No,' she shook her finger at him. 'You will come. You and the doctor and the driver. Two o'clock.'

'I'm not really the shopping type,' Norman warned.

'Two o'clock,' she said, refusing to hear his protests, and swept back out towards the dining-room.

'Who's the doctor?' Norman asked Mark.

'I think she always travels with her personal physician,' Mark said. 'He stays around here somewhere and comes in whenever they need him. He travels with them wherever they go. If you tell the driver he'll pick the doctor up on the way here.'

'You organise it,' Norman said. 'I'm going for some fresh air.'

Norman went out of the back door and made his way to a bench overlooking the ornamental fish-ponds. The sound of the fountains calmed him a little as he rolled himself a cigarette and took a long drag. His ulcers were rumbling ominously.

'I don't think we've been formally introduced,' a voice behind him said, making him jump. His hand was already on his gun before he realised it was the Major.

'Norman Dorset,' he said, taking his hand off the butt of the gun and offering it to Cox.

'I'd like to give you some advice, Dorset,' the Major said, ignoring the extended hand. 'When you're working for royalty, it pays to know your place. They don't appreciate uppity lackeys.'

'What're you talking about?' Norman growled.

'The way you talked to Her Highness, yesterday, at the stables.' The Major stared out at the landscape as he talked, uncomfortable under Norman's cold stare. 'They don't like it.'

'Well, it's kind of you to put me right, Colonel,' he said, his voice steady and quiet.

'Major,' Cox corrected him with an irritated cough.

'But I talk to people the same whoever they are.'

'Then I doubt you'll be here long,' Cox snapped, wheeling round and marching off smartly.

'I doubt that too,' Norman muttered under his breath as he settled back to finish his smoke.

At two o'clock the Princess and two of her ladies had arrived at the front door and the car was waiting outside. Mark was holding the door open and the doctor was already sitting in the front seat next to the driver. Norman waited until the women were safely inside before climbing into the front beside the doctor. None of the men spoke on the journey into London whereas the women whispered and giggled in the back like school children on an outing. When they reached the Brompton Road, the driver drew up at the front door of Harrods. Norman jumped out first. The doctor called him back. He was fishing under the seat and came out with a small stool which he passed to Norman. Norman gave it a distasteful look and walked round to Princess' door, placing the stool on the ground and opening the door. He kept a watch on the crowd as a doorman opened the store door and the women alighted.

'Mr Norman,' the Princess said, 'you take this.'

Norman was so surprised that she knew his name that he took the large manila envelope she was handing to him without thinking. It was surprisingly heavy. She turned and walked into the shop, assuming he would follow her.

'This won't take long,' he told the doorman. 'Can the car wait here?'

'No, sir,' the man replied politely. 'It'll have to circle the block or park around the back.'

'Shit!' Norman didn't have time to argue. The woman he was supposed to be guarding had now disappeared from sight into the store. 'Okay, I'll be back.'

The limousine, carrying the silent doctor, slid away from the kerb as Norman dived through the doors holding the envelope. For a moment he couldn't see the Princess and he swivelled his head frantically from side to side, until he caught a glimpse of her brightly coloured scarf at a leather counter. She waved him over.

'You pay,' she said when he reached the counter, indicating the small heap of leather handbags and wallets which had been piled up.

'Pay?' Norman was beginning to feel irritation creeping over him. 'I don't have any money.'

'There,' the Princess said, gesturing to the envelope in his hand. 'You pay.'

Jarmina was already moving off towards another counter, waving at the assistants who were gathering around her like flies, and ordering goods by the dozen, before he had time to protest. Norman opened the envelope and saw it was stuffed with money. Wads of twenty-pound notes the size of bricks.

'Wait!' he commanded loudly, but Jarmina was not listening. Norman tried to keep an eye on where she was going, at the same time as peeling off enough money to pay for the goods on the counter and giving the assistant the address of Upton Park for the delivery.

By the time he had caught up with her she had already been through the perfumery department, leaving piles of purchases in her wake, and was heading for the lifts to find the glassware. Norman's ulcers gave a volcanic roar in his stomach, the bile seeming to erupt almost to the back of his throat.

'Right!' Norman chased after them and grabbed Jarmina's arm. She recoiled from him, but he held firm. The silk of her dress was soft to his touch and her arm surprisingly slender. She suddenly seemed delicate and vulnerable to him. 'That's it,' he spluttered. 'No more shopping. We're going home.'

Jarmina shouted back, furious that anyone should speak to her in such a way, let alone lay hands on her, but Norman turned a deaf ear, hustling her across the crowded store towards the door they had come in through, leaving the piles of purchases on the counters. She lashed out at him with her foot, the sharp end of an expensive court shoe finding its mark on his ankle-bone. He gave her arm an angry jerk, making her headscarf slide off and allowing her hair to fall free. She tried to repair the damage with her free hand as she was whisked out into the street.

Outside, on the pavement, there was no sign of the car. The doorman approached, with a beaming smile, to see if he could call them a taxi and then recognised them.

'Where's the fucking car?' Norman snarled.

'It just passed by,' the doorman replied. 'It'll be back round in a few minutes.'

Jarmina had given up her struggle. She was now more concerned with the fact that they were stranded on a busy pavement with no means of escape. She tugged her scarf forward to hide her face from the curious stares of passers-by. She was so shocked by the way she had been treated that she could think of no words to express her fury.

They waited for what seemed like an age. Norman's eyes darted from one end of the pavement to the other, critically aware of the bulk of the gun pressing into his armpit and the weight of the money in his hand. A pair of policemen appeared at the far corner of the store and began to stroll towards them.

'Shit!' Norman muttered under his breath, turning his head to look in the other direction. He didn't see the car slide around behind the officers and crawl along the kerb towards them until it had come to a stop right beside Jarmina and the other women, and the driver had jumped out to open the door.

As soon as the women were safely inside, Norman hopped briskly into the front seat, aware, from the corner of his eye, that the policemen were walking past the windows.

'Back to Upton Park,' Norman ordered the driver as they rejoined the flow of traffic.

The moment the car doors were all shut, Jarmina began to shout abuse at Norman and the doctor rummaged in the bag at his feet to find some tranquillisers to pass back to her. Norman stared steadfastly ahead, refusing to respond to the tirade being directed at the back of his head, a slight smile twitching at the corners of his mouth. Eventually she gave up and a silence fell on the small group as the limousine headed out of London on the motorway. It lasted all the way to the front door. Norman waited by the car as Jarmina got out. He did not trouble to put the stool out for her.

'No more shopping trips,' he said quietly as she passed by. 'In future you take someone else.' He held out the envelope. 'Here.'

She looked at it with contempt and then looked back at him. 'You keep it,' she said, 'for your trouble.'

Turning on her heel she strode inside and Norman made his way round to the side door. It had been a bad experience, but it looked as if he had been well remunerated. Once inside the security room, with a mug of tea and a sandwich, he counted the money under Mark's amazed eyes and open mouth. It came to just over fifteen thousand pounds.

Norman passed a few hundred pounds across to Mark. 'There you go, lad,' he grinned. 'And next time you can take her bloody shopping.'

The other women were buzzing around Jarmina like summer insects on the eyes of cattle. She brushed them away without a thought, barely even seeing they were there as she made her way to her room and slammed the door behind her. She stood for a good thirty seconds, incapable of making a decision as to how to vent her spleen. A mixture of anger, frustration and excitement were knotting up inside her. She felt like screaming at someone, anyone. She really wanted to shout at Norman, but she knew he would shout back and that would make her even angrier. She moved as if to throw herself on the bed and bury her head in the pillows, but thought better of it. She didn't quite feel like crying.

She eyed up the crystal vase of lilies which stood on the coffee-table between the sofas, and felt an urge to hurl it through the window. She strode across the room and picked it up. It was heavier than she expected and the water slopped out over her arm and dress. She dropped it back down on the table with a bang and a cobweb of cracks spun out across the glass surface. She was about to kick the table but realised that her foot was still hurting from where she had lashed out at Norman when he grabbed her arm. She had put all her strength into that blow and it had still not stopped him from forcing her out of the shop. The audacity of the man took her breath away. She could still feel the pressure of his fingers on her flesh. They had been like a vice. She felt a little breathless at the memory.

Rolling up the sleeve she found that the red marks were beginning to turn to bruises. It was unbelievable! The man had laid hands on her. He would be flayed alive for such a crime back home.

She limped towards the bed and threw herself down on her back, staring up at the portrait of her father that hung above the fireplace. That's what she would do. She would send a message to her father, telling him what had happened, and he would have the upstart flogged. She remembered an incident when she was about six. She had had a nanny whom she had despised: a stupid, ignorant woman who did nothing but lecture her on how to be a woman and remain invisible. They had been in her nursery at the palace in Domai and she had heard her father's car returning in the courtyard below. She could remember clearly deciding to run out onto the balcony to wave to him, knowing that the nanny was forbidden to allow her to go out there for fear she would fall to her death.

She too could remember the expression on her father's face as he looked up and saw his first-born child leaning over the railings, waving frantically. He had called out angrily and stormed into the palace. She had known that she had succeeded in her mission. He couldn't be cross with her because she was just a child and she was being so sweet, welcoming her father back home. She knew he would never be angry with her. All the consequences would fall onto the bowed head of the nanny who had been pleading with her to come back into the safety of the room.

Within minutes guards had rushed into the nursery and the poor woman was dragged away, sobbing for mercy, to be whipped. A new nanny was in place within two hours and bars were put up at the nursery window to ensure nothing like that could ever happen again. Jarmina would see the poor woman occasionally, hunched in shame, going about humble household cleaning tasks, and she knew she had the power to do whatever she wanted, as long as she kept the men in her family sweet.

If her father found out how Norman had treated her he would be instantly dismissed. They might not be allowed to beat him, this being England, but they could certainly make sure he never worked again.

She pictured Norman being banished from Upton and the feeling of euphoria was replaced by something else, something like disappointment. The emotions that were boiling inside her might be uncomfortable, but they were better than the tedium she had felt before. The day might have made her furious, but at least it had been different. And if Norman was sent away, there would be no one else who would challenge her or make her angry. She would be able to shout at anyone she wanted, even slap and kick them if she felt sufficiently angry, but none would ever hit her back. So, what would be the point? With the realisation that she had actually enjoyed the fight in Harrods, came the far worse revelation that she wasn't enjoying the rest of her life.

As she lay, staring at the silk canopy above the bed, her mind travelled back to the first time she had come to London, and her escape into Bond Street from Claridge's. She remembered the Italian man who had accosted her and who had shown none of the respect she was used to. For years she had fantasised about meeting that man again but, as time passed, the memory had come to her less frequently and she realised she hadn't thought about him for months. She decided she wouldn't make any complaint about Norman to anyone. She would keep him there and she would defeat him herself. She would force him to show her the respect that was her due. She would have to hatch a plan.

To begin with she would confuse him by staying in her room. She would leave him wondering how much trouble he was in, whether he was going to lose his job or not.

CHAPTER NINE

Two days later the Princess came into the security room for the first time since the shopping trip. Occasionally Norman had seen her moving about the landing upstairs, going between her own room and her mother's, where she had taken all her meals. There was something different about her demeanour. She was wearing a mysterious smile instead of her usual frown. Other members of staff were still complaining about the way she treated them, but she seemed to be avoiding Norman. He was quite happy about that. He was only just managing to get his ulcers back under control and he didn't want any aggravation that might stir them up again. At the same time, he was pleased to see her. Whatever happened, she was bound to break the monotony of the security room.

'Mr Norman,' she said in a loud voice.

'That's me,' Norman replied, without getting out of his chair. 'What can I do for you? No more shopping trips, I hope. Because I'm warning you, I'm out of here before I'm going back to Harrods with you.'

'No,' she said. 'You can stay. You are a good soldier.' She laughed and Norman was surprised what an attractive sound it was. And her laughter seemed to make her face light up. 'No,' she promised. 'No more shopping trips to frighten poor Mr Norman. And no more horses.'

'I'm glad to hear it.'

'My mother would like to go on a picnic tomorrow.'

'A picnic? You'd need to talk to cook about that.'

'Okay. But you come to look after us, yes?'

'A picnic?' he repeated with a small smile. 'Okay.' He felt he could handle that. They would be out in the country somewhere, well away from any crowds. It would make a change from staring at the walls of the security room.

'Good.' Jarmina nodded in satisfaction. 'We need four cars tomorrow at eleven.'

'Four cars?' Norman protested, but she had already left the room and was on her way back upstairs. 'Four cars,' he muttered, and picked up the phone.

The following morning when Norman rose and went through his normal security routine, he found the kitchens already in uproar. Extra cooks had been brought in and a moveable feast was taking shape on the table, complete with a full set of china and silver serving dishes, crystal glasses and gold cutlery. Folding tables, which the King had bought for the last Ascot meeting, were being brought down from the stables and piled up in preparation for the arrival of the cars, which Norman had taken the precaution of ordering early. Two throne-like chairs were being brought out, one large enough to seat two people.

As he watched the piles of food and utensils building all around him, Norman began to feel stirrings of unease and a warning twinge in his stomach. This was turning into a major circus and was likely to attract a great deal of attention from anyone who happened to come across them whilst they were enjoying this picnic. He did not like that idea. Dragging the Princess away from trouble was one thing, trying to move her, her mother and their entourage was quite another.

'Maybe you should go on this trip,' he said to Mark as they both watched the proceedings over the screens.

'I'd love to,' Mark said, allowing himself a sly grin at Norman's expense. 'But Her Highness has left strict instructions that you alone should handle the security. I have been ordered to stay here and watch the house, while you're all off enjoying yourselves.'

Norman gave him a stern look and Mark's grin evaporated.

At quarter to eleven the Queen Mother emerged from her room for the first time since her arrival and waddled breathlessly towards the lift. As she descended, the other women scampered down the stairs to be ready to greet her at the bottom and help her on the short walk to the first car. Outside, the tables, chairs and hampers were being loaded into the fourth car. The boots of the first three cars had already been filled. The servants were getting into the third car and the ladies-in-waiting clambered into the second.

'Here she comes,' Mark said, as Jarmina emerged onto the landing upstairs. She seemed to have taken particular care over her appearance, wearing a light, silver-coloured robe that floated around her as she walked downstairs, well aware of the impact she was having. 'You'd better report for duty,' Mark teased.

Norman gave a grunt and pulled himself to his feet. 'Wish me luck with this lot,' he said, and made his way through into the front hall, giving Mark a discreet V-sign on the hidden camera as he went. Although he doubted the wisdom of allowing himself to be bullied into attending this outing, Norman had to admit to himself that he was curious to see what was going to happen.

During the morning he had been consulting some maps of the area so that he could make suggestions should they ask him where they should go. He was hoping they would be willing to settle in the grounds of some luxury country hotel somewhere, so they could make use of the facilities on offer.

Casting a quick eye over the whole caravan as the cars started up their engines and prepared to draw out, Norman nodded in satisfaction and climbed into the front seat of the first car, alongside the doctor, who was dressed in exactly the same three-piece suit he had worn to go to Harrods.

As the cars rolled forward towards the gate, the Princess leaned forward. 'Her Highness, my mother, would like to go to the seaside,' she announced.

'Okay,' Norman nodded. He could think of a few secluded places he could head for in that case.

'She wants to go to Brighton,' she added.

'She could go to Brighton after lunch,' Norman suggested. 'We should be able to find somewhere more picturesque for the picnic.'

'She wants to have the picnic in Brighton,' Jarmina insisted.

'Brighton's a big town,' Norman turned round in order to argue his case more succinctly and was surprised by how pretty Jarmina looked. She seemed to be wearing lipstick, which he'd never seen her do before. 'It's not really somewhere you can have a picnic.'

'Go to Brighton,' Jarmina said, becoming irritated at having a staff member arguing with her in front of her mother. 'We will find somewhere when we get there. It is my mother's wish.'

Norman looked across at the Queen Mother, who was sitting back, nodding with a beatific smile on her enormous face. He had a feeling he was not going to be able to talk them out of this one. His only option would be to stop the cars and get out, but he now felt he had some responsibility for their safety. God alone knew what would happen to such a vulnerable crowd if they tried to eat in Brighton without protection. He made a mental note never to allow himself to be talked into escorting them on any outings any more, and to ring Len immediately he got back to the house to tell him his 'few days' were up.

'Okay,' he said eventually, his ulcers emitting a warning stab of pain. 'Let's go to Brighton.'

He settled back in his seat, hoping that once the royal women saw what the Brighton sea front looked like they would realise the impossibility of stopping there for a picnic. The only people who ate on Brighton beach were families who carried everything they needed in a few Tupperware boxes. He doubted that the reality of the grey sea and even greyer crowds would live up to whatever fantasy the Queen Mother was carrying in her head. As they came closer to the coast, the sunshine which had bathed Upton Park on their departure vanished behind heavy clouds and a wind began to whip at the clothes of the holiday-makers they could see walking along the promenade. Norman felt more optimistic.

'Maybe we should go through Brighton to the other side and find somewhere sheltered, or perhaps a hotel,' he suggested.

The Queen Mother said something and the Princess banged the back of the driver's seat. 'Stop!' she instructed. 'We want to stop here.'

'Here?' Norman looked around as the driver stood on the brakes and the other cars screeched to a halt behind them.

'That shelter.' Jarmina pointed to shelter overlooking the increasingly choppy seas. It must have been designed to double as a bus-stop. A few elderly people, some with small, equally elderly dogs on leads, were sitting, staring out at the view. 'We can set up in there. Then, if it rains, the picnic will not be spoiled.'

'I don't think we're allowed to park here,' Norman protested.

'We won't park,' Jarmina insisted. 'We will unload the cars and the drivers can drive up and down until we are finished.'

Norman looked across at the driver, who let out a sound rather like a tyre being let down, but showed no expression on his face of having heard a word. Norman was about to protest again but realised it was too late. They had made up their royal minds.

Jarmina was preparing herself to step out and Norman climbed reluctantly out with the little stool from under the front seat. He placed it on the ground and opened the back door. Jarmina stepped daintily out and breathed in the damp sea air with every sign of satisfaction. Her hand rested lightly on Norman's shoulder for a second, her fingers brushing his neck, and he caught a breath of her perfume. He readjusted the stool so that her mother could follow, but misjudged the timing. The colossal woman's tiny foot landed on his fingers and, for what seemed like an age, she transferred her entire weight onto it as she pushed herself through the door and landed the other foot on the pavement. All his life Norman had practised taking pain without showing any sign that it was getting to him – it had been the main reason he had managed to survive in the many approved schools and prisons he had spent time in. He had always been able to rise to be a 'daddy' to those around him in any community, partly through his ability to dole out pain and partly by being able to take it. For a moment he thought he might be going to have to break the habits of a lifetime and scream, but he managed to hold it in long enough for the foot to lift and the two women to start directing their ladies-in-waiting and servants in setting up the tables and chairs in the shelter.

The elderly people already there did not need to be asked to move on. They took fright as the army of Filipinos descended and started flapping tablecloths in the wind, slamming down the silver tureens and plates to keep the fine Egyptian linen from flying away. Directors' chairs were brought for the other women, and the thrones for the Queen Mother and Princess. As the lids were ceremoniously lifted from the serving dishes, whole chickens appeared, salads and piles of cold meats, fruit and mountains of chocolates. Loaves of bread and a variety of drinks were dispensed amongst the women by the staff as they sat themselves down, their wrists and fingers jangling with priceless jewels and watches, and allowed the staff to run around them, filling their plates and glasses with the exquisite fare.

'Excuse me, sir.' A policeman's polite monotone made Norman jump. 'Are you in charge here?'

'Yes, officer,' Norman said. He'd never been this polite to a member of the force in his life.

'These cars can't stay here. They shouldn't even have stopped.'

'They're on their way, officer,' Norman assured him, waving the drivers forward.

The cars drew away and Norman had the same exposed feeling he had experienced on the Brompton Road. He was on his own, protecting the biggest sitting target in town, with no means of escape. They couldn't even run if trouble threatened because the Queen Mother would be left behind. He was aware of the bulge of the gun under his jacket and wondered if he would be covered by some sort of diplomatic immunity if the policeman spotted it.

'Make sure they don't obstruct the road, will you, sir?' the policeman said, nodding towards the feasting women.

'Yes, officer,' Norman nodded. He was aware that on the other side of the road a bunch of youths were gathering outside a pub to watch the free show. As the policeman moved off they began to shout across at the picnicking group but their words were drowned by the noise of the traffic. Norman positioned himself behind the shelter, staring hard at anyone who looked for too long at the curious spectacle of a desert feast on a grey English day. The gang of youths increased in size and courage and their catcalls became louder and bolder. The women, jabbering to one another around the table as they pushed food into their mouths, appeared not to notice, but Norman could see the servants were becoming nervous, their eyes darting from their employers to the youths, wondering whom to pay the most attention to.

Norman watched as the bravest of the group started across the road, dodging amongst the traffic. He unbuttoned his jacket so that he would be able to make the gun visible if necessary, and cursed Len under his breath. The moment he got this lot safely back home, he vowed he was jacking the whole lark in. It was too much for his nerves, and he could feel his ulcers churning in his stomach. If these lads made a big scene, the police would be back and would start asking for names and addresses. He needed to get back to the villa in Spain for a bit more of a rest.

'Bloody hell! It's the Arabian fucking Nights!' a voice jeered from behind him. He swung round to find another bunch of swaggering youths approaching from the opposite direction along the pavement. The ones crossing the road were now close to the kerb. Through flickering, narrowed eyes, Norman watched them all, his fingers, still throbbing from the weight of the Queen Mother's foot, flexing at his side ready for action. He could see that Jarmina and the other women had noticed the approaching problem, although the Queen Mother continued to push food into her mouth, oblivious to any danger. None of the women appeared to be worried and he realised that was because they automatically assumed they were well guarded. Norman was less confident. If things turned really nasty, there were now around eight potential assailants. Whilst they were all a great deal younger and softer than him, that was still bad odds.

'This your bleedin' harem then, mate?' one of the lads asked.

'Fancy sharing?' another joined in.

'That big one looks like she could take us all on at once,' a third voice shouted.

'Move on lads,' Norman growled in a voice that men who knew him would have obeyed without question.

'Give us a nibble on yer drumstick, girl!' one of them called out to the Queen Mother. None of them showed any signs of moving on. With one swift movement Norman took hold of the young man's testicles and crushed them so hard he screamed, making the others jump back. Norman didn't loosen his grip, but brought his other hand up to squeeze his victim's face so tightly that his mouth was forced open and his eyes popped.

'I said move on, you little turd,' he snarled, giving the testicles an extra hard squeeze.

The other boys were regaining their bravado after the initial shock of their friend's scream. Norman shoved him back into the midst of them, knocking them aside like skittles. The injured boy fell onto his knees and vomited into the gutter. As they regrouped Norman flipped his jacket back, standing with his hands on his hips and the butt of his gun clearly visible. 'Go, now,' he said.

'Jesus, it's Clint fucking Eastwood,' one brave boy mocked. 'Know how to use that thing do you, grandad?' Norman gripped the butt of the gun as if preparing to draw it. The pain from his ulcers was making him feel increasingly angry and he was tempted to let off a bullet amongst them just to send them packing. He didn't need to. The young men scrambled to escape, shouting some final words of abuse as they went and Norman rubbed his stomach ruefully. This was definitely the last bloody outing he was taking them on.

As he turned back he noticed that all the women were still happily immersed in their eating and chattering, apart from the Princess, who was watching him over the rim of her glass as she sipped at it thoughtfully. When he caught her eye she immediately looked away and said something to her mother, who nodded without stopping her chewing. Looking at her, Norman felt a tightening sensation in his stomach but wasn't sure whether it was his ulcers or not.

When they arrived back at Upton Park, Norman noticed an official-looking Rover parked at the front of the house. He didn't like the idea of unannounced visitors and told the women to wait in the car. He would go inside first to find out who it was. The housekeeper, he noticed, was dithering in the hall, looking uncomfortable and unsure what she should be doing.

'Who's the visitor?' he asked.

'Sir Roderick Salisbury,' she said. 'He's in the library. He wants to talk to the Queen and the Princess.'

'Who's Sir Roderick Salisbury?' Norman enquired.

'Important government man.'

Norman's ulcers gave a vicious kick. Could this man have come down to warn them that their security was being handled by one of the most-wanted villains in the country? It was possible. Maybe the policeman on the sea front had recognised him after all and radioed in the information. Norman considered walking straight back out of the front door and keeping going, but thought better of it. He would try bluffing his way through first. After all, they hadn't got anything on him at the moment, as far as he knew, just suspicions.

He buttoned his jacket up as he walked into the library. The man who rose from one of the leather wing-back chairs by the fireplace looked too old and distinguished to be anything to do with the police. His face was grave.

'Sir Roderick?' Norman enquired.

'Yes.'

'The Queen Mother and Princess are tired from a day out. Can I take a message to them or could we make an appointment for another time?'

'No.' Sir Roderick's voice didn't rise and there was no smile on his face. Norman knew that this was a man who was used to being obeyed. 'It's imperative that I speak to them immediately. Please convey my apologies for arriving unannounced and assure them that I will not take up too much of their time.'

'May I ask what it's about?' Norman made one last attempt to find out if this implicated him.

'It's a personal matter. Please tell them that I must speak to them now.'

The women had obviously grown tired of waiting in the cars and Norman could hear them coming in through the front door outside the library. Sir Roderick raised an eyebrow as if to indicate that he expected Norman to do as he was asked immediately. Norman left the room, closing the door behind him. 'Bloody hell,' he muttered under his breath, feeling he was becoming more like a butler every day.

'Some bloke called Sir Roderick Salisbury wants to talk to you and your mother,' he grunted at Jarmina as she started to go upstairs. He was still cross with them for the sea front ordeal.

The Princess stopped in her tracks and called out to her mother who was waddling towards the lifts. For a second, Norman saw a look pass between them which he could have sworn was fear. Neither of them said another word as they walked across to the library door. Norman opened it for them without thinking and Jarmina stepped back to allow her mother to pass through first.

As the door closed behind them Norman made his way upstairs to his room to pack. That was it, he'd had enough. He'd warned Len he would only be able to stay for a few days and that he wasn't the forelock-touching type, and if he carried on much longer he was likely to do or say something he would regret. He pushed his few belongings into the case he had brought back with him from Spain and made his way down to the security room. Mark was staring at the screens.

'Something's up,' he said.

'What do you mean?'

'The Princess just came out of the library and ran upstairs. I'm pretty sure she was crying. The other women were all crowded outside her bedroom door, calling out to her, but she didn't answer. Then the Queen came out of the library with her face covered in her head-dress and went up to her room and they all scurried along there. Sir Roderick left very quickly after that.'

'Well, whatever it is, it's your problem,' Norman said, pushing the last of his belongings into the bag.

'Why? Where are you going?'

'I've got to get on with my life. I can't stay in this place any longer.'

'You're just walking out? You can't do that!' Mark was horrified at such dereliction of duty.

Norman just looked at him and picked up his case. The internal telephone rang and Mark picked it up. 'Yes, he's here,' he said. 'I'll tell him.' He put the phone down and turned to Norman. 'The Princess would like to see you in her room. Sounds like she's still crying to me.'

'You go,' Norman said, picking up the bag. 'I'm off.'

'The least you can do is say goodbye to the woman,' Mark protested.

Norman stopped in his tracks and turned to glare at the younger man. Mark stood his ground and held Norman's icy gaze. Norman realised he was right. He also realised that he wanted to see her once more, just to let her know exactly why he was leaving. He wanted to give her a piece of his mind.

'Okay,' Norman dropped the bag and walked out of the room. Mark watched on the screens as he made his way across the hall and up the main staircase. Norman strode along the landing and knocked on the bedroom door, disappearing inside.

Jarmina was sitting cross-legged on the bed. She had pulled the scarf she had been wearing off her head and tossed it to one side. Her huge dark eyes were red from crying and Norman could see she was shaking. He opened his mouth to speak but no words came out. He wasn't good with emotional situations.

Jarmina took several deep breaths as Norman stood and waited, unsure what was expected of him, waiting for the right moment to tell her he was going. 'Sir Roderick has informed me that my father is in hospital,' she said at last. 'He has had a stroke. Will you take my mother and me to see him?'

Norman opened his mouth to decline. If the old King was dying there were likely to be police everywhere, and the press. It would be too high profile.

'Here,' she said, interrupting him before he spoke, and climbing off the bed, 'this is for your trouble.'

She walked to her wardrobe and opened it, pulling out a suitcase which was obviously heavy. She opened it and Norman could see it was packed solid with banknotes. She lifted out a wad and gave it to him. For a second her fingers hovered against the skin on his wrist and he fancied he felt the smallest of electric currents pass between them.

'Thank you,' she said. 'We will be downstairs in one hour. Please arrange for a car.'

She looked up into his face, like a small child pleading to be taken to the park.

'You don't have to give me this.' Norman tossed the money onto the bed. 'I'm being paid wages to be here.' He was uncomfortable with the feelings of compassion which seemed to be stirring inside him. He had never experienced anything like it before. 'I'll take you.'

He left the room and went downstairs at a brisk trot. Mark was still in the security room.

'What's happened?'

'The old King's ill. They want to be taken to the hospital to see him.'

'Did you tell her you were leaving?' Mark teased.

'The woman's father is dying. I'll tell her later. Another day won't hurt.'

'Right,' Mark grinned, which puzzled and annoyed Norman.

'I'm still going,' he said gruffly. 'Tomorrow.'

'Okay,' Mark said. 'Whatever you say.'

Norman was busy ordering the car to come back and didn't bother to think about the young man's suggestive tone any more.

The trip to the clinic in Harley Street was silent. The doctor travelled with them, quietly confessing to Norman that he was concerned what effect this would have on the Queen Mother's heart, since it was already under strain from her weight. Norman cast an anxious glance at the back seat. The last thing he wanted was for the old girl to kick the bucket while he was supposed to be looking after her.

As they drew close to the hospital entrance, Norman noticed a uniformed policeman on the door. He automatically glanced around the street and up to the windows opposite, but he couldn't see any sign of a back-up force. He decided to make himself look as inconspicuous as possible, concentrating on the job of being a bodyguard. Passers-by would be looking at the women in their robes, not taking in the faces of the men serving them. He performed the stool operation, deftly removing his fingers before they could be stepped on again.

Having seen his charges across the pavement and into the hospital, Norman went back out to wait in the car with the driver. The doctor had gone in with them. It seemed unlikely that anything would happen to them inside a private hospital, and anyway the old King's bodyguards would already be in there to handle any trouble. Norman swore under his breath. He was beginning to think like a professional security man! He rolled himself a cigarette and met all the driver's attempts at conversation with discouraging monosyllables. Norman was trying to concentrate on working out what was happening to him.

An hour later the royal party came back out and both women had their faces covered. There were muffled sounds of crying all the way back to Upton Park, but no one spoke. The doctor kept his eyes fixed on the road ahead and Norman thought he saw a glint of tears in the corner of the man's eye. He felt an unfamiliar urge to comfort Jarmina in some way, but suppressed it.

Jarmina and her mother went straight upstairs to their bedrooms when they reached the house and the other women went to the Queen Mother to console her. None went to see the Princess. If she had closed her bedroom door it meant she wanted to be alone.

Norman sent Mark to bed and settled down in the security room with a cup of tea. Once everyone was off the ground floor he could close the house down and set the alarms. From then on he was the only one who could walk from floor to floor because he was the only one with a key to the system.

He had decided it was too late to leave the house that night. He sat thinking for a while, planning where he would go the next day and how he would slip back out of the country to Spain for a while, just until Moody and his team had stopped nosing around, or until someone else could be found to carry the can for Sidney Rose's death. His thoughts were interrupted by the sound of the phone ringing. He recognised the Princess' voice as soon as he picked it up.

'Tell the kitchen I want tea now,' she said and hung up.

Norman considered ringing her back to tell her the kitchens had closed for the night, but decided against it. She would only insist that the poor chef was dragged back downstairs just to make her a cup of tea. He decided it would be easier to make it himself. He pulled himself to his feet and walked out to the kitchens. Everything had been tidied away and cleaned in preparation for the next day. He opened a few cupboards and was confronted with row upon row of fine china. He stared at it all for a moment and then shook his head. It was too much to think about. Plugging in the kettle, he drained his own mug, rinsed it under the tap and dropped a tea bag into it. When the tea was made he disconnected the alarm system and went through to the hall, walking upstairs gingerly, afraid he might slop the tea onto the carpet.

He knocked lightly on her bedroom door and she ordered him to come in. She was sitting on one of the sofas in a silk dressing-gown, her legs curled under her. The television was playing soundless pictures. It looked like a video of some state occasion in Domai. He saw pictures of the old King.

'Oh,' she said, when she saw him. 'It's you. Come in. Close the door.'

Norman opened his mouth to protest and then thought better of it. 'There was no one in the kitchen,' he said, 'so I made you a cup of tea.'

She stared at the clumsy mug with a look of puzzlement, as if she had never seen such a thing before. Then laughed.

'Never mind,' she said. 'You drink it.'

Norman shrugged and turned to go. If he hadn't made up his mind to leave the next day he might have told her what he thought of the way she ordered people around, but it didn't seem worth it, not after what she had just been through.

'Don't go,' she said. 'Stay and talk. Sit down.'

She patted the sofa next to her and he did as she instructed, careful not to brush against her. The last thing he wanted was to have her accusing him of making a pass. God knows how many policemen would be swarming through the house if that happened!

'This is my father,' she said, gesturing towards the screen at the regal figure waving to the crowds. 'He did not look like that today.'

Norman wondered if she was going to cry again, but she seemed to have regained control of herself.

'Today he did not even recognise me,' she went on. 'He was just staring straight ahead in the bed, with tubes coming out of him. And one side of his face had collapsed.' She pulled down the flesh of her left cheek to show how her father had looked to her. 'He looked very, very old.'

'I know what you mean,' Norman said. 'My Mum had a stroke. They found her in the bath, unable to get herself out. I went to see her, but she didn't know it was me.'

'Were you close to your mother?'

'Yeah.' He sipped at the tea. 'But I had to make a life for myself. She needed money to live and my father wasn't going to provide it. I couldn't spend time with her. Not like you and your mother.'

'Women have to cling together where we come from,' she said. 'Perhaps you had sisters who looked after her?'

'Yeah, three sisters and my brother, Len. We had another brother, older than us, but he was killed when he was a nipper.'

'A nipper?'

'A kid, six or seven years old. He fell onto some railings and the spike went through his lung. They didn't realise in time and he died in hospital.'

'Your mother must have been very sad.'

'She didn't have much of a life, poor woman.'

As they talked he became aware that her foot was lightly touching his thigh. He ignored it and continued to talk, but he was sure he could feel a growing pressure from her toes, and then the foot slid up into his lap and he knew, without question, that she was the one making a pass. But still he was cautious, unsure what was expected of him; unsure of his own feelings.

'You can cut that out,' he said roughly, but she didn't. 'Listen,' he said. 'If you're serious get yourself over to the bed and we'll do it properly.'

Jarmina stiffened. She had never been in a position like this before. She had made love a few times, very furtively, over the years, but all her seduction techniques had been learnt from watching American films and Norman didn't seem to be obeying the rules of etiquette she felt should apply in this situation. Her eyes flared indignantly for a moment and then she withdrew her foot and stood up with a rustle of expensive silk. She walked over to the bed and lay down.

'Come on then, Mr Norman,' she said, patting the bed beside her. Norman put his tea down carefully on the cracked top of the coffee-table and walked over to the bed, lying down beside her without even taking off his shoes. He put his arm around her shoulders and she turned to bury her face in his chest. He sensed she was crying again. The portrait of her father stared down at them from above the fireplace and the video continued to send its flickering light around the room. He stroked her shining, scented hair. As he felt her warm body pressing against him, Norman held her a little tighter, and his hand moved from caressing her hair onto her neck and the small part of her slim shoulder which showed from her dressing-gown. Her perfect, olive-coloured skin was soft to the touch. She lifted her wet face to look at him and he bent to kiss her on the lips. Her arms went up like a child's and encircled his neck, pulling him down on top of her. He felt an unfamiliar urge to be gentle.

It occurred to Norman that she must have known when she phoned down that the kitchen staff would have gone to bed by this time of night.

The next morning Norman went downstairs at five o'clock to unlock the doors and readjust the alarms. Jarmina did not stir as he disentangled himself from her arms and slipped into his clothes. His heart was thumping as he came out onto the landing, his mind racing as he tried to think what he would say if he ran into anyone. The house remained silent.

He switched on the radio in the kitchen while he made himself a cup of coffee. The news items flowed past him, only half catching his attention, and then he heard the announcement that the old King of Domai was dead. The newsreader gave a brief description of how the old man's son, Najid, had been Sultan for two years and that there would be no disruption over the succession. Then another voice talked of the history of the area and of the great leadership the old man had given to his people at a time of dramatic transition from a nomad existence to a nation of great wealth.

Norman switched off the radio and stared out of the window. He could imagine how upset the Princess was going to be about this. It was obvious she loved her father more than anyone. No doubt it was a merciful release from the indignities of spending years as a stroke victim, but that wouldn't lessen the woman's loss. He decided to postpone his plans for leaving by a day or two. It would make her feel better to have a few familiar faces around. Norman was surprised to find that the idea of staying wasn't as unattractive as it had been the night before. It wasn't that he expected to get laid again – he was quite aware that the Princess had only turned to him for comfort in a moment of personal grief. But he liked the idea of being around her for a little longer. She interested him.

He went upstairs to shower and change for the day ahead. No doubt there would be a stream of visitors following the announcement of the death.

'The Princess and her mother will be returning to Domai with the ex-King's body,' the Doctor told him later, over the phone.

'Is she all right?' Norman asked. 'The Princess.'

'They were both very upset,' the Doctor confided. 'But I have given them something to calm their nerves. The Princess asked me to inform you that she intends to return to England in a few weeks. She wants you to remain in charge of the house until she gets back.'

'I can't make any promises,' Norman said, spotting an opportunity to get away from Upton Park with the minimum of fuss, whilst also seeing that a house with no royals in would not be hard to look after.

'I think it would help the Princess to know the house was safe. She plans to leave many of her most precious possessions here.'

Norman thought for a second. 'Okay,' he said eventually. 'Tell her I'll be here.'

Later, when the women were taken out to the cars to be driven to the airport, Jarmina and her mother both left the house with their heads covered. Norman helped the Princess into the car and she leant heavily on his arm, as if drunk. He wondered how many pills the doctor had allowed her to take. She didn't speak to him or make eye contact. He wondered if she felt guilty about being in bed with him at the time her father died. He also wondered if he was making a mistake in agreeing to stay. Maybe, once she was over the worst of her grief, she would regret asking him.

The arrangements clicked into place with military precision at the airport where Michael was waiting to take control. Norman escorted them to the departure lounge and waited by the window as he watched the two royal women being escorted into the small jet. It seemed extraordinary to him that a plane so streamlined could contain a woman the size of the newly widowed Queen Mother. He thought he noticed Jarmina turn and look back at the airport building as she went up the steps, her robes stirring around her in the wind, and for a second he fought back an urge to raise his hand. He felt a twinge of sadness at seeing her leave. He had never met a woman like her before, someone who wasn't frightened of him. He doubted if he would be there when she got back. He was sure she would realise it had just been a one-night fling once she was away from the house.

When he got back to Upton a few hours later the house was sad and silent. The staff were still there, but there was none of the usual bustle. Norman wandered from one luxurious empty room to another, and eventually, when Mark went out for a run, he put in a call to Pete Chappell at The Country Club just to make sure everything was okay.

'Thank God you called,' Pete said, the moment he heard Norman's voice. 'Moody's made it official. They've got a warrant out for your arrest. The word is there's some evidence to do with Sidney Rose's death, that they're gonna try and pin it on you.'

'Shit,' Norman said.

'I need to be able to contact you, Norman, for Kathy and the girls, if they need anything. Kathy needs more money, more than I can get out of the club without attracting too much attention.'

'I'll call you again in a few days,' Norman said and hung up.

He sat completely still for several minutes, hardly blinking, just thinking through the situation. If it were true what Pete said, then they would have the airports covered by now. So if he wanted to get back to Spain he'd have to find a secret way out. But maybe Pete was playing some sort of game with him, trying to keep him away from the club for some reason. If there was one thing Norman had learned in life, it was never to trust anyone who had anything to gain by betraying you.

After thinking through all the alternatives, he reached a decision. It would be better to do nothing, to stay exactly where he was. No one knew he was there and no one was likely to come looking. As long as he kept his head down he could wait things out for a few weeks and prepare himself properly with a new passport and identity. He could grow his hair and put on a bit of weight so that no one would recognise him. There was also money to be had in the house, which he could draw on in an emergency. He was actually in the best possible position for lying low.

Having made that decision he was surprised by how good it felt. He realised that the thought of leaving before Jarmina got back had been making him feel quite sad. He decided to phone Len.

'Len, it's Norman,' he said when the connection was made.

'Hello, mate.' Len sounded very cheerful. 'I've got good news. I've found someone who can take over from you.'

'Forget it, Len,' Norman said. 'I've decided to stick around for a while.'

'Stick around?'

'It suits me to stay here a bit longer.'

'Have you any idea how hard I've worked to get you out of there?' Len complained.

'Don't give me that shit, Len. I got you out of trouble by coming here, and now you can return the favour by making sure I stay here until I'm ready to leave.'

Something in Norman's tone suggested to Len that he should accept the situation without any further argument. 'Okay, Norm, no problem. I've got plenty of other jobs the guy can do. Business is booming. Can you try to give me a bit of notice when you're ready to move on?'

'There's something else you need to do,' Norman said, ignoring the question.

'What's that?'

'Make sure my name isn't in any of your accounts books. Use the name that I came into the country with, and don't let anyone know where I am.'

'It's already done, Norm,' Len said, uneasy that his brother should feel it necessary to make such a request. 'Are you in big trouble?'

'Nothing to worry you, Len,' Norman said quietly. 'Just make sure no one finds out I'm working for you. Okay?'

'Okay.'

The line went dead and Len hung up. He sank back into his chair and cursed his bad luck at bumping into Norman in Spain that evening. After years of avoiding trouble, and avoiding being involved in Norman's life, he was now implicated in something, and he didn't even know what it was.

Norman went through to the kitchen to make himself a coffee and was annoyed to find Major Cox sitting at the table reading the paper and eating a sandwich the cook had obviously just made for him. Norman waited for a couple of beats to see if the man said anything. He didn't even look up.

'What're you doing here?' Norman asked.

'Having my lunch,' Cox replied, casually turning the page of the newspaper.

'Not in here, you're not,' Norman snapped. 'Your patch is the stables and the grounds. This is my territory and outside staff don't come into the house.'

'You're new around here,' the Major said with a smile that came out more as a sneer. 'When the family isn't in residence I take my meals in here.'

'Not any more,' Norman said. 'Piss off out of it.'

The Major sat firm. It had now become a matter of honour. He could no more allow a man like this to order him around than kiss the feet of a sergeant major. He continued to read the paper and chew methodically on the sandwich, although it had become uncomfortably dry in his mouth.

Norman could see there was no way out of a confrontation and decided to move immediately. He kicked the chair out from under the Major, sending him sprawling across the floor, the sandwich flying into the air. The cook slipped discreetly from the room. Norman stamped his foot hard down on the Major's remaining arm, pinning him to the floor, and pulled out his gun, pushing it painfully into the man's mouth which had sprung open with a cry of surprise.

'I'm in charge of security in this house, and only people who have been cleared to come in, come in. Do you understand me, Colonel?'

The Major nodded, his eyes wide. Norman pulled the gun roughly out from between his teeth and pushed it back into the holster.

'Now, get the fuck out,' he hissed, delivering a mighty kick to the Major's rear and sending him scrambling across the highly polished floor on all fours, his legs skidding out at all angles as he desperately tried to regain his balance and dignity.

Eventually he managed to pull himself up and limp to the door. He turned to Norman, his face purple with rage. 'I'll have you out of this house before you know what's hit you.'

Norman said nothing. He simply pulled his gun out again and levelled it at the Cox's head. 'Fuck off,' he said matter-of-factly, and the Major did as he was told. Norman made himself a coffee and went back into the security room, feeling better for having vented some of his temper. If only he could give Detective Constable Moody some of the same treatment.

CHAPTER TEN

For the next three days Norman stayed in the house, eating heavy meals and sleeping whenever he felt like it. His weight started to build up. When Len rang to ask if he needed someone to replace Mark while the boy had a few days off, Norman told him not to worry. He could handle the house on his own.

'Anyone been nosing around, asking questions about me?' he asked.

'Nobody's said anything to me,' Len said. 'Don't you think you should tell me what the problem is?'

'I just heard they're trying to pin something on me. Best if you say you don't know anything if they do come asking.'

'Sure. You told me.' Len was happy to agree. The more he thought about the situation, the keener he was to avoid anyone finding out he was having to hire his ex-con brother to do security work for his best client. The business was on a real roll at the moment – and mostly because of recommendations stemming from the contract with General Beckett and the Sultan. Len was having trouble hiring enough people to fulfil all the contracts that were pouring in. The last thing he wanted was someone casting doubts over the quality of his people.

'It might be an idea if you tell them you bumped into me in Spain and you assume I'm still down there. That'll put them off the scent for a while.'

'No problem.'

'There's another thing – can you get some money to Kathy?'

'Your wife?' Len was surprised to hear Norman even mention the woman. He was under the impression the marriage was well and truly over.

'She's fretting for money and if you could let her have some it'd quieten her down.'

'I don't know if I have that much...' Len spluttered nervously.

'I'm working for you, aren't I, Len?' Norman kept his tone light, but his brother recognised the cold sound of a threat beneath the surface. 'So take my wages over to my family.'

'Okay, Norman.' Len didn't feel he could argue. He had found something else for the new man to do and once again had no one to replace Norman with should he decide to walk out of Upton Park.

Norman hung up with a growl of irritation. He thought he and Len had reached a better understanding than this. He resented having to rely on his baby brother to provide him with a safe house, even if it was only temporary. He checked each of the screens quickly and then put his feet up for a few minutes' sleep before lunch.

The following weeks passed quietly enough, the staff providing him with meals and the Major staying out of his way. Norman found himself thinking about Jarmina more than he would have expected. He was surprised by the warm glow which passed through him when he remembered how soft she had been in his arms. Her face had tasted salty from the tears and her skin had smelled sweetly and exotically foreign, impregnated by many years of expensive perfumes as well as the foreign aromas of Domai and desert life. He found himself looking forward to her return with something close to impatience. He had never felt like that about anyone, not even Kathy.

There had been no warning given when the car arrived at the gates; the buzzer simply sounded in the security room to tell him it was approaching the house. He stared hard at the screen. He didn't recognise the number-plate and so picked up the phone to the gatehouse.

'Who's in the car?' he wanted to know.

'Princess Jarmina,' the guard replied. 'No one told me she was coming.'

'Nor me,' Norman said. 'Is she alone?'

'Yes.'

'Is she planning on staying?'

'She didn't say, just ordered the gates to be opened.'

On the screen, Norman could see the car had drawn up at the front steps, but none of the staff were opening the front door. It wasn't one of Len's cars – she must have organised this herself. He hung up the phone and pulled on his jacket. The gun was still in the arms cupboard where he had taken to leaving it, but he decided not to bother with it. He went through into the front hall and opened the door to let her in.

'Welcome back, your Highness,' he said, with an expression which was as close to a friendly grin as he ever got. 'I wasn't told you were coming.'

She gave him a stern look. 'The luggage is in the car, please bring it to the room.'

Norman opened his mouth to tell her that wasn't his job, but thought better of it. The housekeeper, suddenly aware that her employer had returned unexpectedly, was scurrying out to greet her and lead her up to her bedroom. Norman decided to return to the security room and leave the household staff to deal with the luggage. He didn't intend to give her the idea that he was at her beck and call. No doubt she would phone down and tell him off later. He looked forward to that. It would be good to have someone to fight with again.

For the rest of the day he mooched back and forth between the kitchen and the security room. The phone rang a few times, but it was always incoming calls to be transferred up to the Princess. She never said anything to him when he announced the callers prior to putting them through, just accepted the calls. Norman tried to read a book, but found he couldn't concentrate on the words, going through whole pages without taking in anything. His mind kept going back to Jarmina, imagining her curled up on a sofa upstairs, or perhaps in bed, and he began to long for her. He didn't like the sensation. It made him feel vulnerable and foolish, like a little boy again. Norman was not comfortable with vulnerability.

By ten o'clock, when she had still not rung down apart from to order food from the kitchens, he told the staff he was going to lock up and sent them up to their rooms. They were watching a television programme in their lounge off the kitchen and were obviously reluctant to leave halfway through, but one look at Norman's face told them he meant what he said and they scuttled up the back stairs to bed.

Norman paced around the kitchen for another ten minutes until he reached a decision. He put the kettle on and made two mugs of tea. He then walked to the main stairs, setting the alarms as he went so that the bedroom floor became isolated. If anyone came in downstairs, or moved down from the top floor before he had opened the house in the morning, the whole place would be alive with bells and flashing lights. He made his way along to Jarmina's room and tapped on the door. His heart was thumping in his chest like a sixteen year old's. What if she sent him packing?

He heard her voice calling him to come in. The hot mugs were burning the knuckles of his hand as he pushed open the door.

'Thought you might like a cup of tea,' he said, gruffly.

She was curled up on the sofa, just as he had imagined, wearing white silk pyjamas and a matching, full-length dressing-gown. She was brushing out her hair and it shone in the dim lighting of the room. The hi-fi was playing Arabic music which made Norman feel he was about to embark on some kind of mystical religious experience. He had smelt her perfume the moment he walked in, mingling with the lilies which stood around the room in vases.

'Hello, Mr Norman,' she flashed him a smile. 'Come in.'

He kicked the door shut behind him and sat beside her, placing the mugs on the table. He noticed the housekeeper had had new glass put on the surface.

'Are you pleased to see me back, Mr Norman?' she asked with a teasing look.

Norman gave one small, silent nod.

'My mother wanted to come back to England too – she says she is tired of the heat – but I persuaded her it would be too much travelling for her while she is still in a state of shock. She doesn't like me going away from her. I had to tell many lies.'

'What sort of lies?'

'I had to tell her Najid needed me over here, that he might get into trouble without me. I said I had shopping to do. I expect she hopes I am meeting a potential husband.'

'Oh, right,' Norman nodded again, still not smiling. 'You want some tea, then?'

She glanced at the mugs and said nothing, just continued brushing her hair, aware that he was watching her, knowing that he wanted her. Jarmina had never felt the urge to lead a man on this far before. She had been brought up to be coy and coquettish with men, and although she had rebelled against much of her upbringing, she had never been able to throw off completely the attitudes to men that had been instilled into her for so many years. Putting the hairbrush down, she slid across the sofa and onto his lap. Wrapping her arms around his neck she kissed him softly on the mouth. With no apparent effort, Norman stood up with the Princess in his arms and carried her across to the immense bed with its silk drapes towering towards the ceiling. He laid her down on the soft sheets, unbuttoning her pyjamas as she stretched her arms above her head and lay, submissive, waiting for him to have his way. Norman was more than happy to take advantage of her unspoken offer. He realised it was what he had been waiting for ever since she left.

Major Cox didn't like London. He wasn't comfortable in cities of any sort – he liked open spaces, the desert preferably, or at least the English countryside. The traffic that roared up and down Park Lane made him as jumpy as a young colt. He had hoped General Beckett would agree to see him at Upton Park, but Michael had made it obvious he was on a tight schedule and that if Cox wanted to talk to him, he would have to come into town.

Michael's new preoccupation was with the apartment. Now that the old King had gone, Najid had expressed his intention to stop using hotels for himself and to have the apartment standing in constant readiness for his visits. He had made it equally plain that he did not want this to be a marital home. If the young Queen Nabila was accompanying him to London, or was there for business of her own, she would continue to stay at Claridge's. The apartment was to be a male preserve where Najid could feel comfortable bringing the coterie of slim young men that he increasingly liked to surround himself with.

Michael was less comfortable with this development in his friend's tastes, but did not feel it was his place to comment. He made it his business to ensure that the apartment was fully secure and constantly staffed – what Najid chose to do there once he was behind fortified doors was his own business. He had suggested that Cox meet him at the apartment that day as he had already planned to be there to oversee the installation of a new alarm system.

If Michael was uncomfortable with the new King's tastes, Major Cox was completely out of his depth. The death of the old King had left a painful hole in his heart; a gap that he knew was never likely to be filled now. He comforted himself by looking after his ex-employer's beloved horses with meticulous care and attention. Through them he felt he still had a connection to the old and honourable world he had been trained to inhabit. He was willing to concede that there was some bond of shared military background between himself and Michael, but the General's relative youth made even that relationship difficult for the older man.

When Cox arrived, Michael was standing over a large hole in the floor of the apartment's marble-tiled hall, staring down at the tangle of wires beneath as an engineer tried to explain to him what was happening. Michael shook hands with the Major without interrupting the other man's flow, and then, when the man's lecture had finally finished, thanked him politely and led Cox through into Najid's study, closing the door behind him.

'Drink, Major?' he asked.

'That would be very welcome,' Cox said, and Michael poured them each a whisky, indicating that the Major should sit down and make himself at home. For a while they talked generally about Domai and about the past.

'There's something I feel I should mention,' Cox said at last and Michael indicated he was listening. 'It's about the security in the house. I'm not sure the people handling it are up to the job.'

Michael's face remained impassive and he sipped at his drink. 'Why is that?'

'The man who's in charge down there at the moment...'

'Norman Dorset,' Michael confirmed.

'He's not a trained soldier, is he?'

Michael laughed. 'No, I don't suppose he is, Major. Ex-military men are harder to get hold of these days. I've been happy to let the company choose its own men. Do you have a specific worry?'

'He doesn't treat the family with the correct respect. I don't trust him. He seems a criminal type.'

'Things are changing these days,' Michael said gently. 'People are not generally as respectful of the old institutions as you and I might wish.'

'I felt I should speak up, sir,' Cox said. 'I have a great affection for this family and I don't like to see them treated badly.'

'No.' Michael's face became serious again and he regretted laughing. He could see the man was sincere in his concerns. 'I appreciate you coming to me, John,' he said kindly. 'I'll have a word with the Princess to see if she has any complaints. Now, why don't we go and get some lunch. The Dorchester is just down the road, shall we wander down?'

'So, where the fuck is he?' the Inspector enquired, staring hard at Moody, who averted his eyes and gazed down at the floor.

'I'm not sure, sir,' he admitted.

'After all these years of following the man around trying to pin something on him, the moment you actually have some evidence that'll put him away for good, you can't bloody find him?'

'No, sir,' Moody muttered, like a tongue-tied schoolboy.

'Have you got any idea at all?'

'He has a villa in Spain. He may be down there.'

'Have you contacted the Spanish police?'

'They weren't exactly helpful.'

'Fuck!' the Inspector muttered. 'You'd better go down there yourself and have an ask around.'

'Spain?' Moody was so startled by this suggestion he found himself looking the Inspector directly in the eye.

'Get yourself a ticket, but don't stretch it out. I don't want you coming back with a bleeding suntan.'

'No, sir,' Moody said.

He left the Inspector's office in a daze. He had never been abroad before. He would have to get himself a passport. How would he manage without a word of Spanish? A hundred doubts assailed him as he made his way down the corridor to the squad room. When the others heard about his orders the room filled with catcalls and jeering. Any one of them would have been happy to take on the extra responsibility for a few days in the sun!

Norman lay in the bed with Jarmina's head resting on his chest, gently stroking her hair, enjoying the feel of the newly laundered sheets on his skin and the aroma of her warm, naked body. The light was still on in the bathroom and illuminated part of the room. He realised how tired he felt and how tempting it would be to sink into a world this luxurious and never leave it. For the first time in his life he felt an urge to settle down, to begin to take things more easily, to make a life more like everyone else's. He wanted things to stay like this, to be with Jarmina all the time. He felt her chest shudder slightly against him and realised he could feel the dampness of tears from her cheeks.

'You all right?' he asked, hoping she would make a non-committal answer. He didn't want to get into any emotional scenes.

She said nothing, but the sobbing increased. Norman reached down and lifted her head up so he could look at her in the dim light. She looked immensely beautiful with her eyes glistening and her lips trembling.

'Why're you crying?'

'Because I will never see my father again,' she replied.

'Oh.' He stroked her face and then lifted the corner of the sheet to dab the tears gently away. 'You were fond of the old man, weren't you?'

'Yes,' she laughed a little. 'I was very fond of him. He was very good to me. Fathers aren't always good to their daughters where I come from. He never made me marry anyone I didn't want to. He brought me up to believe in myself. Usually daughters are just there to look after the men in the family and to be sold off in good marriages. He never did that to me.'

'He must've been a good man,' Norman said, his mind drifting uncomfortably onto his own girls and how they were having to manage with nothing more than increasingly infrequent visits from their father. He couldn't imagine they would ever be saying these sorts of things about him, and he felt a pang of regret. For a moment he imagined what it would be like to start a family with Jarmina and stay around to watch the children grow up. To his surprise he found the idea strangely pleasant.

'He was a good man,' she agreed. 'That was why the British had to get rid of him.'

'Get rid of him?' Norman assumed she meant the old man had been assassinated, a concept he was not unfamiliar with.

'They couldn't get him to do whatever they wanted. They had to put Najid on the throne because he was happy to buy their tanks and their planes and allow them to fill Domai with their soldiers and their weapons.'

'Your father didn't allow that?'

'No, he didn't allow it. He would let Najid run the army up to a point, but he wouldn't allow General Beckett to have his own way in everything. Najid and Beckett are like husband and wife. Najid does everything the General tells him.'

'That's not my experience of marriage,' Norman said ruefully.

Jarmina had no wish to think about Norman's marriage and so kept talking, ignoring the interruption. 'When I was a child, my father used to tell me that maybe one day things would change and I would be able to become a queen.'

'Anything's possible,' Norman said. 'Who would have thought we'd end up with a woman Prime Minister?'

'No,' she smiled wistfully. 'I don't think so. My brother does not share my father's high opinion of me, or of women in general. He would like to see me married off and safely imprisoned in some palace somewhere, like my mother. He just needs an excuse to insist that I accept one of the proposals I have had.'

'From what I've heard, he doesn't strike me as the sort of person who could make you do anything you didn't want to do,' Norman said.

She shrugged. 'He's the King. In the end he can make any of his subjects do what he commands.' She was thoughtful for a few moments. 'What was your father like?' she asked, running her fingers across the stubble on his chin.

'He wasn't around much,' Norman said. 'He was a merchant seaman. He'd come home for a few days and give us all a good hiding and then he'd disappear off again, leaving our mother to bring us up, with no money.'

'You loved your mother?'

'Of course, although I probably didn't let her know it often enough. She was just there, doing the washing and the cooking. She left us to our own devices most of the time. She didn't have the time to do anything different. No royal palaces or silk sheets for her! She worked hard for us. She was a good mother.'

'And her son is a king,' Jarmina whispered, kissing him gently on the lips. Since he couldn't think of a single thing to say in response, Norman pretended not to have heard.

They both drifted in and out of sleep through the night, and Norman slid from the bed at five o'clock to give himself time to open up the house before the servants started to come down from their rooms. He made himself a strong cup of coffee and rolled himself a cigarette as he stared out of the kitchen window at the manicured gardens beyond. This wasn't such a bad place to be hiding out, he decided.

Len picked Michael up from the apartment early that morning. They were to drive out to visit a company that had been invited to tender for a new airport in Domai.

'I gather Princess Jarmina has gone back to Upton Park on her own,' Michael said, as the car pulled out into the Park Lane traffic.

'Yes,' Len nodded. 'They informed me when she got there. She didn't ask me to provide her with a car. I've sent Mark back down to help Norman out. They need two of them there if the family's in residence.'

'I agree,' Michael said. 'I had Major Cox up yesterday. He's not too comfortable with your brother.'

'Yeah?' Len kept his eyes on the road. Although he could easily cover up Norman's presence in England if the police came to the office, he had decided from the start to be open with Michael about Norman being his brother, although he hadn't filled him in on any of Norman's history. Now he knew Norman was definitely on the run from the law for some reason, he wished he'd never told Michael who he was. Len was not comfortable with lies, particularly when he had to tell different ones to different people. He now rather wished Norman would decide he had had enough and disappear back to Spain or wherever. It would be difficult to find someone to replace him, but that might be preferable to facing whatever it was his brother was so keen to hide away from. Len was angry that, just as he was building something really good, his brother was risking destroying it.

'A bit of a personality clash, perhaps?' Michael suggested.

'Norman can be a bit outspoken, sir, but he's a good man in a crisis.'

'I dare say he is.'

'The Major's very touchy about other people at Upton. I've had a few run-ins with him myself.'

'I'm aware of that,' Michael said. 'But the family owes him a lot. There's a history there. I can't get rid of the Major. You might have to think about finding someone a little more diplomatic. These people can be very sensitive if they're not treated with the respect they think they deserve.'

'I'll give it some thought, General.'

'Good. We might just drop into Upton on the way back, check that Her Highness is happy with things. I don't want the Major to think we don't take his complaints seriously.'

'Very good, General.'

Len's eyes were still on the road, although his brain was churning over the ways in which he could persuade Norman it was time to move on.

Later that afternoon they arrived at Upton Park and announced themselves at the gate. Michael went in through the front door and Len strolled round to the side entrance to look for Norman. He found him in the security room and they went through to the kitchen for a cup of tea while Mark watched the screens.

'What's the score with the galloping Major?' Len asked after a few minutes.

'Oh, something and nothing,' Norman replied, waving the subject aside.

'He wants you out,' Len said.

'I had to give him a little smack. He's bound to be a bit sore. He'll come round.'

'Why did you have to give him a bit of a smack?' Len's heart sank. So often in the past he had heard his brother casually utter these little phrases, only to find that the next time he heard about him Norman was back in prison, convicted of causing grievous bodily harm to some innocent party.

'He tried to take over the house, and I know you don't want that.' Norman's face was a picture of innocence.

'I'm trying to find someone to take over from you,' Len changed the subject. 'What do you think of young Mark?'

'Good kid, not ready for responsibility yet,' Norman said, without looking up from his mug. 'I told you, it suits me to stay here at the moment.'

'Yeah, that's what I thought.' Len pretended not to have heard. 'I could find you somewhere else to go where you won't have any problem with the Major and where they won't know your real name.'

'Don't worry.' Norman gave a thin smile that implied the subject was now closed. 'I'm getting quite used to it here.'

Len wondered how the conversation between the Princess and the General was going. If she wanted to get rid of Norman that would take the problem out of his hands. They had been talking for half an hour when Michael burst into the room.

'You ready, Len?' he barked. 'We need to get back to London.'

'Right, General.'

As Len pulled himself to his feet Michael rounded on Norman, putting his mouth close to Norman's ear. 'I've been talking to the Princess,' he said quietly. 'She tells me you're one of the best soldiers she's ever had guarding her. Well done. Keep up the good work.'

Len could neither hear the General's words, nor make out from Norman's impassive face what might have passed between them.

Without a word, Norman went back into the security room to watch his brother and Michael leave the house. 'Keep an eye on things,' he told Mark as the car nosed its way out through the gates. 'I'm just going up to the stables to have a word.'

He walked casually across the grounds, enjoying the views as the evening light created long shadows and illuminated the garden like stage lighting. He could see the Major riding one of the horses back towards the stables after exercising it, and leading another behind. The horses were a beautiful sight, with their heads and tails held high and their feet prancing. Cox sat with the easy grace of an expert horseman.

Norman followed him into the stables. He was dismounting and calling over one of the stable-boys to take the horses away and tend to them. Cox turned as Norman walked up to him and a spasm of anger passed over his face.

'Mind if I have a word with your lad here?' Norman asked, taking the boy by the arm and walking him out of earshot without waiting for a reply.

'These stables are my territory, Dorset,' Cox shouted. 'Just remember that!'

Norman raised a hand in recognition of the fact but didn't turn round. The horses were clopping docilely behind them as they walked towards the stalls.

'Is that your car round the back?' Norman asked the boy.

'The blue minivan is mine,' the boy said. 'Why?'

'I want to borrow it,' Norman said. 'Just for the evening. Are you planning to use it?'

'Not tonight,' the boy said, confused.

'Good.' Norman pulled out a few notes and pushed them into the boy's pocket. 'I might be asking again.'

'Sure.' The boy grinned at the feel of the money. 'The key's always in the ignition.'

'Good lad,' Norman smiled. 'I might even fill the tank up for you.'

Norman spun on his heel and walked straight back towards Cox, watching the man flinch, almost imperceptibly, as he made a concentrated effort not to move out of the way. Norman brushed past him.

'Night, Colonel,' he murmured.

'Major,' Cox corrected him. 'I'm watching you, Dorset. You won't last long here.'

This time Norman didn't bother even to wave, he just kept walking.

At nine o'clock, Norman announced he was closing up the house and everyone was to go upstairs. Mark, who was watching television, gave his watch a meaningful look.

'It's nine o'clock, Norman,' he complained.

'You need some sleep,' Norman growled. 'Maybe that'll make you more on the ball during the day.'

Mark was startled by the unwarranted criticism. He had no idea that his performance during the day had been anything less than a hundred per cent. His feelings hurt, he left the room and went upstairs without another word. The other staff did as Norman told them without any protest. As soon as the ground floor was clear, Norman set the alarms for the top floor and made his way up to Jarmina's room. He found her waiting on the sofa just as she had been the previous night.

'You haven't brought me any tea,' she joked as he came in.

'Come on,' he said, 'we're going out.'

'Going out where?' She looked confused and a little frightened. She was not used to being told what she was to do. 'I have not requested to be taken out.'

'You don't have to. It's a surprise. Get yourself dressed.'

'I can't just go out...' There was a note of panic in her voice – this was not what she had expected. The suddenness of it had knocked the breath out of her. She felt simultaneously excited and nervous. She needed someone to advise her, someone she knew well. She realised she hardly knew this man. How could she just 'go out' with him without any chaperone? What would her father have said? She felt alone and vulnerable and she stopped smiling as she tried to work out what she should do.

'You can do whatever you want,' Norman corrected her, going to the walk-in wardrobe to find her something to wear. 'You're a grown-up woman.'

The rails of clothes stretched for ten yards on either side of the sweet-smelling room, and racks of shoes stood on the floor. He ignored all the brightly coloured Arabian robes and pulled a pair of designer jeans and a cashmere sweater from the shelves that covered the end wall. When he came back out Jarmina had got off the sofa and was standing, watching, with her arms wrapped tightly around herself, as if trying to stay safely cocooned from whatever new experience was threatening to sweep her away.

'It's not safe for me just to go out without arrangements,' she protested, half-heartedly.

'Of course it's safe,' Norman said, dropping the clothes on the bed. 'I'm your bodyguard, aren't I? Anyway, this is England. No one's going to try to assassinate you here. Come on, get a move on or it'll be closing-time before we even get to the pub.'

'Pub?' Jarmina said the word as if she had never heard it before. 'You are going to take me to a pub?'

'Yeah. You don't have to drink if you don't want to. You can have a Coke or something. You'll like it, honestly.'

She thought for a second. 'I don't want to wear those clothes,' she said. 'Find me something better.'

'Just put them on,' Norman growled. 'I'm not your bloody maid. If you're going to make a big fuss about the whole thing we might as well forget it. I'm offering to take you out for a drink. If you want to come, put the clothes on and we'll go. But if you'd rather stay locked in this room for another night, that's up to you. Why do you always have to give everyone such a bloody hard time?'

She pulled herself up to her full height and her nostrils flared. No one had ever dared to speak to her in such a tone and for a moment she thought of slapping his face or calling for security. Then she remembered he was security and she felt the panic rising again. She was trapped. But the idea of going out into the world as an ordinary citizen was taking root in her mind and she began to like it. It would be an adventure. She remembered the time she had escaped from Claridge's and met the Italian man. And Norman was right, what could go wrong as long as he was there to protect her? She liked that idea. Without saying another word she walked to the bed and slipped out of the pyjamas.

Ten minutes later he was leading her out of the side door to the minivan which he had parked there earlier.

'Give me your jewellery,' Norman said as they walked out. 'I'll take care of it.'

She hesitated for a moment and then pulled off her diamond rings and bracelets, and a Cartier watch. Norman slipped them into his pocket. 'There's no point asking for trouble.'

'We're not going in that?' She stared at the rusty, dented little motor. 'It's for carrying animal food and straw! Look!' She peered in through the back windows. 'There is stuff in there now.'

'I'm not unloading all that now,' Norman grumbled. 'And I'm not going to call a limousine out just so we can go for a drink. This is how most people live all the time. The experience will be good for you.'

'It will smell.'

'Oh, get in the car and shut up,' Norman said, climbing into the driver's seat and starting the engine with an angry-sounding rev of the accelerator. Jarmina waited a few seconds, but he obviously didn't intend to open the passenger door for her, so she did it herself, with some difficulty.

Lowering herself into the hard, broken seat, she looked down and saw the ground passing by beneath the floor as Norman took off. 'There's a hole!' she shrieked, but Norman drove on towards the gates without bothering to respond. The guard peered out of his window with a look of puzzlement on his face. Norman leant forward so that his face was lit by the security lights and gave him a wave. The man waved back and the gates clicked open.

'You could be kidnapping me,' Jarmina said, after they had been driving in silence for a few minutes.

'Would you like that?' Norman grinned.

She stared at him hard for a few moments, intending to intimidate him, and then started to laugh. It was a raw, gurgling sound that bubbled up from her stomach like thick black oil and the sound of it made him laugh too.

'So where are we going?' she asked, when the laughter had finally subsided.

'I thought we'd just go into town and find a nice pub.'

'Okay. Let's do that.'

The local town centre was quiet. A group of youths were laughing and shouting around some benches in the central square and the sound of voices could be heard from a couple of nearby restaurants. Norman parked the car and climbed out. He could see Jarmina was nervous as she emerged into the world without her protective layers of clothing and wealth. He put his arm around her shoulders and she snuggled in closely. He felt a small glow of affection for her. They strolled in silence towards a pub at the end of the square. He reckoned he could get used to this feeling of togetherness.

As Norman pushed open the door, a wall of noise and smells hit them. The smoke-filled air made Jarmina blink and the stale smell of beer and ashtrays made her nose wrinkle.

'Not here,' she said, 'this place smells.'

'It's just a pub,' Norman said, his arm firmly around her shoulders as he propelled her towards the bar. 'They all smell the same. Do you want a Coke or do you want to try something new? Have you ever tasted beer?'

She allowed him to steer her onto a bar stool, her eyes darting from side to side nervously. 'No,' she admitted. 'I have never tried beer. I'll have a fruit juice.' It seemed odd to her to walk into a room and have no one take any notice of her, no one rush over to kiss her hand or bow. She wasn't sure if she liked the feeling of being invisible.

'Okay.' Norman ordered her an orange juice and a pint for himself. The noise of raised voices lifted to a roar and there were some high-pitched whistles of feedback as someone switched on the karaoke machine and a group of drunken women began to perform the greatest hits of Abba at the tops of their voices. Norman leant back against the bar and rolled himself a cigarette. Out of the corner of his eye he could see Jarmina was smiling. She was beginning to relax. He held his beer out for her to try. She sipped at it and the foam stuck to her top lip. Norman reached across and wiped it away with his thumb.

At eleven o'clock the landlord called for last orders and Norman led her outside into the cool night air. The youths were still hanging around the benches and had been joined by a couple of girls. Their laughter was uproarious and hearty, fuelled by the contents of the cans of lager which could be heard clanking around their feet as they rushed around one another in a ritual of courtship and horseplay.

'Hungry?' Norman enquired.

'Yes,' she said, cuddling in under his arm, 'I'm hungry.'

'Come on, then.' He steered her across the square to a Burger King where a queue was already forming of people from the pub. They joined the back of the queue. 'Shall I order for you?' he asked.

'Okay.'

They sat eating their food in the window of the restaurant, staring out at the sudden flurry of activity in the street outside as the pubs and restaurants emptied and people made their way back to their cars or across to the taxi rank.

'Glad you came, then?' Norman asked.

'Yes,' she said, 'I'm glad. But this food is disgusting.'

As they made their way, arm in arm, back towards the car, she pulled him over to an estate agent's window. 'Do you want a house?' she asked, gesturing towards the pictures and details pinned on the window display.

'I've got a house,' Norman laughed. 'I've got two houses, one here and one in Spain. I don't need any more.'

'I could buy you a nice one,' she said, peering closely at the pictures. 'There!' she pointed to a large mock-Georgian family house. 'That one! I'll buy you that one.'

'I don't want a house!' Norman insisted, pulling her on towards the car. She pouted for a few seconds and then decided not to spoil the mood and kissed him. They embraced like young lovers on a first date.

'Don't ever leave me, Mr Norman,' she whispered. 'Please don't ever leave me.'

He kissed her again, so that he didn't have to answer. At that moment he couldn't imagine that he would ever want to be away from her, but commitment to relationships had never been easy for Norman.

CHAPTER ELEVEN

The villa seemed to tower above Moody as he looked up from the gates. He had seen bigger ones on his way across Marbella, but this one was still pretty impressive. He pushed open the wrought iron gates and made his way up towards the front door. There was a bell-pull. He tugged it and it jangled, making him jump. He stood, waiting for a few moments, but nothing happened. Cautiously, he made his way round the side of the house, calling out in a small voice in case he came across anyone.

The water in the swimming pool was still lapping at the edges, as if someone had only just climbed out. The body on the sun-lounger made him jump when it stirred and sang a line from 'Avalon'. It was a beautiful body, perfect in almost every way as far as Moody could make out – perfectly slim, perfectly brown, perfectly smooth. The face at the top of the body looked equally flawless, the eyes closed against the brightness of the sun, the ears covered with headphones. He could just make out the tinny sounds of Bryan Ferry's voice coming through from the Walkman that lay beside her. Her thick blonde hair was pulled back to give her face maximum exposure to the sun.

Moody coughed politely but she still didn't hear him over the music. He touched her foot, very lightly, and she shot into the air as if she had been stung, snatching the headphones off and pulling a towel up over her naked breasts in one movement.

'Who're you?' she squawked as the tape continued to play in the distance.

'Detective Constable Moody,' he replied. 'From London. I'm looking for Norman Dorset.'

'Join the club,' she said, pulling on a short towelling robe. 'He hasn't been back here for a few weeks.'

'Do you live here?' Moody asked.

'Nah, this is Norman's place. But since he's pissed off without so much as a thank you, I thought I'd stay on here a bit longer. I got a key off the maid after he'd gone.' She suddenly looked nervous. 'You won't tell him you found me here, will you?'

'What's your name?' Moody asked, getting out a notebook from his jacket pocket. He noticed that his shirt was wet with sweat and there was an unpleasant smell. He closed the jacket again quickly.

'Lorraine Sands,' she said. 'You look a bit hot. Do you want a drink or something?'

'That would be nice,' Moody said.

'Take your coat off and make yourself comfortable,' she said. 'I've got some lemonade in the fridge. Do you want a Pimms?'

'That would be nice,' Moody said again. 'Thank you.'

The blonde disappeared indoors and he quickly removed his jacket, folding it up and pushing it beneath the seat. He fanned the armpits of the shirt in the hope that the smell and damp patches would have gone by the time she returned. She came back a few minutes later with a glass for each of them. She sat down beside him, giving no indication of noticing anything.

'So, Norman didn't say where he was going?' Moody continued the conversation.

'No. We was having a really good time and then he bumped into his brother – at least he said it was his brother – and just vanished for a few days. Then he came back, packed his things and announced he was leaving. Told me to sling me hook. I told him a few things too, I can tell you.'

'What's his brother called?' Moody asked.

'Len. Len Dorset.'

'What did they talk about?'

'I dunno. I told you, he just pissed off for a few days with him, leaving me like I was some stray dog he'd picked up.'

'How long have you known Norman Dorset?' Moody asked, sipping his drink and dabbing at his brow.

'I just met him a month or two ago in a club.'

'The club in Streatham?' Moody asked.

'Streatham?' She looked at him as if he were mad. 'No, a club down here – The Blue Angel.'

Moody made a note of the name. 'What sort of place is it?'

'It's all drug dealers and coke-heads,' she said. 'Norman was in there doing business with a bunch of blokes from North Africa somewhere. They were talking about importing into England.'

'Importing drugs?' Moody's biro was flying across the page.

'Am I giving away too much?' Lorraine asked, with mock innocence.

'You're being most helpful,' Moody assured her.

'Roderick Salisbury here, Dorset,' the voice on the other end of the line announced.

'Good morning, Sir Roderick,' Norman replied.

'The Sultan of Syran has enquired if he can visit Princess Jarmina this afternoon. Will the Princess be there?'

'As far as I know,' Norman replied. 'Do you want me to check?'

'You can put me through to her in a minute. I don't want anyone else on the estate to know who's coming, do you understand?'

'Yes, I understand.'

'Very well. The Syranian security people will be in touch in an hour or two. Put me through to the Princess, would you.'

Norman put the phone through and went back to reading his paper. A few minutes later Jarmina called down and asked him to come to her room. When he got there she was flinging clothes onto the bed.

'Aran is coming to visit me this afternoon and I have nothing to wear,' she moaned, gesturing at the pile of outfits in despair.

'Aran?' Norman feigned ignorance. He didn't like the niggle of irritation he could feel inside as he watched her fussing around for another man.

'The King of Syran. He asked me to marry him about five years ago and I turned him down.'

'Do you think he's going to try his luck again?' Norman asked.

'Are you jealous?' She looked up at him, her eyes flaming and hopeful.

'Jealous?' Norman allowed himself a smile, refusing to acknowledge the slight feeling of sickness in his stomach. Could that be jealousy? It wasn't a feeling he had ever experienced before. 'You must do whatever you think best,' he finished quickly.

'I don't want to marry him,' she laughed and came over to put her arms around Norman. 'You don't have to worry about anything.'

'I'm not worried,' Norman said, returning the kiss and sliding his hand inside her dressing-gown.

'I'll insist you stay in the room throughout the interview,' she said, 'so you can see I behave with perfect decorum.'

'It's not necessary, really,' Norman protested. 'You can behave any way you want.'

'It's decided,' she said. 'You will be there. It's an order from a Princess to her bodyguard.' He was about to respond with an abrupt choice of words and then saw that she was teasing him.

'Whatever you say, your Highness,' he said with an exaggerated bow, dropping her back onto the bed.

At three o'clock that afternoon, as a light drizzle descended from the heavy clouds overhead, four cars drew up at the gates and their arrival was announced in the house. Jarmina waited in the library and Norman made his way to the front steps. The cars drove across the courtyard at full speed and stopped in unison. The doors of all four cars opened simultaneously. Two men who looked like they could be the Sultan stepped out of the back of the first two cars and Norman hesitated, trying to work out which was the real one. Whilst he was still figuring it out, a third man stepped out of the driving seat of the first car and walked quickly around Norman to the door.

'Just a moment, please,' Norman called out, but he was too late, the man was already inside the house. 'No one except the Sultan is to go inside,' he announced, seeing a pair of English policemen getting out of the third car and heading for the door.

'No one except the Sultan has gone inside, mate,' one of them said with a smug smile. 'We'll just give the house a once over, if you don't mind, then stay out of the way.'

'No, sorry.' Norman's voice stopped them in their tracks. 'Only the Sultan inside the house. The rest of you wait out here. I'll have tea sent out to you.'

Before they had a chance to question his orders, he was back inside the house, had closed the door and was walking briskly to the security room. The light drizzle was turning to rain as the bodyguards and drivers drifted back and forth between the porch and the cars, obviously unsure how to react to this new order. One of the policemen was on the radio, no doubt trying to find out if Norman had the authority to keep them out of the house. Norman smiled grimly. While he was enjoying his moment of power over the law, he also felt uneasy at having so many of them so close to his hideaway.

'Wankers,' he muttered. 'Keep an eye on them, Mark. None of them is to come into the house. If they need the toilet they can go to the guardroom. Understood?'

'Yes, sir,' Mark smiled. Some days he liked Norman's style.

'Have the staff take tea out to them in a few minutes.'

'Where are you going?'

'To see if the Princess needs anything.'

'She's in with the Sultan,' Mark protested, but Norman had already disappeared back through the green baize door and could be seen on the screen making his way to the library.

He opened the door and slid silently into the room. Everything was quiet and it took him a second to locate the royal couple who were now seated in two chairs beside the fire.

'We'll ring if we need anything,' Aran said, irritably.

'Don't worry about him,' Jarmina said. 'He's my bodyguard. He's to be trusted.'

The King of Syran looked doubtful but could tell from the Princess' tone, and from the stance of the heavily set man by the door, that nothing he said was going to make any difference. He was used to having servants always hovering in the background, although none that looked quite like Norman. Obviously unsettled, he returned to whatever they had been talking about before they had been interrupted. Norman stood stock still, with his hands crossed over his crotch, staring into space, as he had seen bodyguards do in American movies a million times.

'I've spoken to your brother, and he's given his permission for me to ask you one more time to be my wife. If you refuse it will be the end of the matter,' Aran said, almost as if this was a threat. 'My advisers insist that I marry this year and produce an heir. If I do not marry you I'll have to choose another wife from my own family.'

He paused and looked at Jarmina for a reaction. She said nothing, staring at the floor, her hands lying peacefully in her lap.

'So, what is your answer? Will you respect the wishes of your brother and allow me to become your husband? You will never want for anything as my queen.'

'I will never want for anything whatever I do,' Jarmina said, quietly. 'If I agreed to marry you it would be because I wanted to be your wife, no other reason. I have a great affection for my brother, of course, but little respect.'

Aran was unable to stop himself from sucking in a breath of air in shock at such a disloyal comment from a royal sister.

'He's not the man my father was, and never will be,' Jarmina continued. 'You know that as well as I, but you are too diplomatic to say. So it's useless for you to try to use him to persuade me to marry you.'

'Then will you do me the honour of marrying me for no other reason than wanting to be my wife?' Aran asked, astounded to hear such words coming from his own mouth, even as he spoke them. Who would ever have believed that any Arab woman, even one of the royal blood, would ever make a king beg in such a fashion?

Norman kept staring straight ahead, although he longed more than anything to glance at Jarmina's face to try to guess what she was going to say next.

'I cannot accept your proposal because I am in love with another man.'

The Sultan stiffened with anger and Norman felt the smallest knot of excitement tightening in his stomach, a feeling he hadn't experienced since first hearing Kathy tell her sister that she was in love with him. The two girls had been in the Ladies at a club, reapplying their lipstick and hadn't realised how thin the walls were between the Ladies and the Gents. He had no time for such romantic nonsense, and certainly didn't know how to respond to it, but he liked the glow it gave him inside, like a pilot light bursting into life in a long disused oven.

The Sultan appeared surprised by this announcement. It was not the sort of thing that women were supposed to say when a king proposed to them. In fact, it wasn't the sort of thing he expected any Arab woman to say under any circumstances, whoever the man might be. Who was she to decide who she should give her heart to? Aran was aware that Western women were expected to behave with this amount of stupidity, but surely not someone of Jarmina's background, breeding and intelligence!

'May I ask who this lucky man is?' he said eventually, his voice far from steady.

'You may ask, your Highness, but I will not tell you.' She smiled sweetly, and had the good sense to lower her eyes, so that she did not directly witness his flush of anger.

'I take it your brother knows nothing of this match?'

'I did not say there was a match, your Highness, just that I am in love. I think that is as much as I would like to say on the matter, and I would be grateful if you did not discuss my private life with anyone else, particularly Najid. He may be my brother, and he may be my King, but he is not my keeper.'

'I am as much in favour of reform and modernisation as the next man,' Aran said, his shock beginning to subside. 'I have spent a lot of time in the West and I know that many of their ways are preferable to ours, but not all. There are many traditions which have grown up over centuries because they are good and serve the people well. You would be wise not to break too many of the rules too quickly.'

'Thank you for your wise words, your Highness,' Jarmina said, with a charming smile. 'Would you like to stay for tea?'

Aran said nothing for a moment, gazing at her face and imagining how it would be to kiss. Then he burst out laughing. 'Yes,' he said. 'I would like to stay for tea. I hope, Jarmina, that we will be able to remain friends all our lives and that one day I will be able to hear you say that you made a mistake in turning me down.'

'I, too, hope that we will remain friends,' Jarmina agreed, 'but I think that you will never hear me say those words.' She looked towards Norman, her eyes giving nothing away. 'Please tell them we are ready for tea now.'

Norman gave an exaggerated bow and left the room backwards. Jarmina bit her lip to stop herself from laughing and stared hard at Aran who was now talking about his racehorses.

This time when Moody arrived at Kathy's house he had the right paperwork and several uniformed officers to help him sweep through the rooms and cover all the exits. He had little hope that he would find Norman there, but he was aware there might be other evidence which he had no intention of giving Kathy the opportunity to dispose of before they could get to it.

Kathy, taken by surprise, was furious. She sat on the sofa in the sitting-room with the girls beside her, shouting at Moody as he went meticulously through every drawer in a set of stained black wooden units, which also held some state-of-the-art hi-fi and television equipment. He noticed that her shouting became louder and more violent as he opened a small drawer to one side of a tropical fish-tank. Inside the drawer was a brown envelope. Moody lifted it out and Kathy fell silent. Moody looked at her and then back to the envelope. Kathy hugged the children closer to her as Moody put his hand inside and pulled out a thick wad of notes.

'Got yourself a job, have you, Mrs Dorset?' he asked.

'I sold my old car,' she said, sulkily.

'So who paid for the new one, sitting outside?' Moody gestured with his head towards the street.

'None of your bleeding business,' she snarled.

'I disagree,' Moody said, slipping the money back into the envelope and placing it with meticulous care on the coffee-table in front of the sofa. 'Because if that money came from your husband, it could well be the proceeds of crime, and as such it's very much my business.'

Kathy's lips became a tight, thin line. One of the policemen who had been searching upstairs came down with a plastic bag full of men's clothes which he passed to Moody. Moody peered into the bag and then looked at Kathy with a raised eyebrow. Kathy's eyes narrowed, her lips set firm and she said nothing.

'Whose clothes are these?' Moody asked. Kathy said nothing and Moody transferred his eyes to Teresa, then Rachel and finally Vicky. 'Are these your father's clothes?' he asked.

'They're Uncle Josh's,' Rachel said, in a small, tense, angry voice.

'Uncle?' Moody looked back at Kathy. 'A brother, or a brother-in-law?'

'He's just a friend,' Kathy replied, and Moody noticed the girls move slightly away from her, all with their eyes fixed on their hands. 'Norman hasn't been near us for years,' she went on. 'Josh's been good to us.'

'Where would I find him?' Moody asked.

'He's not involved in anything,' Kathy said. 'Why do you want to talk to him?'

'If he's involved with you, Kathy, he's involved with Norman. Where do I find him?'

'I have someone who can take over for you, if you've had enough,' Len told Norman on the phone. 'He can start next week.'

'No,' Norman said, gently stroking the moustache he had allowed to grow over the previous weeks. 'I'm okay here for the moment.'

Len grimaced. He had hoped that now the Princess was back Norman would have changed his mind about wanting to stay. Len knew how badly Jarmina treated the staff. And ever since his brother had made it clear he was hiding out, Len had become increasingly nervous at the thought of the police finding out where he was. He was also worried that Major Cox would put more pressure on the General to have Norman removed.

'I don't understand you, Norm,' he protested. 'Not long ago you were saying you would only do a few days and now I can't get you out of there.'

'I'm getting used to the life, like you said I would,' Norman teased.

'Are you likely to change your mind again in a few days?' Len asked suspiciously. 'I don't want to commit him somewhere else and then have to pull him out two days later because you've done a runner.'

'Who can predict the future, Len?' Norman said cheerily and hung up.

It was lunch-time and he had the stable-boy's minivan parked outside the door. Mark had been sent on an errand to Najid's apartment in Park Lane and everyone else was busy in the kitchens. Everything was in place for them to start executing the plan he and Jarmina had agreed upon the night before. After Aran had departed, they had fallen into bed together, laughing happily at the mutual realisation that they were truly in love, and started hatching a plan together. Actually it was his plan, but he knew she would do everything he told her. They both now knew that they wanted to spend the rest of their lives together.

On the screen, he saw Jarmina coming down the stairs. He had to admire the way she walked, looking neither to the left nor the right, with no sign of hesitation. No one seeing her would have suspected she was doing anything other than coming downstairs to spend time in the living-rooms or out by the pool. She was wearing clothes which he had bought her in town, clothes that had amazed her with their cheapness and their 'ordinariness' – in them she would never attract any attention. Initially she had complained at their plainness and lack of style.

'Do you want to keep coming out with me or not?' Norman had snapped. She had opened her mouth to reply and then realised he was right. There was too much at stake for her to allow her vanity to endanger everything. If she attracted too much attention on one of their dates and someone recognised her, Najid would have her back in Domai within hours and Norman would never be able to get near her again. Now that their whole future was at stake she was happy to wear the dowdy clothes for him.

As she appeared through the green baize door he joined her and they walked quickly outside and climbed into the car. Anyone looking closely at her would have seen she did not look herself. Her face was paler than usual and she had changed her shade of lipstick from the bright scarlet she had taken to wearing to a more subdued brown colour. They had planned the look together.

The staff in the guardroom were now used to the sight of the battered little car coming and going with Norman at the wheel. They took scant notice of the passenger, her face always in the shadow of a scarf or high collar. They assumed it was one of the kitchen staff going out for some shopping.

The gates opened automatically as they approached and Norman accelerated through them. Keeping his eyes on the road, Norman didn't notice the glint of sunlight on Major Cox's binoculars up beside the stable block.

Neither of them spoke on the journey, both being lost in their own thoughts and plans. This was the day when they began the process of changing their lives forever. Both of them were excited by the prospect, neither of them was completely sure they were doing the right thing, but neither could bear the idea of not going through with the plan now that they had dared to dream it up.

Once they were in town Norman parked in the multistorey car park and they made their way down to street level, arm in arm like any other affectionate couple on a shopping expedition, and walked into the hairdressing salon. The girl at reception gave them a blank look and Norman told her they had an appointment.

'It's Mrs Blackman,' he said.

The girl ran the extended nail of her index finger down the list of appointments until she found the name. She indicated they should sit and wait while she announced their arrival. Jarmina stiffened at such insulting behaviour but Norman patted her hand to remind her to stay calm and act like a normal person and not draw any undue attention to them. A few minutes later the girl who had done the fitting for them the previous week appeared in reception, smiling blankly.

'We're ready for you now, Mrs Blackman,' she said.

Jarmina rose, holding tightly to Norman's hand, making it clear that wherever Mrs Blackman went, Mr Blackman accompanied her. The girl seemed unbothered and led them through to a small curtained area at the back of the salon. She sat Jarmina down and proudly produced the honey blonde wig on a model head.

'There,' she said, her eyes lighting up with pride. 'Isn't that beautiful?'

Norman looked at it and said nothing. He watched as Jarmina caressed the silky hair, as if it were a small animal she had developed a fondness for.

'Yes,' she said, her eyes sparkling happily. 'It's very beautiful.'

'Would you like to try it on?' the girl asked.

Jarmina nodded and the girl started work on her hair, pulling it back and pinning it tightly on top of her head, preparing her to receive her new crowning glory.

'I'll just be over the road,' Norman said, gesturing vaguely towards the pub. 'Come over when you're ready.'

Jarmina gave a little frown of disappointment. She had wanted him to be there for the moment when she changed into someone new, just for him, but she could see he was ill at ease being party to such a feminine ritual. Desperately trying to convince herself that she would be perfectly safe on her own, she decided not to cause a scene by insisting he stayed.

'Okay, darling,' she said, trying the word out for the first time and liking the sound of it, 'I'll see you in the bar.'

When he left, she felt a ripple of a thrill run through her chest at the bold way in which she was behaving, just like a normal, Western woman and not like someone who had been brought up to know her place, albeit a place at the very pinnacle of the pecking order.

Norman was into his second pint when Jarmina walked in as a beaming blonde. He was startled by how different she looked, how westernised. No one would ever have guessed she hadn't lived all her life in England. He noticed that several men followed her across the room with their eyes. She stood in front of him, waiting for his approval.

'Very nice,' he said with a nod. 'Want a drink?'

'Just very nice?' she asked, her eyebrows arching in their normal regal manner. They were more noticeable than ever beneath the glossy blonde fringe.

'More than very nice,' Norman amended his verdict. 'Do you want a Coke?'

'I'll have a glass of champagne,' she said, glaring at him. 'I feel like celebrating, even if you don't.'

'We don't sell champagne by the glass,' the barman chipped in.

'Then give us a bottle,' Jarmina snapped.

'Wait a minute.' Norman held up his hands. 'I can't afford to go buying bottles of champagne every time you have your hair done. Give the woman a Coke,' he told the barman.

Jarmina opened her mouth to escalate the argument but saw the look in Norman's eye. A month earlier and she would never have let any man talk to her in such a way, let alone someone as lowly as a bodyguard, but she had learned a lot since then. She knew Norman was perfectly capable of walking out without a backward glance, and she didn't want that to happen, not now, not when she was on the verge of a new life with him. So she closed her mouth and pretended that the Coke was exactly what she had wanted all along. They drank in silence for a few minutes.

'Quite sexy, actually,' Norman grunted eventually, gesturing towards the wig.

'Do you really think so?' Her joy was suddenly restored.

Half an hour later they came out of the pub, arm in arm, and Norman led her across the road to Boots the chemists. Jarmina's eyes flickered from counter to counter as they progressed down the aisle and she ignored the urge to start bulk-buying everything she saw. Norman came to a halt in front of a passport photo booth. Two young girls were inside, their bottom halves protruding below the curtain as they giggled and shifted their positions and the camera inside flashed. When they drew back the curtain and saw two adults waiting for them to finish, they fell almost silent, their suppressed giggles occasionally erupting to the surface in little explosions behind raised hands as they waited for their pictures to develop. They watched Norman arrange Jarmina on the seat, adjusting it to suit her height, insert the money and draw the curtain.

After Jarmina had finished, Norman stepped into the booth himself. He drew the curtain and pulled a set of false teeth out of his pocket. He slipped them into his mouth, over his own teeth, and they instantly changed the shape of the lower part of his face beneath the new moustache. He quickly ruffled his hair into a different position from its normal neat style, and pushed a pair of gold-rimmed glasses onto his nose. The transformation was dramatic. He could see the face reflected back at him. He smiled widely, as he had been practising in the mirror at Upton Park, showing off the teeth and changing his normally deadpan expression beyond recognition. He inserted his money and the camera did its work. The moment the last picture had been taken he slid the teeth and glasses back into his pocket and straightened his hair. Pulling back the curtain, he re-emerged into the shop.

The two girls had taken their pictures from the machine and had renewed their giggling. Jarmina was sitting on a plastic chair a few feet away, waiting patiently, toying lovingly with her new hair. They sat together. When the pictures eventually came through he gave hers a quick glance and nodded as if satisfied. When his came he attempted to slide them into his pocket but Jarmina, now giggling almost as much as the two girls, forced him to show her.

'Oh my goodness,' she exclaimed. 'I don't think I want to run away with a man who looks like that.'

Norman shot her a quick frown, angry with her for being indiscreet and they made their way back out into the square.

'Come on,' she said, grabbing his hand and tugging him along. 'Let's go shopping in Woolworths again.'

For half an hour she wandered around Woolworths as if it were a local bazaar, picking up every cheap, brightly coloured item that took her fancy. Eventually Norman managed to extricate her, but only after she had filled two bulging carrier bags with her purchases.

'Oh, Norman, look!' She gave a squeak of delight and pulled him over towards the forecourt of a garage on the other side of the road. A brand new convertible BMW was revolving slowly on a turntable. 'I want to buy this car for you. We could have it delivered to our new house in America.'

'I don't need a car,' he protested. 'I don't want you spending your money on me. Anyway, they do have cars in America.'

She pulled away from him and stared angrily. 'Why won't you let me buy you a present?'

'Just leave it, will you,' Norman snapped and walked briskly back towards the car park, forcing her to run in order to keep up with him. She linked her arm through his and remained silent until they were back at the house. She didn't understand him at all – but that was what made him so fascinating.

CHAPTER TWELVE

Joshua Franklin was walking around a brand new car, allowing his customer to drink in the beauty of its lines and the shine of its metallic paintwork, when the doors of the showroom burst open and Moody strode across to him, leaving another man standing at the door. Moody flashed him an identity card.

'Can we talk?' he asked, abruptly.

'What about?' Josh asked, startled by the sudden invasion of the space which he normally controlled so carefully.

'In private,' Moody said, gesturing to the customer.

'I'm sorry about this,' Josh said to the man. 'May I ask one of my associates to take over?'

The customer nodded, his mouth hanging open, and Josh waved over one of his salesmen.

'Follow me,' he said curtly to Moody once the customer was taken care of, and he led him into the back office.

'Are you Joshua Franklin?' Moody asked.

'It seems you know I am,' Josh said, unable to keep the irritation from his voice. 'If I lose that sale because of your bad manners I'm going to be suing someone.'

Moody ignored the threat. 'Do you live with Kathy Dorset?'

'What's that got to do with you?'

'It would be much better if you just answered the question.' Moody hated everything about the man in front of him. He hated the gleaming shine on his shoes and the razor-sharp creases in his trousers. He hated the discreet white handkerchief in his top pocket and the fact that he looked as if he had exfoliated every pore of his face and neck. The man positively shone with good grooming and Moody was horribly aware of the state of his own jacket and shoes, not to mention his badly shaved chin and unbrushed hair.

'Yes, I live with Kathy.' Josh sat down, forcing himself to remain calm. He could see that if he antagonised this little man he was likely to end up wasting far more valuable time than if he co-operated.

'Do you give her money?' Moody could tell he was being patronised, but continued anyway.

'From time to time. Women need things, you know.' Looking at him, Josh suspected Moody might not know too much about women. He didn't look the married type – no self-respecting woman would let her man get this scruffy.

'We found an envelope with several thousand pounds in. Would that be from you?'

'No.' Josh shook his head. 'I never give her more than a few hundred at a time and she always spends it straightaway. If it's a few thousand she must have got it from her husband.'

'Norman Dorset?'

'Yeah.' Josh shifted uneasily in his chair. He preferred not to be reminded that he was sleeping with Norman Dorset's wife. When looked at in the cold light of day, it didn't seem such an intelligent thing to do.

'He comes round to the house with money?'

'No,' Josh was adamant. 'Well, I've never seen him. Various people come. I think his brother Len was the last. But I'm out all day, so I don't really know what goes on.'

'Len?' Moody wrote the name down on his pad and circled it thoughtfully. That was twice in a week someone had mentioned that name to him.

'Yeah, Len. He runs a limo and security business up the West End.'

'He and Kathy close, are they?'

'Kathy and Len? No, I don't think so. I think he's just a messenger.'

'Does Norman Dorset know about you and his wife?' Moody asked, not missing the spasm of discomfort that passed over the other man's smooth features.

'It doesn't matter to me if he does or he doesn't,' Josh said, his voice croaking a little. 'I'm not scared of him. He's just an old gangster, past his time, isn't he?'

Moody didn't reply for a moment. 'If I were to give you my number,' he said, 'would you let me know if Norman makes contact in any way? I would be interested to ask him a few questions.'

'Is he in trouble for something?' Josh was finding it easier to breathe now. It didn't seem that he was in the frame for anything and he could see through the glass that his customer was still there.

Moody didn't reply, just opened the door to leave. Josh leapt to his feet and ushered him out with a broad smile. As they came into the showroom he shook Moody's hand ostentatiously. 'Anything else I can do for you, officer, just let me know. Any time.'

Moody said nothing, his hand remaining limp in Josh's dry, powerful grip. Once Josh was confident the customer had taken in the scene he dropped Moody's damp hand and escorted him to the main doors, before returning to complete his sale.

On the nights when Norman stayed in Jarmina's bed till morning, he would always have to wake himself up at five and slip out to open up the house in preparation for the staff coming downstairs. He had spent enough time in institutions to have no difficulty waking up early, but exhaustion from the combination of late nights and early mornings was beginning to wear him down and irritate his ulcers. He felt nervous at being cut off from the rest of the world, however comfortable his new prison cell might be. He made regular calls to Pete at the club to try to find out what was happening and to make it known that he was still around. If his staff got the idea he was out of touch they might start taking liberties. He wanted to make sure his name stayed fresh in their minds.

Norman was never quite able to relax in the house now, always watchful in case one of the other servants got wind of his relationship with Jarmina. Sometimes, when they lay together after making love, he would be unable to sleep, certain that he could hear footsteps on the landing outside. The last thing he needed was someone getting clever and tipping the Sultan off about his sister's private life. Not only would that put an end to their plans, it would also bring the police down on the house like a ton of bricks. The Sultan would be bound to want to know everything possible about the man about to elope with his sister and, once the stones started being lifted, God alone knew what would crawl out! He knew he would only be able to relax when the whole thing was over and they were safely away. He felt more ready to retire now than he ever had before.

If no other household staff had emerged by the time he had reset the alarms and cameras to their daytime positions, he would make a couple of cups of tea and take them back up to Jarmina. She wasn't as good at waking up early, but, because she enjoyed spending half an hour talking to him before they were forced to go back to playing employer and employee in front of the staff, she was willing to make the effort.

That particular morning, however, when Norman got back to the room with the mugs, she wasn't in the bed and he could hear the sound of retching coming from the bathroom. Norman was distracted, thinking about a phone call he had just put through to Pete. He knew he'd woken the man up, although Pete had been polite about it, and he'd had difficulty getting any sense from him. It seemed, according to Pete, that Moody was not giving up the chase.

'He says he's been down to Spain to check out the villa,' Pete said, with a yawn. 'And he's been sniffing around Kathy. He found some money you'd sent her, so he knows you're around somewhere, but I don't think he has any idea where.'

Norman didn't like the idea that Moody had been to the villa. He liked to think he was completely safe when he was down there. Although he knew the British police could do little to get him out of Spain once he was there, he was still unsettled by the thought of them being there at all. He would have to find another bolt-hole, in case everything went wrong and he had to disappear again. He didn't get back onto the bed as he usually did on these mornings. Instead, he plumped himself down in one of the armchairs, staring straight ahead, lost in thought.

When Jarmina emerged from the bathroom he was shocked by how pale she looked. Her eyes were watery and her hair dishevelled.

'You all right?' he asked as she staggered back to the bed and lay down, groaning.

She didn't respond and he stood up, walking over to the bed. He stroked her forehead gently. It felt cool. Then the penny dropped.

'Were you sick yesterday morning?' he asked.

'Yes,' she said. 'For several days.'

He remembered a night, early in their relationship, when the urgency of their desire had carried them away and he hadn't used protection. He'd forgotten all about it. He couldn't think of the words to say to her. Luckily, she said them for him.

'I think I will have to go away for a few days. I have talked to the doctor. He is making arrangements. I am so frightened. Will it spoil our plans?' There was a look of panic in her wide eyes. Just when she believed she had found an escape route from ending her days like her mother, it looked as if fate might be about to snatch it away from her.

'You're not spoiling anything,' he said, his thoughts spinning. If her family found out about this they were going to want to know who the father was. Maybe they would think it was the King of Syran, but somehow he doubted it. He was going to have to bring his plans forward now that he knew Moody was getting closer, but he couldn't do anything until this was sorted out. For a fleeting second he thought about suggesting they run away now and have the child in America. Then he thought about his girls with Kathy, and how he had let them down over the years by not being there. If he was going to leave them again he had to make sure that everything was arranged for them before he went. He felt a cold chill of panic at the thought of another child arriving before he was ready. There would be other chances to start a family with Jarmina – this wasn't the moment. He shut his mind to the thought of the life that was stirring inside her and what it might become if allowed to survive. Norman was very good at shutting his mind to things he didn't want to contemplate.

'Don't worry,' he assured her. 'I'll have everything ready for when you get back.'

Jarmina nodded as if grateful and watched him leave the room. Once the door had closed behind him the tears came and she buried her head in the pillows. She wanted to have Norman's child more than anything and she had been praying he would tell her it was all right, that she didn't need to get rid of it. But she could see he was right. There would be time to start a family once they were safe.

Len was at home on a Sunday morning when Moody finally arrived on his doorstep.

'Mr Dorset?' Moody asked.

'Yes,' Len replied.

'Mr Len Dorset?'

'Yes.'

'May I come in and chat for a few moments?'

Moody could see Babs in the background in a short dressing-gown which showed off her long, muscular brown legs. He held up his identification card for Len to read.

'Yes, I suppose so,' Len said, reluctantly. He knew immediately what this was likely to be about. He led the policeman through to the kitchen and gestured for him to sit down while he busied himself making coffee. Babs had vanished back upstairs.

'When did you last see your brother?' Moody asked.

'My brother?' Len asked, as innocently as he could manage.

'Norman.'

'Norman and I don't see much of one another,' Len said. 'We fell out a few years ago.'

'When did you last see him?' Moody persisted.

'A few years ago,' Len repeated, concentrating his attention on the coffee-pot.

'You didn't bump into him in Spain a few months ago?'

'What's this about?' Len asked, bringing the coffee to the table and sitting down to pour it. He was playing for time. He should have admitted to seeing Norman in Spain, just as Norman had told him to. He had panicked and tried to distance himself even further from his brother, and now he had been caught in an unnecessary lie.

'I'm just trying to find out when you last saw your brother,' Moody persevered.

'We did bump into each other in Spain, yes,' Len said. 'We spent a bit of time together, talking about old times, you know how it is, and then I came back to England.'

'And where did he go?'

'I don't know. I guess he stayed down there.'

Moody stirred sugar into his coffee and said nothing. Len was tempted to fill the silence but thought better of it. Eventually Moody said, 'So why did you say you hadn't seen him for years?'

'Norman's a bad lot,' Len said. 'I prefer to forget he's my brother.'

'But you spent time with him in Spain?'

'Not my choice.'

Moody sipped his coffee. 'Do you have anything to do with his wife?'

'Kathy? No.'

'You don't give her money?'

Len sighed. He realised Moody knew a lot, but he couldn't be sure exactly how much.

'Okay. When we were in Spain Norman asked me to pass some money on to Kathy. He didn't tell me why, and I didn't ask. There's no point asking Norman too many questions. Never has been.'

'How much did you give her?'

Len shrugged. 'A few thousand. I don't know exactly.'

'So where is he now?' Moody asked again.

'Honestly,' Len said, spreading his palms. 'I have no idea.'

'There's a warrant out for his arrest,' Moody said, 'for the suspected killing of Sidney Rose. If you're covering for him you could end up as an accessory to murder, Len. This could be your chance to put yourself in the clear.'

'If I knew where he was,' Len said with wide-eyed innocence, 'I'd tell you, I swear.'

Moody stared at him very hard and knew he was lying.

The phone call from Claridge's took Norman by surprise. 'It is Queen Nabila, here,' she said. 'I need you to come to the hotel now.'

'I can't leave Upton Park, your Highness,' Norman protested, trying to think through the possible reasons why he would receive such a command.

'There's no one there, is there?' Nabila insisted. 'The Princess is not there. My husband's mother is not there...'

'The house needs to be secure,' Norman blustered, not liking the idea of being summoned somewhere where he had no control. He knew it was unusual for the Queen to make a phone call like this personally. Surely one of her assistants would be instructed to summon him. She must want him there badly. It could be a trap. Perhaps Najid was behind it.

'Your assistant can handle the house,' the Queen snapped, her patience with his insubordination wearing out. 'There's a car coming to fetch you.'

The phone went dead in his hand. He sat for a few moments, thinking. If Nabila knew Jarmina wasn't there, did that mean she also knew where the Princess was and what she was doing? Norman guessed that if a Princess checked into a private clinic for a termination, the news was likely to get back to her family. That didn't mean they would know who the father was, of course. But if they did know, then presumably they would summon him, just as was happening. And then what? Would they offer him a pay-off to leave her alone? And if they did, how much was it likely to be, and would they agree to pay it offshore and under the name of Blackman? Perhaps they didn't realise it was him, but thought he would be the most likely to know who it was, since he was always watching what happened at the house.

All these thoughts were jostling for space in his mind as he told Mark he had to go to London. The car arrived for him an hour later and his mind was still turning over the possibilities as he and the driver headed back up the motorway in silence. If he was about to be paid off, maybe he should agree to it and then meet Jarmina later, once he had established his new identity in another country. It was the first time Norman had ever had to take someone else into account in his plans and it made him feel uneasy. It was going to be harder to move freely around the world with a woman, particularly a woman as noticeable as Jarmina, but the thought of leaving her behind made him unhappy. In fact, he wasn't sure that he would be able to do it.

'Fuck it,' he muttered to himself. 'I've gone fucking soft!'

'Sorry, mate?' the driver said. 'I didn't catch that.'

'Don't worry,' Norman replied. 'Talking to myself.' He turned the radio on to ensure the man didn't make any more attempts at conversation.

John Parsons was nervous and it showed. Moody could hear him humming to himself through the microphone he'd strapped to John's chest. Moody and his colleague were back in the room opposite The Country Club in Streatham. They'd seen Parsons coming down the road from the window but now he'd disappeared into the building and they were forced to listen to the crackling soundtrack of his chest mike.

'Hi, is Pete Chappell around?' they heard him say.

A mumbled response obviously pointed him in the right direction. There was more humming as he went further in search of his prey.

'Hi, Pete.'

'Hello, mate,' came Pete's voice.

Moody and his colleague exchanged looks of relief that the mikes were working as they'd hoped and they could hear everything that was said.

'What have you got for me today?'

'I've got some lovely stuff,' Parsons said, and there was a rustling of plastic bags.

'How much do you want for this?' Pete asked.

'Five hundred.'

'Anything else?'

'I've got these.'

There was more rustling and then silence, presumably while Pete inspected the goods.

'Okay,' he said at last. 'If you throw these in I'll give you five hundred.'

'You're kidding. With those I'd want seven-fifty, minimum.'

'Six hundred and that's my last offer.'

'You drive a hard bargain, Pete Chappell.'

'I'm still the best customer you've got,' Pete laughed, and there was a rustle of paper that sounded distinctly like money being handed over.

'Bingo!' Moody said and picked up the radio, talking excitedly. 'Wait till our man's clear of the building and then go in at full speed. Whatever you do don't let Chappell get to a toilet.'

'Come on,' he said to his colleague and the two of them ran downstairs. As they came out into the street they saw John Parsons emerge from the club door and walk quickly away.

'He's clear, go now!' Moody ordered into the radio. Thirty seconds later they were inside Pete Chappell's office and Pete hadn't even had time to clear the merchandise off his desk.

As he climbed out of the limousine in front of Claridge's, Norman's eyes were darting in all directions. He had put on dark glasses to give himself a little cover. He announced himself and was told to make his way up to the suite where Queen Nabila was in residence. It was the suite which Jarmina and her mother had always stayed in. Now that they used the house when they were in England, Jarmina was no longer able to keep her sister-in-law out of the suite.

There were several ladies-in-waiting in the sitting-room and Nabila made a dramatic entrance a few minutes after Norman was let in. He was impressed by how beautiful she looked. Being married and spending a lot of time in the West had changed her. She was immaculately groomed and dressed in a conservative European style.

She looked him up and down. Her eyes came to rest on the Rolex watch on his wrist. It had been a gift from Jarmina after the argument about the car. He had tried to refuse it but she had been adamant and he had wanted to make it up to her for seeming churlish. To cover the significance of the gift, she had given Rolexes to all the other staff members as well. The man from Asprey's had come down with a case full of them. While he was there, when Norman was out of the room, Jarmina had ordered a diamond tiara for herself, made to a design she had sketched on a piece of paper, and a diamond ring which she intended to give to Norman once they were safely in America.

After a meaningful few seconds, Nabila lifted her eyes from the watch and came forward with a charming smile and an extended hand.

'Mr Dorset,' she said. 'I have heard so much about you.'

'You have?' Norman was genuinely puzzled. He noticed the other women were hiding smiles and averting their eyes.

'I'm told you are the best security man in London.'

'That's very kind of you to say so.' Norman was not flattered. He could smell a rat.

'I would like you to work for me.'

'I'm afraid I already have a job,' he replied. The idea that he would actually have developed a reputation for doing a job he had only taken on as a favour to Len made him want to laugh.

'I'm sure Jarmina would be happy to see you improving your station in life, going from protecting a princess to protecting a queen. She speaks so highly of you, claims you are the best soldier she has ever had working for her.' Nabila's eyes had fallen onto the Rolex again.

'The Princess is very kind,' Norman said. 'And I'm very happy to be working for her.'

'When a Queen offers you a job,' Nabila's voice was becoming less friendly, 'you would be wise to accept it.'

'Are you offering me a job, or just trying to steal me from your sister-in-law?' Norman asked, and there was sharp gasp of shock from the ladies in the room. 'If there is nothing else, I'll be on my way.'

He turned and left the room before Nabila had a chance to think of anything else to say. The limousine was still waiting at the front of the hotel and he ordered it to take him to Euston Station. Once there he told the driver he no longer needed him and walked through to the ticket office. A few minutes later he was on a train to Liverpool, staring out the window, his mind going over every detail of the plans which had been formulating for several weeks now.

When he arrived in Liverpool he took a taxi to the street where he was born. The street itself looked just as he remembered it, although it now stood like an island amongst giant blocks of flats, factories and flyovers. The houses were mostly still run-down, although a few people had made attempts at livening them up with window-boxes or replacement front doors. The children in the street now wore trainers instead of clogs, but otherwise they looked just as he remembered his friends looking.

He gave barely a glance to the house where his mother had lived for all her adult life, and where he and all his brothers and sisters had been born. He didn't want to have to deal with any unnecessary memories. He stopped at another house three doors down. It was one of the ones which looked as if someone cared for it, with its newly painted front door and brightly coloured window boxes. A plastic cat had been stuck to the roof-tiles to discourage the pigeons. The doorbell chimed prettily and was answered by a pleasant-looking woman whose face hardened as soon as she saw who it was.

'Is Billy in?' he asked and she stood back to let him past, without saying a word.

Norman walked into the sparkling clean house, knowing that he would find his old childhood friend in the kitchen. But as he went in, he was shocked to find a man who looked like Billy's father reading the paper at the kitchen table. Last time he had seen Billy he had had hair and he had been about half the size of the man in front of him. His childhood friend now looked like an old man.

'Norman?' Billy looked up from the paper and his face broke into a grin. 'Bloody hell, look what the cat's dragged in, Pat!'

There was no response from Pat Blackman, beyond the slamming of the front door.

'She had some shopping to do.' Billy excused his wife's disappearance and Norman nodded his understanding.

'Do you want a cup of tea?' Billy asked, busying himself with the kettle and prattling on.

Norman glanced around the room. There were photographs on the dresser, displayed amongst the best china.

'Still going to Wales for all your holidays?' Norman asked, holding up a picture of Pat and Billy on the beach.

'You know Pat,' Billy grinned ruefully. 'Never held with the idea of abroad.'

'She's probably got a point,' Norman said, putting the picture back and sitting down at the table. 'I saw Len the other day. He asked to be remembered to you.'

'How's he doing?'

'Pretty good, considering what a pain he was when we were kids.'

For an hour they chatted about old times and then Norman got to the point.

'So you and Pat have never applied for passports?'

'Never needed to,' Billy replied. 'You don't need a passport for Wales.'

'I'd like to make you an offer, Bill, which Pat never need know about.'

'What's that then?'

'I need a couple of passports pretty quickly and I don't want them in my own name. If you could let me have a borrow of your birth certificates, both yours and Pat's, and a marriage certificate, I could let you have a bit of cash.'

'How much cash?' Billy asked.

Norman pulled a roll of notes out of his pocket and put it on the table.

'How much is that?' Billy stared at the fat tube of money.

'Five grand.'

'Don't move,' Billy said, scooping the money into his pocket and going to the dresser.

He pulled out a box full of papers and rummaged through them until he had found the certificates, which he handed to Norman.

'If Pat ever asks where they are I'll profess complete ignorance,' he warned. 'If you get caught I'll deny this conversation ever took place. I'll say you must have nicked them while I was in the toilet.'

'Fair enough,' Norman said, slipping the neatly folded pieces of paper into his pocket as they heard the sound of the front door opening, and Billy pushed the box back into the dresser and stood up.

'Still here?' Pat sniffed as she came in.

'I was just going to take Norman down the pub to see if some of the others are around,' Billy said.

Pat said nothing as the two men made their way out of the house. The less she had to do with a man like Norman Dorset the happier Pat Blackman would be.

Norman arrived back at Upton Park the following morning to find the courtyard filled with cars and vans. A marquee was being erected at the end of the swimming pool and Major Cox was strutting around issuing orders.

'What's going on?' Norman asked.

'You worry about the house,' Cox replied. 'This is my domain.'

Norman grabbed his tie and jerked the man's face close to his.

'What's going on?' he enquired again.

'The King has ordered some musicians to play for him tonight. A private concert.'

'Is he planning to stay in the house overnight?' Norman asked.

'He hasn't informed me of his plans in that direction.'

Inside the house the kitchens were in uproar as the cooks prepared enough food for the growing band of musicians and technicians appearing at their door.

'When did this all happen?' Norman asked Mark.

'Yesterday. I tried to get hold of you. I even rang Len and asked where you were. He seemed a bit funny.'

'So, what's happening?'

'Najid's employed the London Philharmonic to play for him.'

'Jesus Christ! Is he planning to stay here?'

'Apparently not. He's being driven back to Park Lane afterwards. Where have you been?'

Norman didn't bother to answer.

By six o'clock the orchestra was in place beside the swimming pool and a meal had been set up for Najid under the marquee. The musicians began tuning up and Norman went up to Jarmina's bedroom, opening the window and sitting down to watch the proceedings below. At eight o'clock Mark rang up to tell him Najid's car had arrived, driven by Len, and that Len was in the kitchen.

Norman watched for a while longer, lost in thought, and then pulled himself wearily to his feet and went downstairs. Len was sitting at the kitchen table, watching the staff working around him.

'Hi,' Norman said. 'Want a drink?'

'I'll just have something soft, an orange juice or something. I've got to drive him back tonight.'

Norman fetched them each a drink and they walked out onto the terrace to watch the goings-on below. The musicians were being served refreshments while they waited for Najid to finish his meal, and were talking quietly amongst themselves as if at some polite drinks party.

'I've had the police around asking about you,' Len said.

'Moody?'

'I think that was his name, miserable little git.'

'What did you tell him?'

'Nothing. But he knew we'd met in Spain. Seemed to know a lot. You're going to have to get out of here. It's only a matter of time before someone puts two and two together, and now my neck's on the line along with yours.'

'I know. I appreciate it.'

'That's okay, but I'd rather not go down with you on this, if it's all right with you.'

Norman nodded and didn't smile. 'I'll be out of your hair soon, Len. I promise. Give me a couple more days.'

Finally Najid finished eating and he moved to the armchair which had been set up for him on the edge of the terrace, as the musicians took their places. The staff melted away around him, leaving him sitting alone as the music struck up. Norman could see Major Cox standing in the shadow of the trees a little distance behind the marquee.

The music swelled and faces appeared at the windows of the house as the staff were drawn from all over the building by the beautiful sounds in the evening air. Najid closed his eyes and steepled his fingers in front of his bowed head as he listened.

The concert was immaculate, with the musicians giving their all, despite the fact that they were performing before a handful of people, only one of whom was officially there to listen. At the end the applause was tiny and inadequate after the power of the sound that had gone before. Norman saw Najid call Major Cox over and whisper something to him. Cox turned, looked at Norman, and nodded his agreement to whatever the Sultan had whispered. Najid then stood up, thanked the conductor for the entertainment and walked into the house. Norman undid his jacket so that he could reach his gun should he need it.

Cox made his way towards Norman with a self-satisfied smirk on his face. Norman didn't move, his hand ready to get to the holster.

'His Majesty would like you to see him in the library.'

Norman didn't give any indication whether he had heard the instruction or not. He knew Cox assumed he was about to be fired. He turned and went into the house, his mind racing. Had the King discovered their plan? Had he come to tell him that Jarmina would not be returning and he was to forget he ever saw her?

Coffee was being brought to the library as Norman got there and the Sultan was already sitting in one of the armchairs with a bottle of whisky and two glasses beside him. He gestured for Norman to sit in the chair opposite and the waiter served them both with coffee before withdrawing, closing the heavy panelled doors behind him.

'What did you think of the music?' the King asked, pouring Norman a whisky and passing it over without a word.

'I'm not too much of a judge of classical music, but it seemed good to me.'

'Yes. It was good. They are a fine orchestra.'

He lapsed into a thoughtful silence again. Norman waited patiently to see what would come next.

'General Beckett tells me my sister thinks very highly of you,' he said. 'A good soldier, I believe she said.'

'I'm glad she's pleased,' Norman said.

'I gather that my wife sent for you yesterday.'

'Yes, she did.'

Najid waited, obviously expecting Norman to say more, but Norman didn't oblige.

'I have some difficulty where my wife and my sister are concerned,' he said. 'I think you probably understand.'

'I can tell there's no love lost there.'

'No, quite. No love lost at all,' Najid chuckled. 'I think perhaps you are in a position to do my family some harm, Mr Dorset.'

'I'm not sure I follow you, your Highness.'

'The British newspapers are hungry for stories about the terrible Arabs who have invaded their country. They want to hear how depraved we are, how fabulously rich and spendthrift. They like the idea that for all our money we do not know how to use a Western bathroom properly and that we like to ravish Western women – when we are not ravishing our camels, that is. They would love to hear a story about a queen and a princess fighting for the services of a bodyguard.'

Norman stayed very quiet. Things were going in a direction he hadn't anticipated.

'If you were to decide to sell your story to the newspapers I'm sure they would pay you well. I would like to ask you, as a personal favour to me, not to do anything like that; to help me protect the reputation of my family.'

Still Norman said nothing, just sipped his whisky and watched his coffee cool, waiting to see what would come next. He had sat through enough late-night poker games in his life to know when it was best to let the opposition show their hand.

'I would be more than happy to recompense you for any money which you might feel you would lose through doing me this favour. I think, in other words, I can outbid the newspapers.'

Norman waited a little longer, but now the King too seemed to have stopped talking.

'You may rest assured, your Highness, that I have no intention of talking to any newspapers, either now or in the future. I'm honoured that you have talked to me in this honest manner and I hope I'll be able to count on your friendship in the future.'

'You'll always be able to count on my friendship.' Najid took out a small, embossed embassy card and wrote a number on the back. 'If at any time you need help, just ring this number and ask for Michael. He'll always be available for your call. He's my ears and my eyes. He has my complete confidence and will look after your needs, whatever they are. He tells me he has a high regard for your brother.'

Norman took the card and slipped it into his breast pocket without reading it.

'Thank you, your Highness,' he said.

The Sultan refilled their glasses and the conversation turned to more neutral matters.

CHAPTER THIRTEEN

Jarmina returned to Upton Park a week later as if nothing had happened. None of the other servants could have read anything suspicious from her face or her demeanour. Norman had to admit she was a good actress. Unless, of course, she had changed her mind and was going to pretend the whole thing had never happened. He was surprised by just how panicked he felt at that idea. This woman had got to him in a way that no one else had ever managed and he wasn't sure he liked the feeling. He was afraid his feelings for her were making him act irrationally. He was taking too many risks, but he couldn't stop himself.

She gave instructions for her luggage to be taken to her room and rang down to Norman to tell him to come up to her. He was shocked by how pleased he was to see her, and how eager he was to take her in his arms. He was also relieved by how desperate she was for him to take her, after what she had been through. It was as if she wanted to block out everything else in the world and concentrate on her love for him – like she was ending her previous life and thinking only of their future as a couple.

After they had made love, they lay on the bed and she pointed to a large leather suitcase which stood by the door, as if it was waiting for them to leave the room together.

'That's for us,' she said. 'To help us start our life together in America.'

'What is it?' Norman asked.

'Open it.'

Norman climbed off the bed and went to pick up the case. 'Bloody hell!' he exclaimed at the weight of it. 'What have you got in here, gold bars?'

He heaved the case across the room and swung it up onto the bed. He snapped back the catches and lifted the lid. The sight that met his eyes made him laugh out loud.

'Where did you get this?'

'From the bank,' she said, as if the answer was obvious.

The suitcase was packed solid with ten-dollar bills.

'Didn't they want to know what you wanted it for?' Norman asked.

'It's none of their business,' she said, astonished he would think anyone would challenge a Princess making a withdrawal from her account.

'I can't lug this lot through customs,' he said. 'I'd stick out like a sore bloody thumb. Apart from which, I'd give myself a bleeding hernia!'

'Oh well, never mind,' she dismissed the idea immediately. 'I have an account in New York. We can withdraw from that once we arrive.'

'That would probably be a bit more clever,' Norman said, giving the contents of the case a last wistful look.

'Take some now, anyway,' she said. 'To cover the expenses of the trip.'

'No,' Norman said, shaking his head. 'That won't be necessary. I can cover the expenses.'

He snapped the suitcase shut and went to his jacket which was folded neatly over the back of a small gilt chair, and pulled out an envelope. 'I've got something to show you, as well.'

He climbed back onto the bed with the envelope and passed it across to her. She opened it and two British passports fell onto her lap. Picking them up she opened the first one and burst into a delighted laugh at seeing the photograph again.

'Look at me!' she shrieked. 'I look so English! Let's see you.' She opened the other and her laughter brought tears to her eyes. Giving a thin smile, Norman found himself unable to stop himself from joining in with her childish glee. 'You look so cute,' she said. 'Like some happy old professor. Not like my soldier at all.'

Norman took the picture from her and looked at it again. He was pleased with it. No one looking at this passport would ever associate it with Norman Dorset.

'When can we go?' Jarmina asked. 'When can Mr and Mrs Blackman sail away together to live happily ever after in America?'

'Soon,' Norman told her. 'I just have a few more things to sort out. I have to make arrangements for my children.'

For a moment silence filled the room and they were both aware of the child they had just lost. The old Jarmina was on the verge of saying something spiteful about Kathy and the children, people she had never met but hated anyway, but she bit back the words. What good would they do? The children were a reality. She couldn't pretend they didn't exist, not all the time anyway. She took a deep breath.

'Do you want that money for your children?' she asked, gesturing at the suitcase.

Norman hesitated for a second. 'Don't worry about it,' he said eventually. 'I'll take care of everything.'

'I have to go to the doctor for one last check-up the day after tomorrow,' she said. 'We can go after that.'

'Sure, we could go after that. I could arrange to pick you up from the doctor's and drive you myself in one of Len's cars.'

'I would like to see my brother one more time. After I have been to the doctor I will go to his apartment in Park Lane. You can meet me there.'

Norman was happy with that idea. Now that he and Najid were on such good terms he felt confident the King would have no objection to Norman driving his sister around without any other bodyguard or doctor in attendance.

'I need to let someone know what's happening,' he said. 'Tell them what we're planning.'

'Who?' she asked, her face suddenly serious.

'Just someone who can tell the truth about what has happened once we're clear of the country. If I don't do that and they find we've gone, they'll think I've kidnapped you. I need to tell someone to give us twenty-four hours' lead and then to explain to your brother that you've gone voluntarily.'

'I can tell him that,' she said. 'I can telephone him from America.'

'You can do that too,' he said. 'But Najid might think I was forcing you to say you had left of your own free will. It'll be better if we have an alibi over here.'

'You're the man in charge, Mr Blackman,' she laughed. 'My soldier is now my general.'

Pete left the club at three o'clock the following morning. He was tired. It had been a long day and he knew he had been ill-tempered with the staff. He was fed up with Moody's endless phone calls, asking if he had heard from Norman or if anyone else had heard anything. He had told the man he would let him know if he had anything. Why couldn't he believe him? His ill temper was also partly due to losing such a large amount of coke to the police and finding himself in Moody's power. Pete didn't like the idea of having to become a grass, but he liked the idea of a long prison sentence even less.

It had occurred to him that if Moody was successful in putting Norman away for murder, that would leave the path clear for Pete to take over The Country Club once and for all. But the idea of having to double-cross Norman Dorset in order to achieve such an end was not an attractive one.

He had parked his BMW in a small private car park at the back of the club. Every other car had gone by the time he got there. The only movement he saw was a cat creeping furtively behind some dustbins which were waiting to be emptied. As he unlocked the car door, a hand covered his mouth and an arm wrapped itself around him, pinning his arms to his side with a strength which Pete knew he would not be able to struggle against.

'Don't make a sound. It's me, Norman,' a hoarse voice whispered in his ear. 'Just walk back with me to the car.'

Pete nodded, to show he understood the instruction, and was released. He and Norman walked to the large black Mercedes which was parked on the road by the entrance to the car park. Norman gestured for him to get into the passenger seat while he went round to the driver's side. The engine was still running and he accelerated away.

'How are you, Norman?' Pete asked, and Norman noticed his brother-in-law seemed surprisingly nervous.

'I'm okay. How are you?'

'Things are good, Norman, at the club, I mean. I was hoping you would get in touch, so I could let you have some money. We've been making good profits.'

'Give the money to Kathy and the kids. From now on I want you to give her my share regularly every week, until I tell you otherwise. Understood?'

'Of course, whatever arrangement you want. It's your money.'

'Don't ever forget that, Pete,' Norman said. 'Not for one moment.'

'I won't Norman, you know that. We're family.'

Pete seemed to have overcome his initial shock at being kidnapped in a car park and his confidence was returning.

'I need to ask you for a favour,' Norman said.

'Anything I can do, Norman. You know that.'

'I'm involved with this woman. You knew Kathy and I were finished.'

'Yes, I knew that.'

'This woman is high profile. I mean really high profile. Because of the police I'm going to have to skip the country and take her with me. Head for South America.' Norman didn't intend to give Pete any more correct information than he absolutely had to.

'What is she, an actress or a singer or something? She's not a member of the royal family is she?' Pete laughed. He felt relieved that Norman was being so open with him. He obviously still had his trust.

'It doesn't matter who she is, not now. You'll find out soon enough. The point is that when they find she's gone and that I've gone too, they're going to assume I've grabbed her. If they jump to that conclusion they're likely to turn the heat on, and then if they find me they'll shoot first and ask questions later. Do you see what I mean?'

'I see what you mean.'

'I want you to wait until you receive a phone call from me, in about twenty-four hours. By then we'll be safely out of the country. I'll give you the woman's name then and you can go to Moody and explain what's happened. Assure him we've run off together, that she was totally willing. You don't have to say where to.'

'Of course not.'

'Tell him about this meeting and that I told you in advance what the plans were. Do you understand?'

'Sure.'

Norman drew the car round a corner into an unlit side-street. 'I'll make contact with you every now and again after that, once we're settled, to make sure the girls are all right. You're their godfather, right?'

'Right.'

'Make sure they do the right things, grow up to be good girls. There should be enough money in the club to finish off their education. I want you to take care of that. Will you do that for me?'

'Of course I will, Norman. It'll be my pleasure, you know it will.'

Norman held out his hand and Pete took it. The strength of the grip reminded him of just what a formidable enemy Norman would be.

They didn't speak again as Norman drove back to the car park and dropped Pete off.

As he climbed into his car, Pete glanced over his shoulder at his departing brother-in-law, and made a note of the car number-plate.

Len wasn't in the office when Moody and his men exploded through the doors and ordered everyone there to remain completely still. The only people there to take the orders were Len's telephone operators and the elderly Asian man who kept the books.

'Where's Len Dorset?' Moody demanded of one of the women. His adrenaline levels were high. He felt he was close to the final kill.

'He's out on a job,' she replied. 'Driving General Beckett.'

'Who the fuck is General Beckett?'

'One of our clients.' The woman was recovering from the shock and beginning to feel affronted by Moody's manner. 'And kindly watch your language in front of ladies, young man.'

Moody pretended not to hear. He pulled out a piece of paper and read out the car licence number which Pete Chappell had given him. 'That's one of your cars,' he said, accusingly.

'Yes, it is,' she replied.

'It's one of the black Mercedes,' the bookkeeper chirped in, eager to be part of the excitement.

'Who's being driven around in it?' Moody demanded.

The woman referred to a ledger in front of her.

'The Sultan of Domai's family. It's being used at Upton Park for the Sultan's sister, Princess Jarmina. Has it been involved in an accident?'

Moody ignored the question.

'That's who General Beckett works for, too,' the bookkeeper volunteered eagerly. 'They're one of our best customers. Mr Dorset always drives the General around himself, and sometimes the Sultan when he's in the country.'

'What's the Sultan's address? And the General's?' Moody asked.

'We aren't allowed to divulge clients' addresses,' the woman protested.

Moody threw some paperwork down in front of her. 'You are to me,' he snapped.

Jarmina's heart was dancing in her chest as she sat in front of the doctor in his Harley Street clinic. She was dressed in her traditional Domai clothes, but she'd spent the morning with Norman, packing suitcases with dozens of pairs of jeans and sweaters and T-shirts. She was on the verge of changing her life forever, of throwing off the chrysalis of her upbringing and transforming into an American citizen, just like the women she saw in all the American comedy programmes and soap operas. She would become a woman with a big kitchen and a big fridge and a horde of happy children. She was sure they would be able to have children now, just as soon as they were married.

'There is absolutely nothing for you to worry about now, your Highness,' the Doctor was saying. 'I can give you a completely clean bill of health.'

'Is there...?' She paused and lowered her eyes bashfully.

'Is there what?' he asked gently. He was experienced at dealing with women from the Middle East and knew not to put any pressure on them or embarrass them, not if you wanted a decent tip.

'Should I decide I want children in the future...'

'There is no reason why you shouldn't have children as soon as you feel ready, although you would be wise to do it within the next five years. If you do make that decision, do come and see me again and we'll make sure you have a comfortable pregnancy and birth.'

'Thank you, doctor,' she said, forcing herself to talk slowly and move sedately when all her instincts told her to hitch up her silken skirts and run to Park Lane to find Norman and tell him she was now his and ready to start her new life, ready for their great adventure together. A picture filled her mind of the two of them living in a suburban house outside New York somewhere, with children playing on the green lawns and the station-wagon parked by the garage.

She forced herself to go through all the rituals of departure, with the doctor standing on the front doorstep waving as her car disappeared down the street, and then settled back into her seat with a sigh of relief. She had arranged to go to her brother's for tea and then Norman would come to pick her up to take her back to Upton Park, except that he wouldn't. He would have the suitcases in the car and would drive them both to Heathrow. From there they would telephone Mark at Upton to say there had been a change of plan and the Princess would not be back for a few days. Hopefully, no one would think to check where she might be for several days, by which time they would be safely in hiding in America and Norman would have made his call to his brother-in-law.

Najid's face was grave as his sister was ushered into the room where she expected to be served tea. Jarmina was too excited by her own plans to notice anything unusual in her brother's demeanour. They made polite conversation as they normally did and tea was brought in.

'Your car will be here in an hour,' Najid said after a while.

'Yes,' Jarmina said. 'I will be going back to Upton tonight.'

'No,' Najid shook his head. 'You will be taken to the airport.'

Jarmina opened her mouth to speak, but nothing came out. She was confused. Did this mean that her brother knew of her plans and approved of them? She decided to say nothing and closed her mouth again.

'My own plane will take you back to Domai, where you will stay with our mother until further notice.'

'Is Mother ill?' she asked, panicking that all her plans were about to be upset by one of her mother's periodic bouts of illness.

'Our mother is well,' Najid said. 'It is for your own health that you are returning home.'

'My health is fine.' Did he know about the short stay in hospital? Had he found out why she was there? Now her heart was thumping with alarm rather than excitement.

'We think that perhaps you need more protection than we have been affording you recently,' Najid said, his voice even. Now that she looked at him more closely she could see he was angry. She hadn't seen him so angry since they were children together and she had taunted him about her superior intelligence. 'It's my fault; I blame myself entirely. I've given you too much freedom and you've misused it.'

'I don't know what you mean.'

'The London police have informed me of your plans to run away with Mr Dorset and to bring shame on our family.'

'Don't be ridiculous.' She forced herself to laugh but it sounded hollow.

Najid chose to ignore the protest. His mind was made up and there was no way he was going to allow her to dissuade him. He was the King. It was his responsibility to ensure the newspapers did not receive any more sensationalist fodder about the Arab royal families. He was already in enough trouble with his people and their increasingly powerful priests for the westernising of their culture; a scandal like this could do irreparable harm to the whole structure of the country. Jarmina had to have her wings clipped. Although he said he blamed himself, Najid actually blamed his father for being too soft with her for too many years. He should have insisted that she married Aran or one of the other highly appropriate suitors who had come her way over the years. Then Norman Dorset would never have had a chance to win her affections.

'You cannot make me do this!' Jarmina shouted. 'I'm a free citizen. You cannot make me go anywhere I don't want to. The British Government will not allow it!'

'The British Government is fully aware of the situation and backs us completely,' Najid said quietly. 'If necessary you will be taken to the plane by force. I hope that will not be necessary.'

Jarmina stared at him as she sometimes had when she was a child, her eyes full of hate. How could it be that, after she had tasted a little of the sweetness of freedom with Norman, her baby brother could just take it from her on a whim? Her anger was boiling inside her.

'If our father was alive you would not be able to do this to me,' she hissed.

'Our father lived in different times. I am the King now. You will abide by my ruling.' Najid's face remained impassive. Leaping to her feet she threw herself at him, her fists flying, and feet kicking. The doors opened and two of Najid's young companions came in to constrain her and she was dragged away, shouting and crying. Najid sat down with a sigh to finish his tea with a shaky hand.

Years of caution meant that Norman didn't draw the car up outside the apartment as any of Len's other drivers would have done. Instead he parked it round the corner on a meter and circled the block on foot, coming back towards the entrance. Had he not done so he would not have seen the unmarked car with two men sitting inside it. Norman long since knew that whenever two men were sitting together in a parked car they were almost certainly policemen. He turned quickly into a mews without breaking his pace, trusting that neither of the men had been looking in the rear-view mirror. His ulcers emitted a searing alarm call of pain.

At the other end of the mews he walked back to the street behind the block and saw another car with two more men in it. Staying close to the shops, looking in the windows to follow the reflections of what was going on behind him, Norman walked past them, his heart crashing in his ears as he waited to hear an angry shout and the sound of running feet or screeching tyres.

He knew Jarmina would be inside the block by now and the whole place would be surrounded. He kept walking, forcing himself not to change his speed or do anything which would draw attention to himself, looking for other people to walk alongside or just behind, in order to disguise himself a little. In this manner he circled the block completely and knew for sure that every entrance and exit was being watched. There was no way in.

He thought of Jarmina inside and part of him wanted to run into the building, gun blazing at anyone who tried to stop him getting to the woman he was planning to spend the rest of his life with, but he knew enough about the building to know that was pointless. The security doors and windows would all be locked and there would be no way of forcing himself through them.

By now they would know he was armed and they were probably all carrying weapons themselves. His first task had to be survival. With one last look at the great fortress of a building, he spun on his heel and walked back up Park Lane and into the next road where he had left the car. If they were waiting for him there, then no one would be watching the airport, yet. With the tickets and passports in his pocket he might still have a few hours in which to escape.

All the way down the motorway his head was buzzing. He was careful not to exceed the speed limit. He didn't want to do anything to draw attention to the car, feeling sure they must know the number. The miles seemed to go past in slow motion. If he could just get to the airport he could hide it amongst the thousands of other cars in the short-term car parks. It would be days, maybe weeks, before anyone came across it. He could ring Len as soon as he was safe and let him know where it was.

The traffic was heavy, which made him feel less conspicuous but also slightly trapped. England suddenly seemed a very small island, almost a prison, and he longed to be free on the great land mass of America. His thoughts kept going back to Jarmina and how he might be able to get in contact with her once he was out of the country. Already plans were forming in his mind.

As he slid the car into a parking space at Heathrow and switched off the engine, he looked around to see if anyone was watching. There was no one. He pulled the glasses and teeth from his pocket and rearranged his hair in the mirror. No one would recognise him from a casual glance. He removed his holster and gun and secreted it under the seat. Walking around an airport with a gun was the quickest method he could think of for drawing attention to himself.

He made his way through to the terminal. There were several hours to kill before the flight. That made him uncomfortable. How long would it be before Moody and his fellow plods worked out that he wasn't going to show up at the apartment? The airport was bound to be their next port of call, possibly after stopping off at Upton Park on the way.

The check-in desk for his flight was open and he checked in quickly. The uniformed woman didn't seem to give him a second glance and was quite happy with the passport.

'Do you have any luggage you want to check in, Mr Blackman?' she asked.

Norman handed over the suitcase he had selected from the many Jarmina and he had packed into the boot that morning, and placed it onto the conveyor belt. He walked through passport control, without a hitch, and went in search of a coffee-shop.

Finding a dark corner he sat himself down and watched as the travelling world bustled back and forth around him. He tried to remember if he had told Jarmina which flight they would be on. If he had, then it was always possible she would try to make it. He was doubtful that she had become sufficiently worldly-wise in their short forays out together to be able to make such a journey on her own, particularly if her family were attempting to stop her. Half of him hoped she would be able to make it, but the more realistic half knew that if she did get to the airport, she would be followed by Moody and enough policemen to arrest everyone on the flight.

The minutes seemed to tick by in slow motion. He bought a newspaper but was unable to concentrate on it as his eyes continually flickered up to scan the ever-moving crowd around him.

Eventually, he saw his flight to New York appear on the screen. Gathering up his briefcase he ambled slowly in the direction of the gate that was indicated. No one was taking any notice of him. To the casual glance he looked, as Jarmina had said, like a professor on his way to deliver a lecture, or possibly a travelling salesman, specialising in some esoteric piece of engineering equipment.

As he drew closer to the gate he noticed there were people out of uniform standing around watching the approaching passengers. Without quickening his pace he kept walking, and went past the gate. He felt them looking at him and then dismissing him. A quick glance through into the departure lounge confirmed his suspicions. There were more people there, all of whom looked like plain-clothes policemen waiting patiently as each passenger checked in, as if confident they didn't have to look anywhere else to find their man.

He kept walking along the brightly carpeted tunnel until he found himself back in a general area. He knew there was no way he was going to be able to get onto the flight now. His disguise might be good enough to keep him unnoticed as he walked around in the crowd, but once his passport was being scrutinised, he was bound to come under suspicion and it would not take long for them to work out which man travelling alone on the flight was Norman Dorset in disguise. It was time to think of another plan.

He spotted a telephone booth and walked over to it. He pulled a small card from his pocket and laid it on top of the coin box, with a handful of money. He dialled the number and inserted the coins.

'General Beckett,' he said to the voice that answered.

'Who's calling?' the girl asked.

'Norman Dorset. He'll take the call.'

'Just a moment, Mr Dorset.'

Michael was on the line a few seconds later. 'Norman,' he said in a voice which gave nothing away.

'I need your help,' Norman said.

'How is that?'

'I need to get out of the country and Najid told me you would be the man to arrange whatever I needed. I want you to get me to the States.'

'Why would I do that, Norman?' Michael asked after a moment's pause.

'Because I have a story which the tabloids would just love to hear, General, and your boss is very keen that I don't tell it.'

'Just a moment, Norman.'

The line went quiet before Norman had time to say that he was in a call box. The display told him it needed more money. He fed the coins in. They were disappearing at a frantic rate but no one came back onto the line.

A flurry of movement outside the booth caught his eye. He glanced up, just in time to see a Middle-Eastern woman shrouded in robes being escorted towards a door by several men in suits. He opened his mouth to shout, but stopped himself just in time, as the woman and her guard of honour disappeared through the door. He hadn't had time to see if it was Jarmina or not. Although he knew it was extremely unlikely, he still felt his throat constrict for a moment and his eyes stung uncomfortably. Again, the display told him to put more money in and he obeyed, as if in a trance.

'Where are you?' Michael's voice came back on the line.

'Heathrow.'

'We can arrange for a private plane to take you wherever you want,' he said. 'What name are you travelling under?'

'If you double-cross me I'll be telling every detail of this story,' Norman growled.

'We understand that, Norman. You can trust us. We're as keen to get you out of the country as you are to be out.'

'William Blackman,' Norman said, hating the feeling of having to trust another man with his freedom.

'Ring this number again in an hour,' Michael said, 'and I'll tell you what to do.'

As Norman came out of the booth, his eyes fixed on the door which the woman had disappeared through. He could see it had a bell and a speakerphone beside it. He guessed it must be the way through to some private lounge, perhaps on the way to a private flight. He was still aware that the chances the woman had been Jarmina were slight, but that didn't lessen the pain. He guessed they would be spiriting her away to Domai as quickly as possible. So it would have to be there that he would get in contact with her once things had quietened down. He imagined her sitting behind the door in some luxurious lounge, her head bowed, the men all around her respectful of her position but firm in their resolve to carry out their King's orders. Jarmina might be a princess, but she was still only a woman and, as such, would have to do as they told her for as long as they were under instruction from Najid.

He found another corner in a coffee-shop and waited for another long hour, avoiding catching anyone's eye, while watching everything around him. This time when he phoned, Michael answered personally.

'We've organised a flight for you,' he said, and proceeded to give Norman detailed instructions on how to find his way to the pilot who was waiting for him in another terminal.

'Once you're in America,' Michael ended, 'we'll feel we have discharged our debt to you.'

'You won't be hearing from me again,' Norman promised.

Michael hung up. Norman scooped the remainder of his change into his pocket and followed the signs to the next terminal. The pilot was waiting to greet him.

'Mr Blackman?'

Norman nodded but said nothing.

'If you would like to follow me.'

There were no more passport formalities for a man who had had a private plane ordered for him by the Sultan of Domai's private office. The pilot was trained in discretion and asked no questions. As they walked out across the tarmac to the waiting jet, he talked a little about the weather they could expect over the Atlantic and the length of the flight. The co-pilot and steward were already on the plane and within a quarter of an hour of leaving the airport buildings they were in the air.

'Would you care for a glass of champagne, Mr Blackman?' the steward enquired, 'while you look at the menu for the flight.'

CHAPTER FOURTEEN

Moody was sitting in an outer office somewhere in Whitehall, and feeling intimidated by the echoes of passing feet on the marble floors and the height of the pillars which surrounded the shabby sofa he had been told to wait on. The springs in the seat had gone and he had sunk so low his knees were almost up to his chin.

'Sir Roderick would like to see you now,' a young man in a pinstriped suit informed him.

Moody heaved himself to his feet and trotted after his guide, who had already stridden halfway across the hall, his heels clicking elegantly on the floor as Moody's rubber soles squelched hurriedly along behind.

Sir Roderick was busy with paperwork as they came into the office and he signed a few more letters with a flourish before looking up with only a trace of a smile.

'Detective Constable Moody, Sir Roderick,' the young man said.

'Thank you,' Sir Roderick replied, handing the signed letters to his assistant and gesturing for Moody to sit down in one of the low seats opposite his desk.

'Good of you to come in to see us,' Sir Roderick said, his face giving nothing away. 'I know how busy you chaps are.'

'I was under the impression it was an order, sir,' Moody said.

'Oh, I wouldn't say that,' Sir Roderick softened his tone, anxious not to antagonise the prickly young man in front of him. 'Your superiors speak very highly of you.'

Moody said nothing.

'Particularly with regard to the way you've worked on Norman Dorset's case.'

Sir Roderick flicked open a file on the desk and Moody assumed it was Norman's. 'You've shown the most extraordinary tenacity in getting after this man.'

'I believe he should be put away for good, sir,' Moody said.

'I think you're probably right,' Sir Roderick said. 'He would appear to be something of a menace to society. I see he's served a fair bit of time already.'

'Not enough, in my opinion, sir.'

'No, quite. We gather he's in America at the moment.'

Moody's eyebrows shot up but he said nothing.

'You didn't know that?' Sir Roderick pretended to be surprised. 'So it might be time to turn your attentions elsewhere.'

'We could bring him back from America, if we know where he is,' Moody said.

'For a number of reasons we would prefer not to do that. We would rather make him their problem. I think, as long as he knows you're still here waiting for him, he's unlikely to come back to these shores for a while.'

'I have a murder case and he's my main suspect,' Moody said. 'And there are any number of other outstanding investigations into his activities over the years.'

'We're aware of that,' Sir Roderick allowed a hint of impatience into his voice. The man was beginning to annoy him. 'But we would rather you left this case and moved on to another. I've heard you're in line for promotion over this. It would be unwise of you to spoil your chances by blotting your copybook at such a late stage.'

'Blotting my copybook?' Moody could feel his temper rising.

'You're being taken off the Norman Dorset case and you'll be ordered to leave him alone from now on. You've chased him out of the country. You've done your job for the British taxpayer. You're now being instructed to move on to something new. It's an order. Do you understand?'

'Yes sir.'

Moody stood up and left the room.

Jarmina was curled up on a sofa at the foot of her mother's bed in the palace in Domai. Several of her mother's friends were sitting around the corners of the room as the Queen Mother picked at a plate of pastries that lay on the bed beside her.

'You pushed your poor brother too far,' the old woman was scolding. 'You might have been able to get away with it when your father was alive, but Najid will not tolerate such nonsense.' There was a note of pride in her voice as she spoke of her son, the King. 'You never did know your place, Jarmina, and eventually you were bound to fall off your high horse.'

Jarmina was aware that the other women were nodding and clucking agreement under their breaths, although they averted their eyes and fell silent as soon as she turned to stare at them. She felt empty inside. All her hopes had disappeared and she felt that now she would be a prisoner for the rest of her life. The palace staff were all under instruction not to take her anywhere without permission from one of the men in the family and she now felt as helpless as she had almost ten years before, when she had first travelled to London and glimpsed the possibilities of life for other women. There was nothing left to dream for now.

Unwinding herself from the sofa, she glowered at the other women and made her way across to the bed. Sitting down next to her mother she stared at the Queen Mother's bloated face and sighed. Reaching out with a bejewelled hand, she picked up one of the pastries. It was sticky with honey. She bit into it and the sweetness seemed to be some compensation. Her mother smiled understandingly and pushed the tray across to her daughter. She knew how much comfort could be had in life from food.

'Such a beautiful ring,' she said, taking hold of her daughter's fingers and admiring a large pink diamond she hadn't noticed before.

'I had it made in London,' Jarmina said, without adding that she had had it made for the man she had hoped to spend the rest of her life with. The man she had believed, for a short time, would rescue her from the life the other women of the court were forced to live.

The jet put down at JFK airport and only the briefest examination of Mr Blackman's passport and visa was required by the officials before a limousine was summoned and he was whisked down to Manhattan.

Norman knew he would need to make some contacts quickly. He had enough money in his briefcase to keep himself for a few months, but sooner or later he was going to need to find some more. He knew a number of people who could put him in touch with the local faces who would welcome someone from out of town, someone who was not known to the local police.

As well as the grumbling of his ulcers, there was a feeling in his stomach like a lead weight every time he thought of Jarmina. It reminded him why he had spent so many years avoiding emotional involvement with women. This was the last time he would make such a mistake. From now on he would concentrate on business.

Andrew Crofts

Maisie's Amazing Maids

Enter Joe Tye – ghost-writer extraordinaire. Out of work and running up debts, Joe has more than enough to contend with from his demanding ex-wife, their runaway son, an overly-amorous sixteen-year-old beauty, and an assortment of wayward flatmates.

And then he starts running into countless Filipino 'maids', all answering to the name of Doris, and all desperately wanting his help…

OTHER TITLES BY ANDREW CROFTS AVAILABLE DIRECT FROM HOUSE OF STRATUS

Quantity		£	$(US)	$(CAN)	€
☐	MAISIE'S AMAZING MAIDS	6.99	12.95	19.95	13.50

ALL HOUSE OF STRATUS BOOKS ARE AVAILABLE FROM GOOD BOOKSHOPS OR DIRECT FROM THE PUBLISHER:

Internet: **www.houseofstratus.com** including synopses and features.

Email: **sales@houseofstratus.com** please quote author, title and credit card details.

Order Line: UK: 0800 169 1780,
USA: 1 800 509 9942
INTERNATIONAL: +44 (0) 20 7494 6400 (UK)
or +01 212 218 7649
(please quote author, title, and credit card details.)

Send to:

House of Stratus Sales Department
24c Old Burlington Street
London
W1X 1RL
UK

House of Stratus Inc.
Suite 210
1270 Avenue of the Americas
New York • NY 10020
USA

PAYMENT

Please tick currency you wish to use:

☐ £ (Sterling) ☐ $ (US) ☐ $ (CAN) ☐ € (Euros)

Allow for shipping costs charged per order plus an amount per book as set out in the tables below:

CURRENCY/DESTINATION

	£(Sterling)	$(US)	$(CAN)	€(Euros)
Cost per order				
UK	1.50	2.25	3.50	2.50
Europe	3.00	4.50	6.75	5.00
North America	3.00	3.50	5.25	5.00
Rest of World	3.00	4.50	6.75	5.00
Additional cost per book				
UK	0.50	0.75	1.15	0.85
Europe	1.00	1.50	2.25	1.70
North America	1.00	1.00	1.50	1.70
Rest of World	1.50	2.25	3.50	3.00

PLEASE SEND CHEQUE OR INTERNATIONAL MONEY ORDER.
payable to: STRATUS HOLDINGS plc or HOUSE OF STRATUS INC. or card payment as indicated

STERLING EXAMPLE

Cost of book(s):...................... Example: 3 x books at £6.99 each: £20.97
Cost of order: .... Example: £1.50 (Delivery to UK address)
Additional cost per book:............... Example: 3 x £0.50: £1.50
Order total including shipping:........... Example: £23.97

VISA, MASTERCARD, SWITCH, AMEX:

☐☐☐☐☐☐☐☐☐☐☐☐☐☐☐☐☐☐☐☐

Issue number (Switch only):

☐☐☐

Start Date: ☐☐/☐☐

Expiry Date: ☐☐/☐☐

Signature: ______________________

NAME: ______________________

ADDRESS: ______________________

COUNTRY: ______________________

ZIP/POSTCODE: ______________________

Please allow 28 days for delivery. Despatch normally within 48 hours.

Prices subject to change without notice.
Please tick box if you do not wish to receive any additional information. ☐